MASKING

MURDER

By Renee Kumor

ABSOLUTELY AMAZING eBOOKS

To all those who provided healthcare,
support and encouragement
to the rest of us as we learned an altered way of life.

ABSOLUTELY AMAZING eBOOKS

Manhanset House
Dering Harbor, New York 11965

bricktower@aol.com ∎ tech@absolutelyamazingebooks.com
∎ absolutelyamazingebooks.com

Library of Congress Cataloging-in-Publication Data
Kumor, Renee
Masking Murder
p. cm.

1. FICTION / Mystery & Detective / Amateur Sleuth
2. FICTION / Mystery & Detective / General
3. FICTION / Thrillers / Suspense

ISBN: 978-1-955036-38-2, Trade Paper

Other Titles in

The River Bend Chronicles
Series

Chapter One

The River Bend Philanthropies office was running to red. Lynn Powers, the executive director, had invited the River Bend Reads Valentine's dance committee to meet at her offices. The River Bend Reads offices were going through a facelift - painting, new flooring all the things a high traffic, highly successful nonprofit needed to do to keep looking welcoming and successful. The committee was crafting center pieces and decorations for the dance. How many ways could one represent a red heart?

To wash the red out of her eyes, Lynn was staring out the window into the parking lot. Where had winter gone? January had seen the town covered in snow. Ground Hog's Day seemed to flip a switch. The crocuses were blooming and the forsythias were ready to burst. She smiled to herself. Spring always came, no matter what The Weather Channel predicted. She turned back to her guests.

Emily Jacobs, the founder of River Bend Reads, the local literacy program, had helped found and fund the agency over forty years ago. Through her dedication the literacy program had assisted hundreds over the years to learn to read and to learn English as a second language. Emily never got distracted by success. This year she had volunteered to chair the annual Valentine's Day dance. The theme, Being Well Re(a)d, was going to be the usual hit. Tickets were sold out and all was ready. This meeting was the final check.

Emily came up to Lynn, "Thank you, dear. I hope to see you at our dance in that lovely red dress I seem to remember you own."

Lynn smiled at the elderly lady. "Don't pretend that you can't remember. I hope I'm as sharp as you when I'm your age."

Emily's face wrinkled into all the smile lines earned over those years. "Eighty-nine in June."

There was a shuffling as the next group on Lynn's calendar came into the office. Robert O'Hara and Penny Rawlings, the Philanthropies' former board chair and the chair-elect respectively, had scheduled some time with Lynn. Penny, a young mother and practicing attorney, would be taking over the chairmanship from H. Lawrence Grayson, another local attorney. Robert, a semi-retired attorney, had volunteered to take Penny through an orientation. Robert didn't mince words and Penny was smart enough to know everything already. Lynn planned on enjoying a brief meeting. Until. . .

"Robert," chirped Emily, "Just the man I want to see. I've been meaning to make an appointment." She looked around the office. Just Lynn, Penny and Robert were with her. "I want to change my will and the trust."

"Now?" Robert had planned on a quick review with Penny then a card game in the men's locker room at the country club. Emily gave him a look that old schoolteachers always had ready. "Yes, ma'am."

Lynn almost laughed. Robert wasn't much younger than Emily. She offered, "Why don't you two sit in the conference room for your meeting?" She led them to the door. "Penny and I can gossip while you talk."

Emily paused on her way into the room. "Why don't you two youngsters join us?"

Puzzled, the two women followed Emily and Robert, everyone taking seats as Lynn closed the door. She had known Emily for years. As a youngster she had met the older woman as a substitute teacher in the elementary school. She had also known Emily as one of her own mother's mentors when Helene Hoefler took up the role of community nonprofit volunteer and leader. When Lynn took her job at the

Philanthropies, she got to know Emily on a whole new level. As in she was a really, really, really wealthy woman.

Emily had been married to a world-famous mystery writer. The man wrote books and plays and turned many of his books and plays into movie scripts. Emily managed the money and the investments during their tumultuous marriage. Over the years her famous husband had lived large and insulted her with his alcoholic induced antics. They had one daughter who followed her father in his fast lane, full throttle, drug and alcohol hazed life. When the daughter gave birth to a child, sperm donor unknown, Emily and the baby moved to River Bend.

Years earlier her husband had found a small cabin in the county on several acres surrounded by national forest. He called it his writing retreat. He had dropped into that secluded spot several times when he was under pressure to meet a deadline. For a few years Emily and the baby had followed husband and daughter intermittently in their party life, but he soon was slowed by alcohol induced physical ailments. Severe health problems and need for seclusion convinced the family to settle in River Bend for his last months. Once the family had moved to town on a more permanent basis with an infant granddaughter, Emily purchased a piece of land and a home in the countryside, not as isolated as the cabin, but still secluded. The daughter had soon followed her father in death, succumbing to liver failure. Within a short time of moving to town, Emily was left to raise her granddaughter alone. That young woman, Alicia, became a semi-successful artist. In time she married another artist and had three children. A bright and calm future seemed ahead for the young family. That had pleased Emily.

But the family was destined for more tragedy. Alicia's husband died in an airplane crash. Two years later the young widow remarried, but after a year of marriage she was diagnosed with pancreatic cancer. Her death was swift.

As Emily was saying to her friends in the Philanthropies conference room, "My granddaughter died a year ago today." Everyone made sympathetic sounds. "I want to change my will to make certain that her husband won't control the money I will leave to my great-grandchildren."

"Is he proving to be the bum you thought?" asked Robert.

Emily massaged her hands together as they rested on the conference table. "Nothing yet. But I lived with an alcoholic long enough to have developed a sense of someone plotting behind the curtain. If you understand what I mean." They looked at her for a better explanation. "He talks a good game, his relationship with me is kind and protective. He always seems to have the children's best interests at heart, and he makes certain that the children and I are always in contact even though it's quietly under his strict control." She gripped her hands together. "Currently he keeps the children in boarding school. And I've always felt Alicia died sooner than she should have." Everyone gasped.

Hints of murder not withstanding, Robert wanted to get on with his day. "I can restructure the trust so someone else will control the money at your incapacity or death, and the kids will get control when they're a certain age." He looked at his client. She nodded, so he continued, "You just need to name that person."

Emily thought for some time. "I need someone young, and someone familiar with raising children." She glanced shyly at Lynn and Penny. "How about you two?" The old woman held a silent plea in her eyes. "I don't mean guardianship. Alicia's will clearly made Heath the guardian. They never had time to deal with him officially adopting them." She sat straighter, wanting to look like the practical person she usually was. "I want you two to join the trust management board and release the money for the children's needs until they come of age. I want to restructure the future board with you two and one of my relatives advising on funds distribution."

Robert cleared his throat. "Emily's current will gives management and control of the trust to Alicia at Emily's death." He frowned. "When Alicia died, according to Emily's current will," Robert emphasized the words, "Alicia's husband would inherit that control and responsibility of Emily's assets upon Emily's death." Robert looked at his client. "Alicia's first husband predeceased her and my client never changed her will after Alicia remarried and then predeceased her second husband." He gave Emily a pointed look.

She gave the group a sad smile. "I reworked the trust documents when she remarried, reducing her and her husband's involvement in the of management and tightening up funds distribution. I didn't change my will. We were all caught by surprise when she died so suddenly. I've been thinking about this for months." She pulled a file from her big mint green designer bag. "This is that old will. I've made annotations where I want changes. And while I'm making those changes, I thought I should amend the trust as well. You two would take over at my demise."

"Let me get this straight," said Penny going into lawyer mode. "Your old will gives Alicia's husband control of your personal assets and would replace you on the trust board unless the trust managers redefine membership. He essentially inherits the responsibilities that Alicia would have taken over at your death." Emily nodded. "Alicia's will made Heath the children's guardian. As their guardian and her husband, under the original trust organization he, as her husband, joins the trust management at your death." Emily nodded again. "Your new will would redefine who follows you into the trust.

"I organized the trust originally when Alicia and her first husband married. They were so sweet. Heath is not sweet, nor in my opinion, is he trustworthy." She smiled. "Get my pun? He's not to be trusted and he's not worthy of serving on the trust board."

"This sounds more complex than it should have been," concluded Penny. She glanced at Robert. He shrugged.

Emily cleared her throat. "At the time of Alicia's first marriage and the coming of the children, it made perfect sense with the two adults involved." She handed the file to Robert as she asked the two young woman, "Do you accept the role of trust managers?"

Penny took her hand. As a young mother who had lost a child several years ago, she was touched by the request. "Of course, Lynn and I would be privileged to do this for you." Lynn said nothing because Penny was correct. She would do anything to help Emily. Of course, she understood the reality. She and Penny would step in to oversee an iffy guardian of three children should Emily pass on. The thought of Emily's death and the sorrow of the children steeled Lynn's resolve to care for the youngsters and to get to know them. But, Lynn thought optimistically, Emily is strong and will be here for many more years to guide the children herself.

"That's settled," said Robert in a hurried voice. "I'll start on it when I get back to the office. One of my staff may call you for particulars." He turned to Lynn. "Why don't you see Emily out? I'll bring Penny up to date on this job." Both young women rolled their eyes at one another. They knew Robert had other things he wanted to be doing.

Lynn jumped up. "Emily, do you have time to walk down to the coffee shop before you leave town?" Emily's home was situated on ten acres several miles south of town.

"I'd like that, dear."

xxx

The two women had only been settled with their coffees for a few minutes when Penny walked in. "Robert was late for a poker game or something," she announced. "He told me to make notes of your instructions and take your old will to his office." She winked at Emily. "I'll make certain he gets this moving." She pulled out a notebook. "Let me get a better understanding of what you want and we'll figure out how to structure it."

"I'll get back to my office," said Lynn, understanding that this could become a very confidential discussion.

"No, dear, please stay," replied Emily, clasping Lynn's hand. "I want to tell both of you my dreams for my great-grandchildren."

When the women finally left the coffee shop, Lynn was in love with the children. They sounded like a gift for Emily after all the personal tragedies in her life. And Lynn turned to share her thoughts with the older woman while helping her to her car.

But Emily was distracted by something else, tugging at Lynn's arm as they walked together. "If I were twenty years younger, I'd chase after that fellow."

Lynn squinted into the parking lot. "Dr. Noah?" Dr. Noah Pflug had opened his medical practice in River Bend almost forty years ago.

"He's so cute." Emily sparkled at the doctor as he walked by.

"Ladies," he nodded. "Emily, put on some gloves, it's not as warm as you think." He winked and walked on toward his office.

"Isn't he a charmer?"

Lynn looked at the graying doctor. "He's all yours," she said, "I've got my man."

"Your man is handsome, too," agreed Emily. "But a little young for me."

Lynn laughed and hugged her. "Then I don't have to worry that you've set your cap for Dusty?"

Emily gave her a soft smile. "It's been a long time since I set my cap for any man." She became serious. "Thank you for agreeing to help me and the children. Their future has been weighing on my mind."

"We've got your back." Lynn hugged her one more time and helped the older woman off the curb toward her car.

xxx

Jody Donlin stood at the counter of her small stationery and office supply business, head-to-head in deep conversation with a customer. "I see what you mean, Andrew," she said as she pointed to the picture in the catalog they were both studying. "This product looks like it would suit your need better. I'll place the order and take back the other." Jodi slid a pencil into her graying utilitarian bun.

"I'm sorry, Jody," replied Andrew, "I hate to cause you this much trouble. You're always so helpful." He gave the older woman a grateful smile.

Jody patted the young man's hand. "Don't worry. You can't use it, but I think I know someone who can." She quickly wrote up the order, allowed the man to check her jottings, and then emailed the order to her supplier. "It'll be here on Friday." Jody walked around the counter to usher the young man out and move on to greet the next customer just coming through the door.

"Thanks." The young man gave her a quick hug. "Pop always told me to trust you."

"I see you're picking them mighty young," drawled the older man who walked into the shop.

Jody rolled her eyes at him. "Let's just say you've aged out of my field of interest."

"Are you one of those cougars?" the older man asked.

Andrew laughed and the two older people looked at him and frowned.

Jody walked to the back of the shop, saying, over her shoulder, "I'll get your order, Noah."

The older man scowled at Andrew who was still standing at the door. "Are you laughing at my old age?"

"Not me, Doc," he replied, "I'm laughing at the two of you. Ever since I've been coming in here, you two have been flirting."

"Flirting?" Dr. Noah scowled more dangerously, his head of graying curls dancing around his head.

Andrew nodded. "You must come in here once a day because I always see you and I'm here at least twice a week. Both of you are free agents. And you're both young enough to - -"

"That's far enough," growled the doctor, "just remember who brought you into this world."

Andrew grinned at the man. "Just remember neither one of you is dead - yet." He nodded to the doctor and was out the door.

The doctor watched the young man laughing as he walked along to his own business office.

Hmm, thought Dr. Noah, flirting?

xxx

"I saw Emily Jacobs today," Lynn whispered into Dusty's ear. The days were bright and warm suggesting spring, but nights were still chilly. She pulled at the bedsheets and snuggled closer. "She said she thought you were handsome but a little too young for her."

"Hmm," he muttered as he traced circles on her back. "I don't have an age limit for women if they're rich."

"Don't get too cocky. You came in second to Dr. Noah." Lynn chuckled.

"He's dating Mrs. Jacobs?"

"No," explained Lynn, "she was just ogling him."

"Isn't she too old to ogle?"

"I don't think ogling has an age limit," she said, "sort of like you not having any age limits for pursuing wealthy women." They were quiet as they cuddled and he continued to rub her back. Lynn hated to break the spell, but she had a confession. "Sigh."

"What is it?" Dusty was wise to her ways.

"This is going to be a busy weekend."

"Tuxedo busy?" he asked suspiciously.

"Two weddings and a dance busy." He released her and threw himself back on his pillow. She laughed. "Don't be so dramatic. Friday evening, your friend Doug Fiore marries Connie Trumbull."

"That was fast." Dusty calculated back to the incident when Doug's son shot Connie's ex-husband.

"At least he didn't throw her in a car and race her to the magistrate," Lynn reminded him. Because that was how Dusty had organized their wedding. "Besides, Connie and Doug have three kids to consider and ex-spouses and Child Protective Services because of that shooting. And they wanted to attend Zeke and Barbara's wedding on Saturday afternoon with their kids at River Dog Brewery."

"Zeke's wedding? That's the second event?" he asked. "That doesn't sound like a bad weekend."

"Did you forget the dance?" Lynn laughed again as he swore.

"You said no tux." His voice threatened a revolt.

She rested her head on his shoulder. "It's the River Bend Reads Valentine's dance. We attend every year. They organize it for donors and graduates of the program."

"That's right," Dusty said, "Will," Lynn's brother, "calls it the GED prom."

"That's why it's always at the Elks. It's big enough to hold a mob and not too fancy. The literacy students feel comfortable attending." She kissed his cheek. "So, no tux but a lot of socializing this weekend.

"I was thinking we should do a little socializing now." He wrapped her in his arms. Lynn liked his idea of socializing.

Chapter 2

Heath Dawson swore as he surveyed the damage vandals had done to the secluded cabin. In years past, the cabin had been the workplace for some old relative of his dead wife. The old guy was a mystery writer or something. The only good thing Heath knew about the man was that he left his family very wealthy.

As his wife had matured as an artist, she had used the cabin to follow her muse. He scoffed, "What the hell is a muse?" He kicked over a broken chair. For years his wife and her first husband had used this cabin for an art studio. The first husband died, or as Heath liked to think, met his muse.

Heath, aging male model handsome, had been fortunate enough to meet and marry Alicia. The young woman had been dazzled by his good looks and unfazed by his lack of social finesse, intelligence, or artistic sense. He had been attracted by her family fortune and was willing to accept her three kids in the bargain. He could fake anything to be close to her wealth. Good old Alicia, always an accommodating wife, got sick and died within less than two years of marriage. Heath used that time during her sickness to try to cement his control over her wealth. Was he wrong! He hadn't counted on her grandmother being so clever and distrustful. As the young woman was dying, that old woman tightened the controls of the trust. The old bag had made certain that Alicia had no control over the trust fund and limited financial responsibilities to pass on to her husband. All Alicia could control was guardianship. She gave responsibility for her three children to the man she loved, and whom she thought loved her children. Ha!

Over the Christmas holidays, when he had traveled to River Bend to give Emily a ride back to Hilton Head and the kids, he had spent a day searching her office for information. Always wanting to stay ahead of her schemes against him, he found her current will with a note to *"talk to Robert after the holidays."* He did learn that, in the current will, control of the trust would pass to him when that old hag died, if the children were still minors. And after some legal mumbo-jumbo, he figured out that, should those precious kiddies not reach majority, he won the trust lottery. Essentially, he was heir to the snotty trio. Finding Emily's note suggesting her intention to rewrite her will became Heath's impetus to cement his status as the last heir standing. He had spent his time since Christmas planning his path to control the wealth because he was uncertain how fast Emily would move on her new will.

He picked up a small sculpture that had been thrown out a cabin window and flung the offending artwork high into the trees. His wife had been dead for a year, and he had finally developed a plan to gain control of all the wealth. This cabin had a role. But first he had to make some repairs and improve security. He wanted no more vandals getting in and he wanted no one, once locked in, getting out.

He spent the rest of the day cleaning the mess, organizing the repairs, and making a list of needed materials. Tomorrow he would be back and start on his project. Anticipating all that wealth was a great motivator. He'd get this place ready in no time. The young mother died thinking Heath loved her and her children and that he would spend his life caring for them and managing the income from the trust. Today he stood in a forest in North Carolina planning their deaths.

xxx

Lynn and Dusty sat in the small church enjoying a happy occasion. Doug Fiore, a highway patrolman, and his son, Toby, were marrying Connie Trumbull and her two daughters. Some folks were surprised at the quick marriage, but Doug had told everyone who leered or snickered that there were three kids involved and it was easier and more appropriate that he and Connie be loving and parenting instead of sneaking around trying to find private time. He was pleased to be setting a good example for the kids as they got older. He was also pleased to be getting Connie in his arms.

It was an interesting, restructured family. Connie's ex-husband and his mother seemed delighted to be present at the ceremony. Connie had confided in Lynn that her ex seemed to have matured in these last months. As Connie had hypothesized, "Maybe getting shot by little Toby was a wake-up call." The fallout of the shooting had hastened marriage because both Doug and Connie wanted to create a stable family life for all three children. Through it all her ex-mother-in-law had adopted Toby as a grandson. The woman had always been hostile to Connie, but had become a champion for the little boy who had wanted to protect Connie and her daughters in a situation he had misunderstood. Shooting Connie's ex had made Connie's ex-mother-in-law a fan of the little boy, willing to include Toby as one of her grandchildren. Instead of the woman moving to the fringes of Connie's life, she was now close and supportive. Odd, how sometimes loving families defied sanity, common sense, or logic.

Several members of Connie's support group also attended the joyful event. The group of sexual assault survivors celebrated success and healing. It was an uplifting time for all of them. And they could hardly wait until tomorrow when a second member of the group would wed.

Many of Doug's law enforcement friends were in attendance, including Dusty's staff. Teniquia, Mars and Danny were there with their spouses. They had promised their children that tomorrow they would all attend a celebration at River Dog Brewery. Tonight was just for parents.

There was a joyful reception for the new couple and their children in the church family center after the ceremony. The Reverend Tilson Butler, Tilly to his friends, greeted Lynn and Dusty. "Great new family." They all watched as Toby was hugged by all of Connie's friends. Connie's daughters carried small trays of cake around the room for guests to take.

As she entered the reception Lynn was surprised to see Emily Jacobs enjoying a chat with Connie's daughters as they passed cake. "Emily," cried Lynn, "you're adding weddings to your social calendar?"

Emily said something to the young girls, and they moved on to pass the cake to other guests. "This is family."

"Family?"

"Remember the other day you asked me about the others on the trust board?" Lynn nodded. Emily tilted her head toward the bride. "Connie's mother, Babs, is my niece, really my husband's niece. She moved to River Bend to help me when I decided to raise Alicia. Babs was nineteen or twenty at the time and at loose ends. She moved in to help me, took classes at the community college and met her husband, George Ballentine. His family owns that air conditioning repair and installation business."

Lynn squinted to bring Babs and George into better focus. "Ah," she said, because she recognized both of them as former board members of the literary program, River Bend Reads. "I've met them. They've helped you for years at River Bend Reads. I didn't know you were all related."

Emily laughed. "George always tells me that being related to me is like having his pocket picked on a regular basis." Babs, this evening known as the mother-of-the-bride, threw Emily a kiss from across the room. Family.

The wedding reception was small but as Lynn circulated, she was delighted to see her friends, Lee Stahlmeier and Beth Seymour. Lynn knew Connie's story and understood her relationship with Lee, the woman who had facilitated the sexual assault survivors' group for years. She was surprised to see Beth, though. Then she thought about Beth's notoriety as a popular attorney with her classmates and figured Beth had attended North Consolidated High School with Doug or someone in his family.

She waved at them across the room. Beth panicked as she whispered to Lee, "What if she asks how I know Connie?" Beth had met Lee and Connie a few months ago when she joined the support group for sexual assault survivors. She appreciated being welcomed in the group but had only told her father and stepmother of the assault she experienced as a child. She was not eager to share her story with her sisters, or Lynn, or anyone else.

Lee patted her hand. "Just say you're old friends. If she gets really curious, we'll just give her a piece of cake." Lee lowered her voice in conspiracy. "She has a crippling sweet tooth."

Beth grinned and Lee hoped she was worried for nothing.

Lynn settled into a vacant chair. "Good to see you two. Are you going to be at Barbara's wedding tomorrow?"

Beth looked at her, confused. Lynn said, "Sorry. I meant Lee. I figure you're here because you went to school with Doug." Lee handed her a piece of cake. "Thanks." Beth handed her a fork. "Thanks. This is my second piece. This frosting is delicious."

Lee cut a glance toward Beth, and they hid their smiles. But the smiles faded as Lynn asked, "How do you two know each other?"

Lee said, "Rita," referring to Beth's stepmother.

"Ah," said Lynn as she licked frosting off her plastic fork. And Beth learned a lesson in how cake can protect privacy.

CHAPTER 3

The River Dog Brewery wedding was a late Saturday afternoon affair. The guest list for the ceremony was limited, only close friends and family were invited to the small Church in the Pines. The wedding party included the two brewery partners and their wives as attendants. Allowances had been made to accommodate Eddie Erhardt, wheelchair bound brewmaster, as the best man. Tuxedoed and gowned, the joyous group carried out the ceremony with quiet dignity. Barbara's brother, Rev. Gavin, from the Church in the Pines, conducted the service with unrestrained joy. He had watched his sister lift herself up from the trauma of sexual assault to become a successful business manager and, finally, to blossom into a happy bride. What more could a brother want but to have his prayers answered in such a delightful, loving way?

But the reception would include everyone who could fit into the brewery. And the reception met all Lynn's expectations. Everyone in Portage came to celebrate. When the three disabled veterans had opened the microbrewery, they had unleashed an economic boom in this derelict community known in the past as the seat of all crime in James County. The brewery had helped small local shops and food trucks prosper. Just recently a local health clinic had opened a small satellite office providing medical and dental care three days a week. Bernice's Beauty Boutique had gone from two semi-vacant chairs to a busy three chair operation with a growing mani-pedi clientele. And the local preacher had a hard time convincing his congregation that alcohol was evil when it had ushered in prosperity and increased his Sunday collection. Lynn and Dusty were frequent patrons of the brewery and were greeted by their many friends as they joined in the wedding celebration. Granny Masterson, grandmother of the groom, dressed as usual in her finest housedress and shiny gardening boots, hugged her friend. Lynn had lived up to her promise and had helped Granny organize and deliver the groom's responsibilities for the wedding celebration.

It had been another of Lynn's wedding planner challenges. Granny wanted her grandson to marry in style. Lynn had to walk a fine line between Granny's idea of style and the bride's idea of style. But it had worked out with the traditional ceremony at the church - Granny walked down the aisle as the grandmother of the groom, seated in her place of prominence by Kane Solomon, respected brewery partner of her grandson. Then, through negotiation and interpretation of Granny's wedding dreams, Lynn and the bride had fashioned a brewery reception that Granny paid for with delight. Barbara's small family, happy to be relieved of the cost of the reception on their limit resources, made certain that they showed their appreciation and affection for Granny and her grandson.

Lynn and Barbara had worried over the expense until Granny's long-time attorney, Mr. Hutch Dunn, had whispered to Lynn that money was no object for the Masterson family. Mr. Dunn was the long-time attorney for many of River Bend's wealthiest residents. And he counted Granny Masterson as one of the quietly wealthy. He concluded his whispered conversation by saying, "And don't you bug her with some fundraising ideas. She has all she can handle helping these boys succeed." Lynn understood. Granny was a silent partner in River Dog Brewery.

Another old acquaintance Lynn greeted was Darwin Masterson, one of the heirs to the Masterson crime legacy in Portage. They had met a few years ago when Darwin brought a video to Dusty showing the murder of his two criminally minded Masterson cousins. They had been running an illegal gaming house disguised as a fake church. Their mistake had been cheating a fellow who had mean friends. The experience had scared Darwin and started him on the road to alter his genetic bent toward crime. His evolution to a law abiding, productive citizen accelerated when he joined the brewers as security and IT director. And life became perfect for the hapless geek when he met Shonda Tindall and her son as the brewers helped protect her from a vindictive ex-husband.

All of Portage anticipated Darwin's wedding soon. And Lynn asked the question as she hugged Shonda and Darwin. "When's your wedding day?"

Darwin blushed and Shonda, the realist, said in her sweet Southern way, "Lynn, honey, we're fine. I like my independence. I have a good job." She did the mani-pedis at Bernice's. "I told Darwin we do just fine, and he visits us when he can." Which Lynn translated into Darwin almost living with her and her son. "And we have time to save money." She stopped, touched Darwin's sleeve. "Darwin, honey, I could use a drink of that cider." He was off. She turned back to Lynn. "He is so sweet. I am so lucky. But I just got over five years of a terrible relationship. I was almost murdered. I want to enjoy single life a little. Besides, Lynn, honey, he almost lives with us, and he is so good with my son Cooper." The young woman watched her man return with the cider. She sighed. "What more could I want?" Lynn gave her a hug. What more, indeed!

As Lynn looked around the brewery, she could feel the old warehouse building vibrating with music and laughter. Children ran through the crowd giggling. Older adults hoisted themselves onto the tall chairs at the bistro type tables. Danny's small combo played in an alcove. The crowd appreciated the duet Johnny Perez and Jin Luft crooned as a special dedication to the loving bridal couple. Shouts came for an encore.

Throughout the evening the celebration continued until Kane as the bridal party emcee, whistled the couples to the memorial wall. Once there, the crowd became silent as Barbara placed her bouquet on the shelf next to the flag and photos and medals of one of the veterans' fallen comrades. A member of their platoon, alone in the world, had made the trio his beneficiaries. Those funds helped start the brewery. The wall had been dedicated to this man. But over time, many River Dog supporters brought in photos, medals and other memorabilia from their own service or the service of fallen family members. It was a living demonstration of love and long-lasting memories.

After Barbara placed her bridal bouquet along the ledge, she was followed by her two bridesmaids. Once the flowers rested at the wall, each woman stepped back and embraced her spouse. Someone in the crowd said, "God bless America and our heroes." Several folks shouted, "Amen." A huge cheer rang out.

Lynn had to drag Dusty away from the brewery for the last stop of the evening, the River Bend Reads Valentine's dance.

xxx

Dusty slumped in a chair against the wall of the Elks' gym. Music blasted as many of the literacy students danced to the DJ and the contemporary sounds. Was he getting too old? He had never heard any of these songs. Lynn placed a glass of cola in front of him. "How long do we have to stay?" He almost shouted to be heard. Lynn smiled at him. "Emily said she's leaving in fifteen minutes and that we could leave after she did. She said the literacy students are waiting for the old folks to leave so they can really cut loose."

Dusty rubbed his eyes. "My ears already hurt. How much more noise can they make?"

As they sat in chairs out of the way of the crowd and noise, Lynn smiled as she watched Will and Piper stroll arm and arm through the crowd of literacy grads. Will took time to introduce his wife to three of his employees. By the smiles, Lynn could tell that they were pleased that Will was congratulating them. Piper was perfect in her role as the supportive spouse, charming each person and introducing herself to their friends and relatives who had come to celebrate this education milestone.

Between the introductions to Will's staff, Piper took time to greet several parents of her students, also literacy graduates. Lynn could tell by Piper's demeanor that she was delighted to meet the parents. And Will, as Piper had done with his friends, greeted and congratulated each elementary school parent.

Lynn brushed a tear from her eye. Dusty leaned over. "Is something wrong?"

She shook her head and pointed to Will and Piper. "They are being very gracious to the students they know here. Will told me when we walked in that he spotted some of his employees. I'm guessing Piper has found some of the parents with children at her school

Dusty located them in the crowd and smiled. "They're letting all those folks know how proud they are of the work these grads have accomplished." He threw an arm around his wife. "I guess this evening isn't all bad."

When Piper and Will found them, Will said, "I gotta get out of here before my hearing goes."

"I'm with you, pal," agreed Dusty.

Lynn and Piper followed the men to the car. "I love this event every year," said Piper. She grabbed Lynn's arm as they walked carefully through the gravel parking lot. "Each year I see more of my parents. I've invited this year's grads to come to the school for a special parent's read day so their kids can show them off."

Lynn grinned. "Are they all interested in coming?"

"Of course," replied the determined principal. "We have cookies and everything. Who can say 'no' to Umberto's special cookies?"

"Special cookies?"

"He makes small cookies with happy faces for all the students and several big cookies for the new parent readers decorated with big yellow seals like a diploma." Piper slid into the back seat of Dusty's car and continued, "I even send big cookies over for Will to give his employees who have graduated."

"It's pretty cheesy," offered Will, "but they all love it. And this year Piper included a cookie for Sean."

"Because he paid for it all," concluded Piper.

"What?" laughed Lynn.

Piper explained, "When he heard what I usually did for the parents and Will's workers, he liked the idea so much he suggested we increase the order." She sighed. "He told Nathan and now Taft Manufacturing does the same thing."

"Cookies for knowledge?" asked Dusty.

"Yep," yawned Will. It had been a busy weekend.

xxx

Once back home, Dusty took the dog out for one last inspection of the yard. On his return, he turned out the lights and locked up. He found Lynn in the den watching a TV news report. She looked up. "This virus talk is getting serious. Folks are suggesting we all quarantine or something."

He sat beside her and put an arm around her. "That's what the emergency manager and the county health director are saying. So don't be surprised."

"What would happen?"

"It's a little vague. We're waiting for CDC and the federal government to outline directions. I think we'll see some sort of national shutdown as people try to control its spread. I'd go shopping during the week and stock up on some staples." He hugged her. "Just think, you and me alone for a few weeks."

"I heard they might send kids home from college. Jason would be here."

"He eats a lot. You really better stock up." He kissed her. "I don't think we'll see anything for a few more weeks."

"What did you think about the weddings this weekend?" She cuddled into him.

"I was glad to see Doug find a good woman. I don't know Zeke well, but Mars says Barbara turned him into a focused and successful businessman. I know Miz Masterson is pleased."

"She wants the best for her grandsons," agreed Lynn. "She just has to get Shonda and Darwin married. They don't seem to think it's urgent. Shonda tells everyone she likes her independence."

"Yeah," laughed Dusty. "Darwin doesn't care because her definition of independence is letting him be her live-in boyfriend."

"I can understand why she's marriage shy," said Lynn in a thoughtful voice. "Her ex-husband almost killed her and her son."

Dusty pulled her into an embrace. "All those folks happily married. I think we should celebrate marriage." He gave her a kiss that left her breathless. She slumped into him. "I see you agree," he said as he pulled her to her feet and led her upstairs.

CHAPTER 4

"Should I call him?" Piper asked Lynn as they met for an early breakfast. "Doyle has to present his big report today. Should I call and wish him luck? Or call later? I want to let him know I'm interested." Doyle was her middle son, a junior in engineering at the state university.

Lynn looked around the elementary school cafeteria. "How many kids do you feed every morning?" There were youngsters crowded at tables eating scrambled eggs and drinking milk. Bookbags were scattered against the walls. Teachers and cafeteria workers were on duty containing the morning energy.

"About seventy-eight percent of my students qualify for free or reduced meals." Piper scanned the room and smiled at all the youngsters. "You haven't answered my question. Should I call?"

Lynn shook her head. "You'll probably wake him up if you call now. Besides, you know how he worries, talking to you will just add to his angst." Lynn played with her breakfast. "Why am I here? It isn't to talk about Doyle."

"My staff and I want to know if there is more we can do for Sharing Shelter." Piper was interrupted as she turned to grab a youngster running past the table, holding him until the teacher could take him off her hands. Piper had a brief word with the student, then returned to Lynn.

Sharing Shelter was a program Piper helped initiate to find shelter for homeless families with school aged children. The Philanthropies offered funds and local churches offered space while the Board of Education led the way in identifying needy families. Piper picked up her tray and said to Lynn, "Let's go to my office."

Once settled, the tiny principal began, "My staff has conducted an informal, but informative, study that shows how kids' grades improve when they're given shelter in the churches and the benefits of finally getting semi-permanent housing. We can track improvements through reading scores and through behavior." She sat behind her desk and Lynn saw the care and concern Piper had for her students. "We want more shelters. How can we get it done?"

xxx

"Hey, Doyle," greeted the dark eyed young woman as she placed her breakfast tray at his table in the campus cafeteria. The young man had been a million miles away. Lori Santiago studied him and asked, "You still worried about that presentation this morning?"

"Yeah, and they pushed it back an hour, so now I have more time to panic." He hadn't touched his breakfast. Lori began attacking her yogurt and fruit. As she ate, the blond and blue-eyed engineering student delineated his concerns, "I'm worried that the projector will eat my flashdrive and my presentation will bomb. Maybe the power will go out and I'll have to draw diagrams on the white board. Maybe I'll throw up in mid-sentence. Maybe I'll trip and bash my head then forget everything." He toyed with his cereal. "And I didn't get a haircut." He threw himself back against his chair and stared at his old friend.

Pushing her dark hair behind her ears in an automatic gesture, Lori laughed at his monologue but stopped when she saw the distress on his face. "I can give you a haircut," she offered.

"What do you know about haircuts? You're a computer geek." They laughed at Doyle's usual jab at her major course of study.

"My uncle's a barber and I used to help him, you know, sweep the floors and things."

"By sweeping the floor you learned how to cut hair?"

She looked at Doyle's blond, curly hair. "You can get away with just a trim at the back of your neck. Then you can go to your own barber later. Where do you go?"

"Some guy in the dorm cuts it."

"Then why aren't you going to him?"

"He got drunk last night and I was afraid of what he might do." Doyle shrugged and Lori laughed again.

"Come to my apartment. We'll get you ready for this big event." They finished breakfast and walked through campus to the student apartments a few blocks away.

"Why do you eat at the cafeteria if you have this place?" Doyle asked as they entered the apartment with its durable, but unstylish, furniture.

"Because," Lori said as she closed the door, "I don't want to cook and the other girls don't either."

"You'll have to learn someday when you get married." Doyle flopped on the couch and watched as Lori pulled a hair cutting clipper set from a hall closet. "Whatever happened to that guy you were seeing last semester?"

"He was a jerk." Lori brought a chair from the kitchen into the middle of the living room and motioned Doyle to take a seat. "He had no--"

"Dick?" offered Doyle. She popped him on the top of the head, then draped a plastic protective cover over him.

"He was too interested in getting into my pants and not interested enough in anything else," explained Lori as she prepared the clippers. "He thought I should do his laundry and clean his apartment."

"What?" Doyle moved his head and Lori popped him again.

"Do that once more and I'll shave your whole head."

Doyle sat quietly as he imagined himself bald along with all the other disasters that could happen today. Lori shaved his neck and trimmed around his ears. Then she blew on his neck. Doyle drew his neck down into his shirt. "What's wrong?" she asked.

"My barber doesn't blow on my neck." He could see the goose bumps on his arms from the sensation of her breath.

"I'll get some powder. I was just trying to clean the hair off your neck." She sounded disgusted with his attitude. After all, how long had they been friends?

"Powder?" he squealed. "Then I'll smell like a girl."

"Here, smell. It's called 'Sea Breeze.' You'll smell like a surfer."

"I just want to smell like a competent engineer," he moaned. The way he hung his head and the sound of his voice pulled at something inside Lori. She looked at this young man who had been her friend for several years, ever since they had met when his mother married her father's best friend. She stared at his neck, all shaved and powdered; she looked at his head hanging down as he contemplated his presentation. She thought about kissing him. As she moved to place a gentle kiss on his neck, Doyle raised his head and bumped her brow. He jumped from the chair.

"Are you okay?" He moved quickly and all the hair resting on his plastic cover slid to the floor. They looked down at the small pile of blonde curls.

Lori took his hand. "You sit and calm down. I'll vacuum this up then we can walk back to campus for your big meeting." She checked her watch. "I have a class in twenty minutes anyway." She vacuumed up the hair, replaced the clippers and returned the chair to its spot in the kitchen. "Come on."

As they walked back to campus Doyle said, "Thanks. What do I owe you?" He turned to her and smiled.

Lori wasn't prepared for the impact of his smile. She immediately dropped her gaze to the sidewalk as though she were thinking. Finally, she said, "How about dinner, Friday night?" Then she panicked. "I mean, if you don't have a date or something."

"What date? I'm an engineer, remember?"

xxx

Sean Hennessey found his good friend Lynn Powers sitting at a table in the coffee shop staring at nothing. She was deep in thought, not even noticing when he took a seat at her table. "Got a big problem to solve?" he asked.

She was startled and bobbled her coffee mug, grabbing it before it tipped over. "Sean!" She dabbed at the few drops of coffee on the table. "I didn't. I mean I wasn't. . ."

"You were a thousand miles away." He stirred his coffee. He was retired from the Coast Guard, a tall man with fading red hair touched by the morning sun streaming through the coffee shop skylight.

"I'm awash in success." Lynn frowned. He waited. She continued, "A year or so ago several preachers helped our community address the issue of homeless families by offering space in their churches as shelter."

"Your Sharing Shelter program!" He grinned, happy to be in the loop. Lynn squinted at him trying to remember if she had asked him for donations to the program. Then she panicked. How could she forget a donor? Was she losing it? Then she calmed. If he knows about the program, he must be a supporter! She smirked to herself. She was married to a detective; she could detect or deduce or something. She pulled herself together to respond to one of her generous donors.

"You read my mind." She sipped her coffee, now cold. "I just met with Piper. She wants more places to shelter families. She told me that her teachers have done an informal study that shows once the kids at her school enter this program, their grades and behavior improve."

Sean hung his head. He volunteered at Piper's school twice a week. He was certain he knew many of the children benefiting from this program. He blew out his breath. "What can I do?"

Lynn wanted to hug him. He was such a generous man. "Nothing yet. We need to find more shelter space. I could use an empty motel." She smiled at her favorite donor. "I told Piper I would bring some folks together."

"I have plenty of space at my house."

She did hug him. "That's not a good idea. It might even be dangerous. Don't worry. I'll find a way to get your money for this program."

He nodded and stood up as his friend Nathan Taft came into the shop. "I see you and Nathan have a meeting. I'll be on my way."

"It's not a meeting. It's just coffee." Sean smiled. It hadn't been so long ago that he had no friends to share coffee. Now he had plenty. Caffeine and friends - what a drug!

Lynn greeted Nathan then left the shop, taking her problem with her. Nathan ordered his drink and soon settled at the table with a plate of fruit and something lo-cal to drink. Sean sniffed in distain. One of those half-latt, skim somethings. He squinted at the fruit plate, another insult, and waved to Chen Lee, who quickly brought over a plate of orange-cranberry scones.

"What do you make of this virus talk?" Nathan asked his friend, trying to ignore the high calorie temptations.

Sean pushed the scones toward Nathan and slid a few grapes from the fruit plate onto his napkin. "It's above my pay grade," said the retired Coast Guard chief. "If it gets here, I'll try to avoid it. In the meantime, I got things to do."

Nathan chuckled. He loved these coffee breaks with his newest friend. "I'm just worried about little Olivia and the baby." Nathan lived with his nephew, Buck Rawlings, and his wife and children.

"If things get really serious," offered Sean, "You can come live with me so the kids are safe from your germs."

Nathan scowled at him then began to laugh. "Thank you, my friend. I'll stay where I am. I don't want to give up Cook's dinners."

"You got me there," confessed Sean. "Uncle Chicken is my chef in residence. If he can pack it to carry out, I order it."

And that's how two good friends spent a morning while the daffodils pushed their heads up for spring.

Chapter 5

It was quiet in the Philanthropies office at the end of the day. Amelia's Maids had arrived to do the weekly cleaning. Lucia and Juan, the regular cleaners, had just moved into the conference room to begin their evening work. Lynn and Nelda were finishing up their work of the day when they heard frantic cries from Lucia. Racing into the conference room, they found Juan covered in glittery hearts and Lucia sprawled on a chair laughing.

The sight was enough for Lynn and Nelda to join in her mirth. Juan was holding the long hose of the vacuum, standing at the window blinds looking forlorn as dozens half-inch glittery hearts clung to his clothing. His mother continued to laugh, waving her arm at his hair and the hearts clinging to his dark curls.

Nelda, ever the unflappable assistant, cleared the laughter from her voice. "Those literacy people left that behind."

It was obvious to Lynn that the hearts were the remnants of the River Bend Reads decorating committee efforts. She nodded. "I remember Emily telling them to use up all the supplies."

Sagely Nelda nodded. "That committee rebelled."

Lucia finally caught her breath. "Juan was cleaning the top covering of the blinds and he knocked a small lid to the floor. It was filled with hearts." She pointed and laughed again. Juan continued to stand in heart felt silence. Lucia took the vacuum hose and cleaned his clothing and hair.

Nelda suggested, "We better look at the other windows." Juan nodded and dragged a chair to a window. Once on the chair he gently felt along the top of the cornice. Grinning he pulled down another small lid filled with hearts.

At that discovery Lynn said, "We better look for more decorations. I guess they got tired and hid things from Emily." Everyone nodded and grinned.

After a search of the room they surveyed the treasure. Five small lids filled with glittery hearts, three rolls of red crepe paper, two shiny big mylar heart balloons, deflated, and seven Styrofoam hearts about five inches wide. Nelda sniffed, "They had so much no one noticed or missed these things."

"Let's throw this all out," said Lynn. Then she scowled at her conspirators. "And no one tells Emily." They all nodded.

xxx

Detective Teniquia LaMont sat at her desk exhausted. In anticipation of this virus, the county health department was getting everyone briefed and ready. She had been assigned as the Sheriff's representative to the meeting. She had learned more than she wanted to know about viruses, quarantine, health precautions and potential government responses to this outbreak based on projected severity. Ugh!

She looked at the clock. Only four-thirty. She still had work to do. But her mind felt like mush. She stared at her desk and noticed the thick folder that had been pushed to the bottom of her in-box. Bill Halstead, hmm.   Last year Bill, at that time a hobo, had helped find little Holly Hardesty who had wandered off. During the search Bill had confided that he had left home when his daughter died. He felt responsible because she had run into the street on his watch and had been killed. Dusty had suggested that Bill's effort to protect Holly was sort of his redemption. With that thought the hobo had agreed to let Tee find his family and facilitate a reunion. All very heartwarming, a made-for-TV movie type reunion.

Until Bill's daughter, Wanda, a very pregnant police officer from Huntington, Indiana, became suspicious. As fellow officers Teniquia and Wanda had kept in touch, Tee

36

remembered the conversation as Wanda had confided, "There's something about him that isn't true."

"True?" her new friend in River Bend had asked.

Wanda had sighed into the phone. "I remember my father's brother, Uncle Henry. Daddy should be similar, but he's different somehow. He seems smarter."

Tee had laughed. "That's not a crime. What does your mother say?"

"That's interesting. She seems happy, almost content."

"That's what sex will do for you."

Wanda had gasped. "I don't think they do it."

"How would you know?"

"I'm a detective, even though I'm twenty months pregnant. He sleeps in a separate bedroom, my old room. From what I had heard about Daddy, he used to be a real handyman. This daddy can't seem to fix things now that he's returned. He does do a wonderful job taking care of the yard. But if something breaks, he's lost."

"The world has changed since he dropped out. Things are more complex than they used to be." Wanda had heard Tee munching on her lunch as she spoke. "You could always run his prints."

There had been a pause. "I don't have any prints. But I can send you Daddy's old prints from when he was hired by the school board and had to have a background check."

"We printed him here when I brought him to the jail. Send me the old prints. I'll follow-up here."

And Tee had followed up. At the beginning, she had investigated Bill and compared fingerprints with Wanda's father, Wayne. It was easy enough to find out that Bill was not Wayne and had been a professor at Drake University in Des Moines, Iowa. Bill had verified all the information with Wanda. They all learned that Bill had traveled with Wayne for a long time and was with him at his death. But Wanda's baby arrived and nothing more happened. Then one day Tee received additional information. She had had the report for almost four months now. She blamed her inaction on crime in River Bend, but the truth was that she couldn't believe that Bill, the gentle hobo, and as she now knew him as the fake father to her friend Wanda, was wanted for questioning in a murder investigation. She pulled out the file and reviewed all that she had discovered. Now it was time to find out why William Garner Halstead aka Bill was a person of interest in a murder.

Tee knew what that thick file contained. Throughout the last months as time allowed she had started detecting. She soon found that William Halstead had been an English Lit professor with a minor in philosophy. He had taught, until his disappearance, at Drake University in Des Moines. Tee knew that was a prestigious university, so William must have had talent, but had destroyed himself and his career with drink and drugs. So sad.

She had next delved into the archives of the Des Moines Register to get some background on a twenty-year old murder. The murder victim had been a woman, Darla Somerall. She was referred to by the reporter as 'a woman with suspicious links to the underworld.' Apparently she had been found dead in her home and information on her answer machine suggested that William Halstead, a professor at Drake, had called and indicated he would be stopping by.

Tee was conflicted, recalling that she hadn't given Wanda this information. Bill was building a great life in Huntington. Everyone was happy. She didn't want to cause a problem. In fact, maybe the murder had been solved. What a great thought! She smiled at the obvious idea. Of course, crimes were solved. Her unit did it every day. They probably had the resources in Des Moines to do it faster. With that happy thought to encourage her, she checked the office clock and placed a call to the Des Moines police.

xxx

Doyle was delighted with the outcome of his presentation. His research advisor had praised its organization, one of the other panel members suggested that he offer his report to the school's engineering magazine. He looked forward to dining with Lori to share his success and decided that this evening was a perfect time to find someplace off campus. In spite of all his recent academic success and all that he had to think about, he kept having random thoughts and shivers as he recalled feeling her breath on his neck.

"Where are we going?" asked Lori as she expected to hear the name of one of the local student eateries.

The state university was in the state capitol which made sense to everyone affiliated with either enterprise. That's why there was a somewhat cosmopolitan air around the fringes of campus, like restaurants with interesting food, cluttered with political hangers-on while the legislature was in session and frequented by real people and occasionally by students at other times.

"Over to Leo's. You know the place?"

"Wow, you must have had a great presentation!" Lori patted his arm as he opened the car door.

"Yeah." He smiled to himself as he trotted around to his car door.

When he settled into the driver's seat, she said, "Tell me everything. Did they mention how great your hair looked?"

"That was the first thing my advisor said." He made a face at her. As they drove away from campus, Doyle told her everything, every word that he could remember. His excitement and enthusiasm mounted as he continued his report through dinner, not allowing Lori to do more than ask a question or two.

39

As they left the restaurant Doyle asked, "Would you like to walk around this neighborhood for a bit?" Lori noticed that as night settled, lights had come on, and the neighborhood around Leo's was alive with people walking dogs and children playing in the park at the end of the block. Everyone was enjoying springtime in Raleigh. "I like this place," offered Doyle. "It reminds me of River Bend and the park and stuff."

Lori put her hand on his arm as they walked. "Did you call your mother and tell her about your presentation?"

"No, I thought I'd do it in the morning when I usually call." Doyle walked along finding that he had nothing more to say because he was distracted by too many sensations all focused on Lori. Walking through the small park, they sat on a bench to watch the people who had also come out for an evening stroll. A small child ran over to them, following a ball that skittered toward their seat. Doyle reached under the bench and got the ball, holding it out for the little boy to take back.

"Can you throw it, mister?" the youngster asked moving away from Doyle. He tossed the ball gently into the air and they watched as it arced lazily overhead, and the boy caught it. They applauded and he waved as he returned to his friends.

Lori moved closer and Doyle raised his arm to place it around her shoulders. "That was sweet," she said. "You're sweet." She put her head on his shoulder. They sat without speaking. Doyle took the hand she had resting on her lap and then he tilted his head to rest on hers. They sat in silence for some moments and then they both sighed.

Startled by the moment, Doyle stood, "I thought we could get some dessert." He threw out his arm indicating a coffee shop and an ice cream parlor.

Lori looked up at him from the bench, took a deep breath and said, "I like just sitting here with you." He thought about her remark, searching her eyes to see if she was teasing. She gave him a shy smile but didn't turn away from his gaze. Returning to the bench he slowly put his arm around her again. They watched their little friend chase his ball. They watched an elderly couple walking their dog. They watched some parents put their little toddler on a small swing. Finally, they looked at one another and Doyle kissed the lips of the most beautiful girl in his world. It was a slow and gentle kiss. They both seemed to know that there was no hurry, they would have the rest of their lives together for all the kissing and loving to come.

CHAPTER 6

Lynn waved as Juan pulled his old truck into her yard. He worked with his mother for Amelia's Maids during the week and picked up extra money on weekends doing gardening. "Thank you for coming by this morning," Lynn said as he walked with her to the old barn on her property. "We keep our gardening things in here." The old barn was filled with all the equipment Bri Llewellyn needed to work on Will's vineyard. It also contained all of Lynn's gardening tools, Jim's old office files, Dusty's old police equipment, and an old motorcycle that everyone used. In fact, every spring Lynn thought about a clean-out, and every spring no one could part with anything. The mess just expanded. She was certain that one day the barn would explode.

Juan stood at the door and frowned. "I have things in my truck." He knew better than to forage in this sacred space of iconic memories - or, as the professionals call it, junk.

Lynn nodded. She didn't want to move all of the vineyard equipment and the newest filing cabinets to get to her rakes and shovels. She walked out of the barn and closed the door. "Let me show you what I want done today." They walked together toward the garden Lynn had created as a memorial to her friend Susan Carmichael, who had been murdered. Lynn had promised to keep the perennials for Susan's daughter to claim once she had her own garden. "Let's clean the debris out of these azaleas so we can enjoy the blooms in a few weeks. And look for some early hostas that we can separate and plant in some other spots along the edge." Juan nodded as she spoke.

While they worked Dusty walked into the yard. "I have to go out to the farm."

"Dusty, I want you to meet Juan. He's helping me garden today."

Dusty shook the young man's hand, gave a tepid smile and said to his wife, "I'll be home for dinner. My mother wants us to clean stuff out of her attic."

As he pulled away, Lynn said, "Sons are sons forever." She looked at Juan. "I watch how you help your mother when you clean my office. You work very hard."

Juan cast his eyes down in embarrassment. "She needs someone to look after her." He took a deep breath. "She always stayed by me, even in my troubles." Lynn looked puzzled. He explained, "I was in prison for eighteen months. It was stupid. I mean I was stupid. I didn't listen to my mother. I thought I would listen to my friends instead. They ran and I got caught. Only my mother stayed with me."

Lynn patted his arm. "And in the long run, you'll always look after her. She's very lucky. You learned a hard lesson."

"*Si.*"

"You aren't very old." Lynn thought he might be only a year or two older than her son, Jason.

"I am twenty-three."

"How long have you been out of prison?"

"Six months." He avoided her eyes because he knew she wanted to know what he had planned for the rest of his life. He knew he didn't want to be a maid with his mother.

"Did you take any classes in prison or learn a trade?"

"I got my GED." Now he really was embarrassed. She knew he was a high school dropout. He rushed on, "I also took some college classes so I could save money and continue with some schooling when I got out." He anticipated her next question. "I would like to be a CNA or an EMT. But I need tuition."

"You're a hard worker. Something will turn up." Lynn felt helpless quoting a stupid platitude. It was the best she could do. Her mind was racing. She was wondering if she could convince Amelia Rawlings, owner of Amelia's Maids, to establish an employee scholarship fund. Lynn slapped her working gloves against her thigh. "Come on, let's finish this work."

xxx

"Doyle finally called," announced Piper as she and Will walked into Lynn's house. "He usually calls in the morning but said he had too much to do this morning. His oral report went well." She settled at the table in the kitchen. They were waiting for Dusty to finish dressing for dinner.

"You were worried about nothing," said Will as he opened a beer.

Piper was thoughtful. "He sounded different. I hope he wasn't lying to me. He sounded like he was keeping a secret."

Will chuckled. "Did he hint at her name?"

"Don't be silly," answered Piper. "Doyle always tells me if he's had a date. Usually he wants to know if he did anything wrong." Piper shook her head. "How can Jason date every girl on his campus and Doyle be such a wall-flower?"

"Jason dates all the girls on his campus?" Lynn was surprised at this information.

Will laughed at Lynn. "He keeps that information from you, eh? You should hear him talk at our house."

"He tells you?"

"No, we just eavesdrop," admitted Piper. She took a sip of Will's beer.

"Eavesdrop about what?" asked Dusty as he entered the kitchen.

"They said Jason dates a lot at school," said Lynn still puzzled at the knowledge.

"Yeah, Mars is always laughing at his exploits. My staff take bets on what stupid thing he'll do next." Dusty caught

Lynn's squinty-eyed look and said, "I mean what fun-loving antics he'll try."

"What do you mean?" Lynn challenged her husband.

Dusty got a beer and sat at the table. "Mars says Jason dates everyone once. Not many girls come back for a second round." Dusty used his hand to signal Lynn to calm down. "He doesn't do anything wrong. He just has a way of making an impression. You know, spilling a drink on a girl's dress, taking a girl hiking and getting them lost," Dusty drank his beer, "running over a girl's cat, setting fire to a girl's hair."

"He's never told me any of this," frowned Lynn.

"Don't worry, honey," consoled Piper, "the girl's hair grew back, and the cat was old. Where are we going for dinner?"

xxx

Heath had spent the last week working at the old family cabin. Someone had broken in. He had planned to stay there while in River Bend spying on Emily, but he had to spend time making repairs and securing the cabin first. After a long day of work he came out of the forest into the town of Portage looking for something to eat. And there it was, River Dog Brewery. Hmm, he thought, things are looking up. New people to meet, opportunities to explore.

He sat at the bar. It was an interesting place, seemingly filled with locals. Then he noticed the children. It was a family bar where everyone seemed to know everyone else. Heath figured that they started their kids drinking early in these parts. There was a big military memorial on the wall opposite the long bar while big barn doors swung open and closed on another wall as patrons entered and left.

"Damn police," muttered the woman on the next stool.

"I ain't the police," Heath replied.

"I know you ain't," countered the woman. "That there Healey." She nodded to a good-looking man talking with a man in a wheelchair. "He killed my boyfriend last summer. No remorse. Never told me he was sorry." She took a long gulp of her beer. The woman looked close to sixty, puffy with age and carrying extra weight. Her hair was a gray-orange combination balanced on top of a colorless face.

"I'll have what she's having," he told the bartender who slid a drink and a bowl of pretzels his way. With his plans it would be good to have some information on the local cops. Turning back to the woman he asked, "What did your boyfriend do?"

She gave Heath an appraising look, found him interesting. "He did a lot of things. I just think shooting him was too much. A little jail time would have been okay." She took another long drink. "At least I still keep getting my money."

This conversation sounded like it could be entertaining as well as informative. "How do I get some food around here?" he asked, ready to settle in for a good listen.

She shifted in her seat to give him a good look over and said, "You just order from these menus using your phone to order and pay. Some youngster will deliver." She gave him another long look. "I ain't had dinner."

"You just show me what to do and I guess I can buy you something, too." He leaned against her shoulder. "I want to hear about this boyfriend of yours and how you deal with loss. I was just widowed myself." He tried to look sad.

Over Thai food and beer Heath got to know Yetta Masterson. He enjoyed listening to the story of how her boyfriend, Rupert Rutledge, got chased through the hospital in his attempt to kill someone and jumped off the hospital roof to his death. To Heath the man sounded like a fool, but Yetta assured him that her man had money stashed away that still supported her. She also admitted that in her role as a CNA she had prepared the lethal dose for his victim. "I got them drugs and made a little cocktail for the syringe. He was going to sneak into ICU and jab the needle into the IV hose. I even told him how to get in and bought him some scrubs." She finished off her beer and Heath signaled the bartender for another. Yetta continued, "And damn that Healey," she nodded to the policeman again, "He interrupted the whole thing in ICU, the mark didn't get the poison. My man died for nothing."

He nodded toward the police officer. "Why didn't he come after you?" She looked puzzled. He continued, "You had a part in that murder attempt. Why didn't he arrest you?"

Yetta shook her head. "He didn't know about me. He never figured out where the man was staying, or where he got them drugs." She ate the last of her pizza. "I guess Healey never apologized 'cause he don't know about me. And all that money."

Heath made all the appropriate sympathetic remarks and finally invited himself to Yetta's small cottage in South End. After all that time at the cabin, a visit to Yetta's place was a good way to be in town and not be seen by Emily. Besides, Yetta seemed to have some skills he might need, like knowledge of local law enforcement, access to lethal meds, and the bonus of a queen size bed she was willing to share. She might be fifteen years older than he was, but she would be useful for a lot of his needs. And maybe he would learn more about this money she mentioned.

CHAPTER 7

"You're pretty healthy, based on your charts, Jody," said the doctor as he ambled into the examination room. "What are you here for? Some Botox?"

Jody scowled at him. She was a prim lady with a stylish bob that made no apologies for the grey in her hair. Sitting on the examining table with her examining-room-hides-nothing gown clutched in front of her, she asked, "Why would I want Botox?"

"For pouty lips," Dr. Noah grinned, "you know, in case you want to vamp someone."

She gave him a look that she had practiced for all her sixty-five years whenever she dealt with silly men. Something seemed to change as she stared at the doctor she had known for thirty-five years. His eyes sparkled, or something, and he leaned in and kissed her.

Stepping back Dr. Noah looked as stunned as his patient. "I guess," he said after he found his voice, "your lips are just fine the way they are." They stared at one another and were both startled when the nurse rushed in.

"There you are, Doctor," she announced, "I'm sorry but I was distracted by that man in room C. I didn't hold you up, did I?"

"No," replied the doctor as he moved to lean against the small desk in the room. "I was just telling Jody that now that she's a Medicare patient, she has some choices as to what she has in her physical." He cleared his throat, "She's decided to delay her pap test this year. So I'll mark her chart to make certain it's done next year." He scribbled something into the folder he had spread out on the desk. "Other than that, your lab work looks great, get your mammogram next week at the hospital and we'll see you in a year." He closed the file, slipped it under his arm and walked out.

"Okay, sweetie," smiled the nurse, "you're good to go." The nurse bustled around helping Jody off the examining table. "How long have you been coming to this office? I've only been with the doctor ten years and you were already a patient, along with that sweet husband of yours. I bet you miss him." She studied Jody, then said, "I like your new hair style. It makes you look young and cute." The nurse was flustered, "I mean younger and cuter."

Jody laughed. "I was thinking last month that Henry's been gone three years. I thought something had to change."

The nurse nodded in agreement. "It's time to move on."

"So I got all that hair cut off. Wearing it in a bun or twisted on top of my head just took too much time." She shook her head and her hair moved in the breeze and settled charmingly back down on her head.

"It makes you look different than the woman I've seen all these years," admitted the nurse.

"I've been a patient in this office for over thirty years. My husband and I were one of Noah's first patients when he came to town." She looked around for her clothing, keeping her dignity under wraps. "Thank you for remembering my husband."

The nurse said, "It doesn't seem that long," shaking her head at the mystery of time. "Get dressed and come to the desk. We'll schedule that mammogram for you." She closed the door to the room as she exited.

Jody gave a big sigh to all the empty space in the examining room and wondered at Noah's action. He and her husband had played golf together for years. Noah's wife had left him a few years ago. Jody never understood what ended their marriage. Maybe he golfed too much. Or maybe he doctored too much. She knew why her husband was dead. He worked too much. He left her with a family business to run and now she was trying to figure out what to do - retire, close it down, sell it? The kids didn't want it. But it had been a good idea. Buying a shop in the business park and then evolving into everyone's back office. Thirty years ago no one understood the concept of back office and now she was one.

She smiled to herself. Her small business enterprise provided copying, mailing, a little IT hardware support and other services for all the small business offices in the business park as well as for many others in surrounding towns. It was a good company, had sent all the kids through college and even helped them start out on their own.

She sighed again and heard it echo around the small room. What should she do with the business now?

xxx

Collie Maddox met his attorney Beth Seymour at the piece of property he wanted to use. "Beth, my pop put in a septic system and dug a well. These are six cabins he used for migrant labor. Then government regulations got too much. After that he made a few improvements and rented them for years but didn't do much upkeep. Then that murder." She gasped. He gasped. "Oh, Beth, I'm sorry. I'm such a fool for even bringing you out here."

She was wearing sunglasses and grateful for the cover. He might not be able to see her watery eyes. And he couldn't see the pain, thought Beth. Her mother, Lily, had lived in one of these cabins for years because Mr. Maddox had been a friend to Hank Seymour. Hank had at least wanted a semi-clean and safe shelter for his ex-wife to see their children on her visitation weekends. Lily's boyfriends had changed almost monthly - but the cabin was Lily's most constant homesite, especially when not in demand for farm laborers.   It   was the cabin where Beth had been molested by Mace, one of her mother's many boyfriends. It was the reason she was now

51

attending group sessions for sexual assault survivors. It was the reason she was who she was - fat and unhappy.

She pulled herself together. Adjusted her dark glasses, a delaying gesture. "Collie," she cleared her throat, "I appreciate your concern." Another adjustment. "Let me recap your land issues. You understand that this property represents an investment by your father. You think he got some funding through an agricultural program that made loans to farmers for migrant and seasonal farmworker housing." He nodded. "You wonder what restrictions are tied to the cabins and you wonder what you can do with this land."

"Yes." He took as deep breath. "I can fix them up and rent them. But must I restrict tenants to farm workers. I can tear them down. But are there restrictions or requirements that apply or repayments that I would have to make?"

Beth looked over the six sad cabins. "It's off-season. Are you renting them now?"

"I am. Lots of itinerants." He shook his head. "But they want reliable plumbing. And I don't know if it's worth updating and repairing things." He shrugged.

The attorney took one last look around. "Let me do the research. Give me a week and I'll call you with some ideas. In the meantime, you can rent but don't deal in leases."

"I never do," said Collie. "I ask folks to pay before I give them a key. One week at a time. Most only stay a few weeks."

xxx

Lynn had given a lot of thought to Piper's information about student success for those whose families were given shelter. She finally decided to invite some of her bigger donors to listen to Piper's report. Sean Hennessey, Nathan Taft, and Emily Jacobs sat in the Philanthropies conference room. Piper had just finished with her brief, but passionate analysis of students who receive Sharing Shelter housing. The attendees looked at Lynn.

Lynn frowned. "That's where we are. I don't know what to do next." She stared glumly at her friends. "Let me give you some thoughts and context. I asked the ministers to canvas their group to find more shelter space. I've investigated some old warehouses down by the river. They're empty because the last several high-water events weakened foundations. The owners plan to tear them down. On the upside, two families are working with Habitat and will move into their own homes this summer." Her listeners cheered. Lynn shrugged, "I've run out of ideas."

Emily wiped a tear from her eye. "As an old teacher I can appreciate Piper's findings. But I never dealt with the numbers of homeless students we seem to have today."

Almost to himself Sean asked, "Whatever happened to all those old labor camps the farmers used to have on their property for seasonal workers when I was a youngster?"

Nathan responded. "The federal government set out regulations that mandated clean water and better living conditions. Most farmers dismantled those old huts and let the workers or their crew chiefs take on housing responsibility."

"How did that work?" asked Sean. He had been gone for many years.

Nathan shrugged. "I don't know. In recent years I know local farmers have had to search for labor. They relate it back to the federal government tightening our borders and restricting illegal immigration."

They all stared at one another befuddled by federal policy, lack of farm workers and homeless children. Emily summed it up. "No problem is ever single faceted, and no solution is ever simple."

"Amen," breathed her listeners.

The tiny principal was not to be ignored. "I don't care about the federal government or foreign policy or even this virus everyone is so keen about," Piper almost pounded the table. "I want more housing for homeless students."

"Are any of those camps still standing?" asked Lynn. "We could pay the farmers the same way we pay the churches."

They all looked at her as the River Bend Oracle of housing solutions. "By golly," smiled Nathan, "I think we might find at least a dozen adequate shelters still standing."

Sean had an idea. Sort of two birds, one stone. "I have an old friend who farms. I could go out and visit him. He might know something." And, he thought to himself, I can stop by to visit his sister, Lee.

Emily smiled in approval; Nathan nodded as though a weight had been lifted. Piper and Lynn gathered closer to hear the rest of his proposal. Sean gulped as he realized they had expectations. He moved his hands in a calming gesture. "I'll just go talk with Jasper and see what I can learn. I haven't seen any labor housing on his place." They frowned. "But he may know of some old camps and things." They smiled. A tiny thread to unravel as they worked toward a solution - which they all knew wouldn't be simple or easy.

xxx

Beth Seymour had started the new year on a mission. She was going to lose weight and learn to fly. She had her father's promise that he would fund the flight lessons. February ended and she felt good about herself. She was dieting, enjoying the report from her bathroom scale that pounds were slipping slowly away. Her legal skills were in demand, and she had joined a sexual assault survivors support group.

Today was an emotional challenge, testing her resolve, courage and determination - meeting her client at that cabin, the scene of all her nightmares. It was all she could do to keep herself together and wrap up the meeting with Collie Maddox. She needed to be alone for a few hours to recalibrate or recommit or have a meltdown. If she didn't get control of this panic attack, Beth was certain she would lose all the ground she had gained and gain all the weight she had lost.

The farm! On the outskirts of River Bend was the Seymour family farm. Her father rented the farmable acres and kept the house clean and available for family gatherings. She smiled as she remembered the recent Christmas holidays and the great days of snowmobiling. But, gasp! There had also been that harrowing attempted escape on the snowmobile when she and Lynn Powers had been chased by some drug guys. Beth sighed. That was over. She and Lynn were safe and maybe she needed to spend an afternoon out at the farm just to enjoy its reliable calm.

She walked into the old farm kitchen. Memories, warmth. Then she noticed a photo of her mother. She wondered why her father kept those photos. Her mother was dead, and he had a new wife. Maybe he wanted his daughters to remember their mother. She studied the photo and groaned. The photo had been snapped at that old cabin where that man had molested her. She shuddered. Wouldn't she ever be free of those memories? She had been so proud. With the support of Lee Stahlmeier and Dr. Rita, her stepmother, she had moved forward, new year - new Beth. And now this. She clutched the photo and tears streamed down her cheeks. She began to shake.

And two of her sisters walked into the kitchen.

"Beth, no wonder we didn't see your car when we drove by the apartment." Michelle, the oldest Seymour sister, tossed her coat on a chair, tossed car keys on the table, and fluffed her hair. She froze as she noticed Beth's tears. "Honey, what's wrong?" Ronnie, the second sister already had her arms around Beth even as Michelle asked the question.

When Beth had finally opened up to Dr, Rita and then explained the trauma to her father, she had asked both of them to help keep the secret from her sisters. She had endured the pain as a child because the perpetrator had threatened her sisters if Beth revealed his actions. She was drawing strength from counseling and group support, but she was not ready to talk to her sisters. And here she was facing the sisters she loved and wanted to protect. She cried harder - deep sobs as Ronnie and Michelle held her and whispered their love and concern promising to make everything right in Beth's world. Then they waited for an explanation.

Beth looked at them, saw the love and concern. It was time. They were together. She had to tell them. Taking a deep breath, she began, "Once when we were visiting mother one of her boyfriends molested me." It was out. It was said. The young women processed what they had heard.

"Mace!" growled Michelle. Mace was the man who had murdered their mother.

"Why didn't you tell us?" Ronnie demanded.

"He said he would kill Patti Ann." They embraced her again, confirmed their love, and marveled at her bravery and long silence.

"Does Dad know?"

She nodded. "He and Rita have been helping me. I don't know how they knew but they suspected something, and Rita took me to meet some people and I go to a survivors' group, and I was doing so well."

"Was?" Sisters didn't miss much.

"I met a client out at those cabins today." Beth took a deep breath. "It was all I could do to finish the meeting and get here to have a panic attack." She gave them a weak smile.

"Who would do such a thing?" Michelle demanded.

Beth made a calming gesture. "It was business. Collie Maddox wants advice on what to do with the land."

"Burn the cabins," snarled a militant Ronnie.

Beth did laugh at gentle Ronnie's ire. "I'm doing okay. This was just a blip. Things are working out for me."

"You have been smiling more," said Michelle as she brushed Beth's hair back from her face and dabbed her tears with a kitchen towel. "And you've lost weight." Michelle stepped back to give Beth the once over.

"Rita put you on a diet!" declared Ronnie.

Beth smiled, chiding herself for being worried about her sisters' response. And here they were wrapping her in love and support. How could something so sad and traumatic turn out to feel so good! "And I'm going to take flying lessons as soon as I lose a little more weight. Daddy said he'd even pay for them."

Now the sisters had all sorts of questions. Most of all they wanted to be reassured that Beth was okay. They didn't ask for details but assured her that they would do all they could to help.

"But why are you all here?" Beth asked as she threw her arm out to indicate the old farm kitchen.

Michelle rolled her eyes. "This virus thing. Patti Ann says if she gets sent home from school, she should quarantine here for a bit so she doesn't make anyone sick, especially Sophie Grayson." Once Michelle married H. Lawrence Grayson, Patti Ann, the youngest Seymour sister had moved in with his mother during breaks from college. It was a solution that worked for everyone, especially Hank Seymour and his new wife, Dr. Rita, and H. Lawrence and his lovely bride, Michelle Seymour.

"She's coming home?" asked Beth.

Ronnie shrugged. "No one is certain when we'll all go into lockdown. But Patti Ann thinks senior pre-med students may be sent home for a few weeks and then asked to work hospitals where they are assigned to medical school if things get serious."

Michelle added, "She's just asked us to make certain the house is cleaned and filled with food." They looked around the kitchen. With the telepathy sisters seem to have, they nodded to one another and began to ready the house for Patti Ann.

CHAPTER 8

Emily Jacobs stopped at the grocery store before going home. All those weeks of working on the Valentine's dance had been so tiring and then the dance itself. She had hardly had time to eat right. She loved her independence even as she aged, but maybe she should give some thought to that retirement community where her friend Thel Bergman had moved. Thel and her husband, the old sheriff, seemed to enjoy life there and Bergy found it very accommodating for his new life in a wheelchair. And as Thel always reminded Emily, "Someone else does the cooking." In her fatigue, Emily thought that not having to cook sounded like a favorable argument.

She also had to admit that it was lonely out in the country, that big house on all those acres. But she had reliable help. Amelia's Maids came in twice a week and Lucia, the regular maid, brought her son, Juan, to help with big things. Juan even came sometimes to help with gardening. Her life wasn't so bad.

Balancing her recyclable grocery bag on one wrist she juggled her key fob and clicked the car door open. She dropped the bag in the back and gave some thought to stopping at the nursery. This was perfect weather to get some pansies into the ground. And she could always reconnoiter, see what Tyrell's was going to have for later spring plantings. She smiled. Mr. Tyrell always saved a few special items for her to experiment with each spring and summer. Maybe staying at her place was best. Her garden was such a joy.

As Emily drove toward the nursery, she had no idea she was being followed. A dark SUV had been watching her for several days. The driver was her grandson-in-law, Heath

Dawson, the second husband of her deceased granddaughter, Alicia.

Alicia had been dead for a year. When Heath had married Alicia and moved into an easy life in Hilton Head, he had accepted the responsibility for her three children. Their father had died several years earlier. When Alicia was diagnosed with pancreatic cancer Heath had stepped in, urging Alicia to enroll the kids in a Charleston boarding school. He had argued that they would be close enough to their Hilton Head home to visit often but they would be away from the daily drama of her sickness. Once she died, Heath kept the children in boarding school explaining to them and their great-grandmother that he was not an appropriate father figure. However, he encouraged a shared vacation and frequent contact with Emily. She might not trust him, but he seemed to do all the right things and she couldn't complain.

Heath had a plan to gain financial independence and part of the plan was to make certain Emily accepted that he was reliable. His plan was playing out now. After Alicia's death, he thought he would control his late wife's money, but he learned that Emily, the matriarch of the family, controlled most of the money. In her will Alicia had named Heath the children's guardian. He received generous funds from the family trust. It kept the kids in boarding school while he led a leisurely, indolent life with few responsibilities. But he wanted it all - all the money, all to himself.

The sad truth for him was that until Emily died, she controlled everything. Once she died the kids got the money and as their guardian, he would control the funds until they reached a specified age. At that point, when the eldest reached twenty-one, she and her advisors would control the trust and Heath would be out of money and out of luck. Ergo, Emily and the kids had to die - soon - before she changed her will.

Heath would have worked through his inheritance problem over time, but he had found Emily's will during the Christmas holidays. He had driven to River Bend to bring her back to Hilton Head for a real family holiday. As he liked to do whenever he visited Emily, he found time to go through records and private papers. He was stunned when he came upon her current will covered with edits and notes to her lawyer. He had searched her desk and found a note on her January calendar to contact the guy about redoing her will in the new year.

Fortunately for Heath, he was able to drag out the holidays and misplace the file containing the annotated document, so he felt confident that Emily hadn't had time to get the information to her attorney. But he knew he had to hurry his timetable.

He had given this a lot of thought. Emily was old. He could wait her out and then as guardian of three pre-teens, take the money and disappear. Or he could eliminate Emily and then over time, eliminate one kid after another. No, he thought, someone would get suspicious. So his plan, the one he had been working on, was to get rid of everyone at once. He'd start with Emily, which would make the kids her heirs. Then any time after Emily's death they would have some sort of accident. He had a vague idea of helping Emily take a fall that would break her neck while he was here in River Bend. The kids were another story. He was planning on using that old cabin that their mother had used as an art studio, the one Emily's husband had purchased years ago. It would be easy to explain it as a sentimental place. An explosion or poison from old art supplies - something would come to him. Next summer would be the time.

But first Emily.

xxx

61

The doorbell chimed. Jody was startled out of one of her reveries while sitting in her kitchen staring out the window. They seemed to happen hourly - those reveries. She was distracted by so many possible decisions these days. Padding to the front door in her stocking feet, she was startled when she opened it to find Noah.

"I came to apologize," he said. She stepped back and allowed him to enter.

"For what?"

"Kissing you."

"That was three days ago. You must not be very sorry."

He moved closer to her and pecked her cheek. "I don't think I'm sorry at all. But it was the only line I thought you would accept and let me in." He kissed her softly on her lips. "You looked different in my office."

She stared at him. "I got my hair cut. It took you three days to realize I looked different?"

"Are you offended? Do you want me to leave?"

She sighed and reminded herself that she was doing that a lot lately. "Come in. We can talk." She led the way into her kitchen, flipped on some lights and grabbing the remote, turned off the little TV on the counter.

Noah looked around the room. A glass of wine sat on the table beside a newspaper crossword puzzle. "Did you get thirty-six down today?"

"I was just trying to figure it out." She squinted at the puzzle grid, then said, "Sit down. Do you want some wine?"

He settled himself in the chair and pulled the newspaper closer so that he could study her progress on the crossword. "Do you think better with wine?"

Jody got another wine glass and turned toward her guest. He was her age, about medium height, but slender and he had grey-black hair that curled around his ears because he always seemed to need a haircut. After pouring wine into his glass, she sat in her chair across from him and the crossword. "Have you had dinner?"

He looked at her over the top of his glasses. "It's nine-thirty. Haven't you eaten yet?"

"It must not be too late if you're at my front door." She scowled at him.

"I just left the hospital." He sighed. It was the same sound Jody had been making for the last few months.

"And you're wondering if you should continue," she said.

He gasped. "How did you know?"

"We're the same age, Noah. I have the same questions about my life."

"Have you made any decisions?" He looked eager for answers.

"Why? Will my answers help you?" Her look challenged him.

"Maybe, because I can't seem to organize my thoughts, but I feel something has to change." He sketched some letters into the crossword grid.

"I know what you mean." They sat there in the kitchen listening to the ice maker drop cubes into a bin in the freezer.

"I think that's why I kissed you." He was sixty-five and confused.

"Three days ago, or tonight?" She was sixty-five and curious.

"Both. It's time for some changes." He threw himself back against the chair.

"You're going to start kissing your patients?"

"No, just you." He tilted his head and reminded her of a puzzled puppy.

She stared at him wondering if getting old explained his attitude. "My challenges are more along the lines of what to do with the business, not kissing people."

"You haven't thought about kissing any one since Henry died?" Noah was curious and interested.

She blushed. "Every now and then." He grinned at her. "Are you volunteering?" she asked, "Is that why your wife left you, you kissed other women?"

His face saddened. "She left because she was tired of waiting for me every evening. I was at work more than I was home. Sometimes I think I worked because I didn't find anything at home."

"She wasn't faithful?" gasped Jody.

"She was. But after those early years of waiting, she developed a lot of interests that didn't include me." He played with his wine glass.

"Where is she now?"

"She moved to one of those Florida retirement cities and seems to have a grand time, playing bridge, riding her bicycle, dancing. Her life is filled with activity and a man or two who seem to have as much time as she has." It was a painful confession for Noah to make and it showed on his face.

"Do you see yourself retiring and moving to one of those places?" asked Jody.

"No, do you?"

"I don't know what I see me doing. The kids are all settled. The two that are married are up to their eyeballs in jobs and kids' activities. They're close enough for quick visits, but I don't see them returning to take care of me in my old age."

Noah laughed. "I'm your doctor. Your old age is a decade or two away. What do you plan to do in the meantime?"

"That's a good question. And I think it's the same one you have." Jody challenged him to deny it.

"You're right. We're two lost souls. You wanna be lost together?" He grinned at her with a puppy's eagerness.

She had to smile. "I wouldn't mind finding someone my own age to talk with about my old age choices." He opened his mouth to argue, but she held up her hand to silence him. "I know I'm not old in your professional opinion, but I think I should be making some decisions for myself for some long-term solutions so that my kids aren't making them for me because I'm too old and senile."

"What kind of decisions?" He reached out and took her hand.

"What should I do with the business?" With great effort she held in another sigh.

"Is it successful?" He massaged her fingers.

"Yes. I think more than Henry ever imaged. But the kids don't want it. How much longer should I keep it up? How would I sell it?" She poured more wine into their glasses.

"How many employees do you have?"

"Five. I could expand the hours and hire two more. But I don't know if that's a good move." They were quiet as Jody placed some crackers and a tapenade spread on the table. "Are you thinking of retiring? And how do you close down a medical practice? What about your patients?"

That did it! Noah flooded her kitchen with his concerns, retirement, a future to do what? His children, an ex-wife, and one very old parent. By midnight they had finished two bottles of wine, the tapenade, several leftover pieces of cheese from the refrigerator, a can of mixed nuts and half a box of crackers.

Walking him to the door, Jody said, "I still can't believe how late it is. But I'm glad you came by. I needed some help organizing my thoughts."

He kissed her cheek. "Me, too. Can I come back to talk some more?"

"Any time. But next time you supply the wine."

"It's a deal." He kissed her lips. "And I like the haircut." Another lingering kiss and he was out the door.

CHAPTER 9

Sean found himself driving along the barren countryside on a sunny, crisp afternoon. In a few months the crops would be pushing out of the earth. But today the fields looked ignored and abandoned. He had promised Lynn and her friends that he would meet with his old friend Jasper Stahlmeier to inquire about possible old farm laborer housing. Although he had interest in helping find solutions for homeless families, Sean also wanted to track down Jasper's sister, Lee. Since December he and Lee had shared intermittent intimate evenings but pinning Lee down to a permanent relationship had proved a challenge. Sadly, Sean had to resort to subterfuge.

He found his friend, Jasper Stahlmeier working on an old tractor in a chilly barn. "Howdy," Sean called, "Your wife told me I'd find you here."

Jasper stood, rubbing his back. "This damn thing." He kicked the tire. "I just wanted one more year."

Sean who could never resist putting his hands on a piece of machinery sauntered over and gave the old John Deere an envious glance. "Maybe I can help."

"You're no farmer," groused his old friend.

"And you're no mechanic."

For the rest of the afternoon two old friends bantered and worked. Finally, the old tractor hiccupped and sputtered, then seemed to take a deep breath and began to hum with renewed energy. As the two men wiped their hands and faces with old rags, Sean's ulterior motive walked into the barn.

"Jasper," called Lee, "dinner is ready." She stopped when she saw Sean. It was too late to run. Besides how would she explain her action to her brother.

"Sean," said Jasper, "you join us for dinner and we can talk about your problem."

"Problem?" sputtered Lee, hoping she wasn't the problem. She had been ignoring Sean for weeks. After several nights spent together, she had told Sean that she could not pursue a relationship with him. She wondered if he had come to the farm to force her to talk.

He gave her a look that said he could read her mind. "Thank you for the offer. I would like both of you to help me with a project I'm working on with the Philanthropies."

Brother and sister were both puzzled. Jasper spoke first. "Don't you come asking me for money. I got kids and bills."

Sean looked at Lee. She said nothing. He then explained, "I'm sort of on an exploratory group looking for housing for homeless families with school children."

"Sharing Shelter," said Lee, almost relieved. This was a topic she could discuss without getting personal.

"That's right. Can I explain my problem over that dinner you promised?" he asked Jasper.

Sean spent an enjoyable evening talking with Jasper and his family. They gave him a list of farmers with old farm worker housing. "I don't know what they did with those places," advised Jasper, "but if you have rent money they might listen."

Sean nodded. "Thank you for your time and for a fine meal." He smiled at Jasper's wife. Then he turned to his objective. "Can I offer you a ride home, Lee? It's gotten late."

As her mind scrambled for an excuse, her phone rang. Just listening to her side of the conversation, Sean knew she would be rushing off to see one of her hospice patients. She ended the call. "Thank you, Sean." She waved her cellphone. "I would appreciate a lift. My patient's family needs me. The care team has advised them it's time to say their farewells."

He nodded. Once they were in his truck, he asked, "Are you going to return my calls?"

She sighed. "I'm still thinking about it." She didn't say, *and I'm always thinking about you.* When they arrived at her trailer, she hopped out, "Thanks," slammed the truck door and dashed to her own car.

Sean watched her little Prius tumble down the old farm lane toward the highway. "Damn."

xxx

"Come in," Jody shouted from the kitchen in response to a bang on the front door.

"Do you always keep your door open so anyone can walk in?" barked Noah as he ambled into the kitchen. "And what are you doing on that step stool? Don't you know about old people and falls?"

He grabbed Jody's hand and helped her step down. Then he stood with his hand on her wrist checking her pulse. She scowled at him. "What are you doing here?"

"Why was your door open, expecting me?" He wiggled his eyebrows.

"No, I'm expecting guests."

"Who?" He frowned at her.

"A whole football team." She counted the glasses she had lined up on the kitchen counter. "Are you staying? I need another glass." She hopped back on the step stool and retrieved one more glass.

Noah helped her step down again, then held her hand - again and said, "You only have four glasses. That's not enough for a football team." He massaged her fingers.

"Lynn Powers and Dr. Rita are stopping by."

"Are you all planning some new nonprofit?"

"It's none of your business." Jody pulled her hand away. "But I asked them to talk with me about my future."

"You could have talked with me." Noah almost seemed to pout.

"I think I already did, and you know less than me about planning a future."

"What does Rita know? She's married to that recycler. And Lynn's a lot younger than you."

She started laughing. "I asked them over to listen to my concerns about my business and selling the house and things. I've been talking with several of my friends. Each one of them seems to have ideas and perspective to add to the discussion."

"Not me."

"Not you what?" She leaned against the kitchen counter. "You're not talking to your friends? You'll figure it out all by yourself?"

"No, I mean you aren't talking to me." Now he did pout.

"I did. Remember, you sat here until after midnight."

"Jody," came a shout from the front of the house.

"Come on back to the kitchen."

"Is someone else here?" asked Lynn as she walked into the room. "Hey, Noah. Are you joining us?" She looked at the two older people. Her gossip antennae vibrated.

"Yes." He pulled up a chair and sat at the kitchen table, pulling the crossword puzzle page in front of him.

"You seem mighty comfortable here," observed Lynn, unable to ignore that he seemed to know his way around Jody's kitchen.

"Yes, I am." He filled in a word on the puzzle. "I like to check in with my older patients. You know, do an assessment to make certain they're still capable of living alone." He glanced at Jody who seemed to be boiling.

"You are so full of crap," snarled Jody. "You come here, do the puzzle, kiss me and eat all my food."

"Kissing?" asked Lynn, always interested in clarity.

"Jody?" called Dr. Rita from the front of the house. She sauntered into the kitchen with a bakery box in one hand. "Umberto was just closing. I got some good not-quite-day-old stuff. Hey, Noah."

"Kissing?" asked Lynn getting the conversation back on topic.

"Kissing?" repeated Rita.

Lynn explained, "Jody was just complaining about Noah's kissing." The two women looked at Jody for an explanation.

She rolled her eyes. "He," said in a tone that made Noah shirk, "comes in here kisses me and talks all night. When I say I want to think about what I should do with my future, he tells me I'm not old yet. Then he comes in here telling me I shouldn't climb on my step stool. Then he tells Lynn he's here to do an assessment of my senility."

"I never said senility," countered Noah. Then he grinned at Rita and Lynn. "But I did kiss her."

The women looked back at Jody. She ignored them all and proceeded to open a chilled bottle of white wine. "This should go well with stale pastry. It's a dessert wine." She poured wine into the four glasses and carried them to the kitchen table. Rita opened the bakery box and took a small dish from a cupboard to serve the cookie assortment.

Once Jody was seated at the table, she began, "I invited some of you here to talk about my business and my situation."

"What situation?" asked Lynn.

"Do I sell my business? Do I sell the house and size down? How do I do it? This is a good time for a transition, I think." Jody looked at Noah and dared him to speak.

"Don't you have a financial advisor?" demanded Noah.

Jody scowled at him, then spoke to the women. "Henry left all our finances with a firm that handled our business and personal money issues. They did, still do, taxes and everything."

"Aren't they answering your questions?" Noah wanted all the facts.

Jody gave him a withering glance. "They're all men and their office is in Asheville. They act as though I have no brain and never answer my questions with anything but a pat on the hand and tell me that I should trust that Henry had a plan."

Noah turned his attention back to the crossword puzzle while Lynn suppressed a grin.

"I can solve your problem right now," said Rita. "Make an appointment with Michelle Grayson," Rita's stepdaughter CPA. "She'll analyze everything and give you solid information to make your choices." Rita nodded her head. "And she'll talk to you like you have a brain." She sniffed with disgust, looked at Noah and concluded, "Men!" He settled lower in his seat, raising the newspaper to read the crossword clues better.

"That's a great idea," agreed Lynn as she reached for her second piece of biscotti. "She's been at her job for ages and really knows numbers."

"There's more to life than numbers," scowled Noah, placing the newspaper back on the table.

Jody looked at him. "Please excuse Noah, he doesn't know what real life is since he works twenty-four hours a day."

"I know life," he snapped back. "I just leave it alone."

"And I don't want to leave it alone," replied Jody, "I want to travel and relax and do things." She stared at him.

"I think," said Rita, "that Lynn and I have given you a good starting point. And I promised Hank I'd be home early." She gulped her wine and, giving Jody a quick wink, ran for the door.

"Me, too," said Lynn as she grabbed another cookie and trotted after Rita.

xxx

"Rita, wait," called Lynn as she raced from Jody's house.

Rita laughed and tilted her head back toward the house. "I didn't think you could wait until tomorrow to chew on this gossip."

"Do you know something?" asked Lynn, wondering if she had missed earlier signs of a Jody-Noah pairing.

"This is a surprise to me," replied Rita, "I know Jody has had something on her mind. And to be honest, I think she's still in the dark about Noah's intentions."

"He was like a neon sign," said Lynn, surprised. "How could she miss it?"

"She's a widow."

"I was a widow," Lynn reminded her, "but I certainly knew when Dusty wanted to change my status."

"You were much younger. Jody's sixty-five. But I think as I recall some of our recent conversations, she wants something more than widowhood for the rest of her life."

"What about Noah?"

"Since his divorce I've watched him insulate himself from any potential relationship." Rita laughed, "Every nurse in the hospital has tried to get his attention. I guess he finally noticed Jody. I guess he's ready to un-insulate."

"So, do you think it will blossom into a romance?" Lynn grinned at the thought.

"No, I think it will explode because they are both so ready."

"Gives me something to think about while I grocery shop," said Lynn as she unlocked her car.

"Grocery shop? Isn't it too late in the day?" Rita hated shopping at the end of the day. She was always hungry and tired and made dumb purchases.

"Dusty says I should be stocking up if the government says we have to shutdown. And if that happens Jason will come home." Lynn shuddered. "I'll need lots of food."

Rita nodded. "This virus may move us to a whole new way of living."

Lynn shuddered again just thinking about trying to keep Jason fed and virus free.

xxx

Noah and Jody sat in the quiet kitchen. "Why'd they leave so soon?" he asked.

It was all Jody could take. "What is wrong with you? I was leading my quiet, simple life then one night you came in and now I can't get rid of you? You're at the store all the time. You manufacture reasons why I should make appointments at your office." She dashed a tear from her eye. "What do you want, Noah?"

"You." The house was silent around them as the single word seemed to echo through the kitchen.

Jody looked shocked, unable to reply for a few minutes, until, "Well, I don't want another old man in my life." She swiped at another tear.

"I'm not old." He reached across the table and took her hand.

"I was widowed by a man your age who, well who couldn't, didn't . . ."

"Are you talking about something specific or just that he wasn't as young as he used to be?" Noah ran his fingers along her knuckles. "Are we talking about him slowing down, or not hearing as well as he used to, or are we talking about him distancing himself from you?"

She gasped and tears ran down her cheeks. "All those things. I think he became very depressed about . . . about aging and he withdrew." She swallowed a sob. "He quit touching me in those last years."

"Why didn't he tell me? There are medicines."

"I think he thought it was normal. I asked him to check with you and he refused. He said it wasn't something he could talk to you about."

"I'm sorry. I'm sorry he didn't ask. I'm sorry that you felt so isolated."

"How do you know that's how I felt?" She reclaimed her hand.

"You're not my only patient married to an old man. Some men seem to get older sooner than others. I think it has to do with stress and other medications and exercise and, frankly, as much as men are sold as sex crazed, I think men follow a normal distribution curve and some aren't as interested as others. Some want to get their game back and ask for help and some don't." He played with a cookie on the plate. "I'm sorry," he told her again.

They sat without speaking for some time. Noah refreshed their glasses with the remaining wine. Finally he said, "Is that what you're doing? You want to move on? Maybe go to a retirement community and find someone?"

"I want to feel alive again," she said, "I want to love, I want to have a man smile at me across a room and know we share secrets and affection. But first, I want to sell everything. Then I'll think about my next step." She glared at him. "Are you going to charge me for a house call?"

"I was hoping I could tell you my dreams in exchange for listening to yours," he whispered, "because I want exactly what you want. Affection, friendship, not being alone anymore." They sat in the quiet house.

"Look at the time," Noah gasped, "I'm missing the news." Jody was lost in thought sitting across the table as Noah asked, "Don't you have a bigger TV for me to watch the news, and probably the sports and the weather?" He nodded an insulting stare toward the tiny TV on a shelf near the table. "I like to keep up on things."

"Don't you have a TV at home?" she asked coming back to the present.

"Look how late it is," he explained, "if I leave now, I'll miss it all."

She rolled her eyes at him. "Come to the den. I have one of those large screens. I don't usually watch it. It's too big and makes me feel lonelier." She led him to another part of the house. "You can sit on the recliner. That's where Henry always sat."

"I'd rather sit on the couch next to you, in case I find the news too scary tonight." He took her hand and settled them side by side. Jody handed him the remote. He clicked on the local news then put his arm around her, put his feet up on the coffee table and sighed, but it was a contented sigh, not the hopeless sigh of a lost man.

Jody snuggled closer and rested her head on his shoulder. She was asleep in minutes.

When the news was over, Noah watched about thirty minutes of one of those late-night talk shows. Same old jokes, he thought, but he smiled to himself and pulled Jody closer. She was still asleep. As her physician, he knew that she wasn't sleeping well. She'd never admit it though. She'd been his patient a long time. He knew that she kept her health to herself. If he couldn't figure it out, or if it didn't show up on a blood test, it stayed her secret. So, yes, he knew, just by looking at her, that she was tired, stressed and, God help him, the cutest Medicare patient in his practice.

"Jody," he whispered, "Let's go to bed."

"Are you still here?" she asked in a sleepy daze. "Did you watch the news?" She pulled herself up to sit away from him, now fully awake. "Why are you still here?"

He took her hand. "I was thinking I could stay the night."

She gasped.

"I told you how I feel," he said, "I don't want to be lonely anymore. I want the same things you want." He pulled her back to his arms and kissed her forehead. She started to cry.

"I guess I'm too pushy," he sighed as he released her.

Jody stared at Noah, studying his face in the reflected light from the TV. His was a good face, lived in, always filled with concern and affection for his patients. She liked the way his hair curled around his ears. He smelled minty and looked tired. She reached out and let one of his small curls wrap around her finger. It was gray and black and seemed to cling to her finger ready to pull her into his arms.

"No, you're not pushy." She kissed his cheek. "I like being held. I like being kissed. I just didn't expect it again. I was so worried that I would look for someone and never find him."

"Do you know that Andrew accused me, accused us, of flirting?"

"What? He thinks we flirt?" Jody was shocked.

"I guess he noticed that I'm always in your store. And I guess he noticed that I wasn't flirting by myself."

"You mean he thinks I lead you on?" Jody felt a blush.

"Are you, have you been leading me on?" She looked at him for a long time while she thoughtfully played with the curls that tickled his ear. "Please, can I stay the night?" he asked.

"Yes."

CHAPTER 10

She opened her eyes on Saturday morning and Jody was glad it wasn't a workday. She thought over her plans for the day and was glad her calendar was empty. Because she had a man in her bed and didn't know what she should do now. At least she didn't have to get out of bed and be anywhere. She stared at the ceiling. She smiled to herself. She wasn't as old as she thought, and Noah didn't seem to be too old either. She smiled again. She felt him shift beside her.

Noah dug himself out from under the blankets and blinked at the morning. Then he reached for her. "This was a great idea." He nuzzled her neck running his hands down her back. "You got dressed."

She shrugged in her comfortable nightgown. "I got up to go to the bathroom last night and was cold." She lifted the sheets. "You're wearing something, too."

He nodded, sadly. "I got up last night, too. I found my shorts on the floor and slipped them on. I'm not young anymore." He frowned. "I didn't want you to see me in my morning . . . There's a medical term for it."

"Limpness?" she offered.

"That's the medical term I was looking for." He smiled at her. "I saw you last night, sitting in that chair," he whispered. "I couldn't see your face. Were you sorry? Do you want me to leave?"

"I was thinking." She looked over her shoulder at the chair. "I often sat there late at night when Henry was alive, wondering why."

"Why?"

"Why he was so distant?"

"Did you reach any conclusions?"

"Yes, I had to lead my life. If he wanted to distance himself, I had to keep moving forward. We had the business, the kids." He felt her shrug. "It was a solitary marriage in our last years."

Noah held his breath as conflicting thoughts raced through his mind. "Are you sorry?"

"About my marriage?"

"No. About me, us?" He pulled at the bedcovers.

She reached out and caressed his face. "No, I'm not sorry."

He heaved a grateful sigh. "Can I stay here again tonight?"

"We can talk about that over breakfast," she replied. "Aren't you hungry?"

He nodded. "You're right. There are some things we should talk about, you know, like condoms." He looked so serious.

"You think I'll get pregnant?" She almost laughed.

"No, sexually transmitted disease, you know, S-T-D's." He turned on his side to face her.

"You think I have STD's?" She pulled away from him, the sheets clutched at her breast with one hand as she balanced herself on her elbow. "Or you have some disease?" She was somewhere between angry and confused.

Noah threw his head back on his pillow, blew out his breath and confessed, "A few months after my wife had settled in her new home and we were divorced, everything final, she showed up on my doorstep. I was thrilled. I thought she had second thoughts. I thought she had come back. Well, she had come back . . . to ask me for medication to cure her STD."

Jody gasped and moved a little further away.

"I don't have anything," Noah admitted, trying to erase the panic he saw in Jody's eyes. "I had to teach her how to have safe sex with old men. When I look back, I was really hurt, first that she wasn't returning and second that she had found someone else. But once I gave her medication and a supply of condoms, I felt released. It was over - the marriage was buried. She calls frequently to check in about her health and ask medical questions that she says she's too embarrassed to ask her doctor. It's usually a quick medical chat and some comments about the kids. She doesn't even ask about life here or any of her old friends." He stared at the ceiling, took Jody's hand and kissed it softly. She moved a little closer. He turned on his side to face her. "Was I okay?" he asked in a whisper.

Jody reached out to touch those curls that were rioting across his forehead. She brushed them back from his face and leaned in to kiss his brow. "It's been several years for me," she began, "but it seemed to be what I remembered . . . . except the part where you held me tight and called my name."

"You don't like calling?" He scrambled to a sitting position.

She smiled. "I like the calling, I like sound, I like letting you hear how I feel because just moving doesn't seem to be enough." She stretched up to sit beside him, their backs against the headboard. "Henry didn't like noise. He was always telling me 'Shhh' like I would wake the dead or something. He never seemed to enjoy it as much as you did last night." She drew the sheet to her face to catch a tear. "That's what I was thinking last night as I sat in that chair. It made me wonder if he ever enjoyed sex with me or whether he loved me." More tears streamed down her face. "What a thing to worry about!" she scolded herself. "I can't change it now, but it makes me feel diminished. All those later years with no affection. Was he just living with me because he was too lazy to make a change in our life - divorce me?" She wiped at more tears.

Noah put his arm around her as he felt the despair she had experienced in her marriage. He wondered how many

81

other of his patients shared these lonely secrets. But he had secret concerns of his own today. "I can't answer any of those questions. But I need you to answer one of my own. The question, was I good enough for you? Did I make you happy and satisfied, all those things I seemed to fail at with my wife?"

"Yes," Jody replied, "you did all those things. It just makes me sad to wonder what Henry and I missed as we grew old together and grew further apart. We have a lot to talk about over breakfast."

He kissed her and caressed her. "I was thinking we should work up an appetite." He ran his hands over her body as he pulled her back under the sheets.

xxx

Heath Dawson was in River Bend living in the South End district with his new girlfriend, Yetta. He was intrigued by the news reports of this virus. If, as the talking heads predicted, the President would be closing down the country and all functioning institutions, it might create the kind of opportunity he needed for his plans. It would allow him to move quickly instead of dragging out accidents to get to the inheritance. This virus and mandated lockdowns were just the cover he needed. It pushed up his timeframe a little, but he had the big stuff in place.

The children's boarding school had notified him that they were processing their response to the anticipated virus mandates. He had responded by telling them he was out of town but would be ready to react to their decision. He suspected the kids would be sent home soon. The cabin was ready with the assistance of his new girlfriend. She knew everyone in town with a criminal background and illegal talents. And the best part was that no one asked questions. All that was left was to rig the explosion.

He had been in River Bend since mid-February working on that cabin. The old lady didn't know where he was.

He had orchestrated a Christmas holiday with her and those damn kids. The old bag had been thrilled. The kids had enjoyed the two weeks with her at their home in Hilton Head. Then he got them back to boarding school and Emily back to River Bend. They all saw him as Mr. Perfect. He was glad he had convinced their mother that they should board once she became so ill. He had argued that she wouldn't want them to see her decline and die. Of course, he had helped hurry death along. And in a few weeks, he would partner with death again.

He lounged at the small rental house with Yetta. She was real accommodating and real dumb. It was time to get organized. He was certain it was a matter of a day or two and he would hear from the boarding school. Show time! "I'd like you to do for me what you did for your old boyfriend," Heath explained to Yetta. He had a good idea that she had abetted in a murder scheme with the dead boyfriend.

"Do what?" Yetta had enjoyed the sex the last few days. Other women might grow too old for a good romp. But she thought she would be ready to her dying day.

He adjusted the sheets. "I need some help getting this old lady out of my life. She has all this money, but until she dies, I can't get it." He massaged and stroked.

Yetta almost fell asleep until he tweaked her nipple. "What?" she moaned, "you want what?"

"I need something to put her into a deep sleep."

"How much?"

"I don't know. You know doses."

"No," Yetta raised up on her elbow. "How much you gonna pay me?"

"She's rich. Her dying makes me rich. How much you want?" Heath decided right there she was getting nothing.

"Five thousand, cash." Yetta muzzled his ear. She liked mixing business with pleasure.

"You have some stuff here?" The plan was coming together, but Yetta had just become a liability.

"I keep a supply of things. Folks always need a little something." With that enigmatic reply, she yawned, then asked, "You got anything left for me or you too tired?"

Why not, he thought, she wouldn't be around much longer. One murder, five murders, the punishment was the same. They just had to catch you. He was ready. And this quarantine garbage would help him get it done quick and anonymous.

xxx

According to the news the world was in for a major catastrophe - a pandemic. It was a word not many had ever heard before and many didn't understand its implications. But one day soon the country would shut down. Every state had its own interpretation, and every town distilled the information further into their own local translation. And River Bend was no more confused than the rest of the country.

"Bars might close?" moaned a disbelieving brewer at River Dog Brewery.

"No school!" shouted happy kids until they faced the reality of online learning.

"Masks to go to the grocery store?" grumbled every old codger who stared at the empty shelves in the pantry.

The President announced that all should prepare for quarantine. "I told you," said Dusty as he helped Lynn carry groceries and other supplies into the house. "We got this weekend to get us organized."

"Us?" She was distracted wondering if she had enough toilet paper.

"No, our department." He shrugged. "No one knows if we arrest folks who don't comply with all these virus rules."

"Just shoot them," said Will. He was also helping unload the supplies. Piper and Lynn had stormed the grocery store together.

"We have been told to prepare for online teaching." Piper huffed as she threw another giant pack of toilet paper onto Lynn's kitchen table. "What are you going to do with all this?"

Lynn looked dazed. "I don't know. I heard someone in the grocery aisle mention running out of TP. So I grabbed what I could."

"Are you sure they didn't mean toothpaste?" asked Dusty.

"Oh, no," cried Lynn. "I forgot toothpaste."

"But you bought three jars of fig and olive jam?" Dusty stared at the jars all claiming to be a product of Greece.

"They were on sale." Lynn stared at the jars and couldn't remember why she had tossed them in her cart.

"And four bags of cauliflower pasta?"

"All the whole wheat was gone." She hung her head. "I don't think my mind is ready for a lockdown."

"Or for long range meal planning," muttered Dusty.

"This stuff isn't bad," opined Will. While Dusty had been complaining about Lynn's purchases, he and Piper had opened the fig and olive jam. Piper was making her own concoction, a wheat cracker, a little cream cheese, a little jam.

"Not bad," she nodded as she agreed with Will. "I bet it would be great with ouzo."

"Nah," disagreed Will, "I never cared for that anise taste." He thought a moment. "Didn't we have some other drink at that Greek festival in Asheville?"

Piper made another cracker and passed it to Dusty as she said, "Yes, something spicy. But I don't remember what it was."

Dusty devoured his cracker and made himself another. "I remember, but I don't know what it was called." He turned to Lynn, "Are these all the crackers you bought?" The box was empty. She didn't want to tell them she had forgotten something else.

CHAPTER 11

Emily drove into the river park and saw Penny Rawlings with her children. Penny waved. "Thank you for meeting us here." She held a small infant and was watching her energetic toddler pick spring flowers. "I thought this would be safe for you."

"I appreciate your concern, dear." Emily was paying close attention to the CDC warnings and kept her distance. She voted for keeping distance rather than masking up like some bank robber.

"I've got your will." Penny sat the baby on the grass and pulled papers from her bag. "Robert has read it. Here's your old file and the new will. You read it and sign it." Her daughter cried out. Penny whirled around to rescue the toddler, shouting back at Emily, "Watch the baby." After a quick chase toward a tempting mud puddle, the breathless mother returned with little Olivia. Coming back to Emily, she said, "Sorry. We're all learning how to work from home while our kids need attention."

Emily scanned the park giving Penny a teasing look. "So this is how you work from home?" She threw her arm out toward the small play area.

Penny rolled her eyes. "Working from home means that I take the kids to client meets." She wiped mud from the little girl's fingers. "We're all so worried about Uncle Nathan getting sick that Cook sends in meals. I do a little cooking and Amelia and Zachary are staying at her old condo, just checking in by phone."

"Nathan's a lucky man," said Emily. "I wouldn't mind having family close during a quarantine."

Penny nodded. "Emily, you know you can call us if you need anything."

"I know, dear. Lynn called yesterday and made the same offer." She thought a moment. "If this lasts too long, I may just take advantage of your offer."

Emily stuffed the envelope with the new will into her mint green designer bag, but the old will's file was too large. She held on to it. "I'll drop the signed copy at Robert's office tomorrow and we'll be done."

Penny agreed. "Just put it in the mail slot. His paralegal is working at the office. She'll take care of everything." The two women parted.

Emily arrived home and gasped. Juan and Lucia were there. She had forgotten that they were scheduled. Lucia was to do some light cleaning while Juan helped her in the yard. She waved to them as she hurried to the house, unlocking the door. "Sorry, I'm late. I'll change and we can get to work." She was clutching her bag and the file.

Her first stop was her small office. She dropped the file into a desk drawer. Rushing into her bedroom, she tossed the designer bag beside the bureau, planning to read Robert's offering this evening in bed. Moving as quickly as an old woman could who was anxious to get into her garden, she finished changing and hustled to the kitchen where Lucia was already at work. "I'll be in the garden with Juan."

Lucia nodded as she pulled on a mask per the new protocols at Amelia's Maids.

"Don't worry about masking, dear," said Emily, "I'll be outside gardening." It would be a busy day for everyone.

xxx

Amelia Rawlings came into Lynn's office, slipping on a very colorful face mask that highlighted her dark eyes. "I haven't seen this place since you finished decorating." The Philanthropies office had been enlarged, an elevator installed, and Lynn's office and additional work and meeting space added on the second floor. "Bonita," Dusty's sister-in-law and an interior decorator, "did a nice decorating job," Amelia commented with approval.

"Did you need something?" asked Lynn, always happy to see Amelia, and adjusting her own face mask as part of the new reality. The Philanthropies board had opted to have a sign placed on the front door saying, 'Masks Required.' They didn't care if Lynn and Nelda unmasked alone, but when visitors were in the office, masks were on.

Amelia tugged at her face mask. "I hate these things, but I'd hate to be responsible for anyone getting sick." Lynn nodded, silently acknowledging her own confused attitude toward the new reality. Amelia continued, "I'm visiting my clients to assure them my crews will be taking every precaution to sanitize their workspace and respect social distance." She took a quick recon of the new rooms and stopped at Lynn's office. "The CDC has sent out some sanitizing guidelines." Amelia shrugged, thoroughly mystified at pandemic germ abatement. "Are you happy with my crew?" She often did some informal customer surveys about the Amelia's Maids' staff as she spoke with customers.

Lynn smiled. "Lucia and Juan are great." And she related the story of the hearts.

Amelia nodded. "Lucia told everyone. The other maids have been teasing him about losing his heart to someone. He's a good sport and takes it graciously."

Hmm, Lynn thought, a perfect opening for her scholarship idea. She cleared her throat. But Amelia spoke first. "I know that sound. You want my husband's money." Amelia had married Zachary Rawlings several years ago. He was a retired international banker.

"Not me," Lynn smirked. "But have you ever thought about funding scholarships for your workers, or their families?"

"Scholarships?" Amelia hadn't expected to hear that idea. Lynn usually wanted money for basic needs like food and shelter.

"Several companies in town," began Lynn, "offer employees funds to get more training or to improve skills. And sometimes they offer scholarship funds to employees' children. It's a common employment perk."

Amelia was thoughtful. "I should pay my maids to get more training and leave me?"

Lynn was stopped by that logic. Scrambling for a rebuttal, she said, "You can only pay them so much an hour before you have to raise your customer rates. And if you can't pay the maids more, you'll feel bad for keeping their wages low." Amelia cocked her head at that thought. Lynn rushed on, "So helping them learn other skills allows them to get better jobs and allows you to bring on new people who need entry level jobs and the opportunity to learn a work ethic." Ta da, she thought.

Amelia leaned back on the office settee in deep thought. She gave Lynn a suspicious look. "You have someone in mind, don't you?"

Even though Lynn was wearing a mask, Amelia knew that she blushed. "Juan." Amelia waved her hand inviting Lynn to spill her guts. "You know he was in prison?" Amelia nodded. "Well," Lynn began to feel more confident, "he took classes while there and would like to train as a CNA, and as money is available work toward becoming an EMT. I know that the CNA training is much shorter so that may be his first goal and then move on to EMT training or even nursing training with an RN." She took a deep breath. "But it all takes money. He even works on weekends helping folks with their gardens to make more money." Reading Amelia's receptive body language she continued with confidence, "If you created an Amelia's Maids' scholarship fund, say, to pay for community college training, or pay half of the tuition or match tuition or something, he could get his training. And some of your maids, especially the younger single moms, could see the scholarships as opportunities to get more education and better paying jobs." She rushed to her conclusion, "Because we both know there will always be women and even men who need that first job. You'll never worry about employees to fill your slots."

Amelia sighed and sat forward to look Lynn in the eye. "That's quite an idea, but not why I came here." She smiled to herself because when you wore a mask no one saw you smile at them - ugh! "Zachary heard about the Sharing Shelter program and wanted to help out." She almost laughed at Lynn's consternation, sheltering folks on the one hand, or scholarships on the other.

"Rats," said Lynn then covered her mask with her hand, "sorry that thought just escaped."

Amelia did laugh then. "Why don't Zachary and I talk things over and see if we can't help with both of these ideas?"

Lynn gave a relieved sigh and fell back in her chair. She was getting too old for fundraising drama.

xxx

"*Señora!*" Juan came running to assist Emily. "Why you not wait? I would get that statue." Emily Jacobs and Juan were working in her garden while Lucia cleaned the house. Emily was grateful he was there. She had reached for an old gnome that had been buried in the garden for years. Stepping into the tilled soil, she had tripped and tumbled. The ground was soft and when she had raised her head that old gnome was staring at her. Was he laughing? She didn't even remember when she had placed the ornament in the garden. He had been unearthed almost like an archeological dig.

She nodded to Juan. "You're right. I should have waited." He pulled her to her feet, and she leaned on the young man. "I

91

think I twisted my ankle." They were working on the secluded patio garden by Emily's bedroom. "Help me into my room." She nodded toward the patio doors. As he helped her, Emily thanked her lucky stars that the fall had not resulted in a broken hip or twisted knee. Old folks could become incapacitated in an instant when old bones gave out.

Juan held her waist and slid the door open. Once he had Emily propped on her bed, he went to find his mother. Lucia came scurrying into the room in a panic. "*Señora!*"

Emily sat up against the headboard and waved her hand trying to calm the other woman. "I'm fine, just embarrassed. I need ice for my ankle and then we'll wrap it."

And that's what happened. As Emily thought, a person doesn't live this long without knowing a little basic first aid. Once tended she sat in her kitchen sipping tea elevating her swollen ankle on a footstool. She nodded to herself. That gnome was getting even for being ignored and covered in dirt and moss. He had tripped her. He was laughing. She just knew it.

Sadly Emily wondered how she would get by alone with this troublesome foot. She didn't want to bother Lucia. She was too proud to ask for help and admit the toll a small crisis took on a person her age.

Lucia was concerned. "*Señora*, I will stay the night."

Emily waved away the offer. "No, no." But Lucia did stay the one night.

xxx

It had been a few weeks since their first kiss. Neither Doyle nor Lori could believe the speed and depth of their relationship. Sure, they had known each other for years, but this was something real and warm - and Doyle seemed to have tumbled into a depression. Lori had no idea what was bothering him. School work was going well. They were in the spring semester of their college junior year, and everything

92

was on track for graduation in another year. She hoped it was on track for more than that, but recently Doyle had become spooked about something.

Finally, one evening as they again sat on their favorite bench at the park near Leo's he asked, "What will we tell Jason?"

"About what?" she asked. She scowled at the restaurant, closed for the lockdown duration.

"About us." Doyle was confused about everything. The world was changing - lockdown, pandemic, a beautiful woman who seemed to love him.

Lori sat forward on the bench and looked back at Doyle for a long moment. "What should we tell him about us?" Doyle looked stressed and helpless. She continued, "First you have to tell me what us is."

Doyle swallowed and she could see the movement in his neck. "I thought that we--" She waited. He continued, "I thought we would be something permanent."

"Are you proposing?" Her question hung in the air, mingling with the aroma of spring blossoms. She couldn't believe she asked. This was not some interim step, like weekends together or moving into the same apartment next school year. This was marriage. And this was the guy. And much to her amazement, she was ready. She waited.

He swallowed again. "Yes," he whispered.

"Yes," she whispered in return. He kissed her with the same slow sweetness that she had come to adore.

"But, Jason?" he asked as he pulled back from her lips.

"Do you, do we, need his approval for some reason?" This quarantine was making everyone crazy.

"I thought he called you all the time and stuff." Doyle didn't know what he was asking.

She laughed. "Of course he does. Someone has to tell him when he's stupid." She planted a kiss on Doyle's cheek. "He is a really smart kid with no sense when it comes to dating. He asks for advice."

"Advice?" The young man was shocked. "He's so cool."

"He's a dumb cluck." She was definitive. "One of the sororities at his school has a blog dedicated to his, well, his lack of finesse." She rushed her explanation when he started to speak. "They all like him. They all think he is really smart. But no one wants to be his next victim. Er, I mean, date." She went on to relate stories. Doyle had heard some of Jason's stories but had never realized that each adventure had started out as a date, you know, with a girl. He listened in stunned silence.

Finally, he gave her a slow triumphant smile. He had the girl and Jason had no finesse. He put an arm around Lori and settled back on the bench to enjoy the evening. Cleared up Jason, check. Proposed, check. Yeah, he had proposed. He wanted to run through the park and tell folks. She accepted, check. He wanted to run through the park and tell everyone that, too. He decided to get on with his final agenda item. "They asked me to stay in town and keep the lab functioning when everyone goes home next week."

"Functioning?" She was puzzled and pulled back to look at him. "No one will be in classes."

"Keep the equipment from deteriorating and make sure no mice eat things." He shrugged and smiled.

She loved that smile. "My news is the same."

"You're staying in town to watch labs?"

"Almost." She snuggled close again. "I have been offered a job to help maintain the online systems since some classes will be available twenty-four seven. They need round the clock tech support. And live online class instruction will need support, too." She took his hand. "Going virtual is going to require a lot of tech support." She played with his fingers and let him think about things.

"You'll be in town, too?" Bingo!

"Yes." It was a whisper.

He stood up. "Ah, we, ah." He ran his fingers through his hair. "My department said they will quarantine our campus staff."

"Us, too," she explained. "They'll sanitize some dorm rooms and want us to move in next week to begin quarantine."

"Us, too." He mentioned the dorm. She nodded. He grinned. Life was going to be fun in the quarantine bubble. "My boss said they're making this up as they go along, so be prepared for anything. He wasn't sure how we would be fed, or do laundry and stuff, but he said we'd figure it out if they didn't."

Yeah, pandemic!

CHAPTER 12

Closing plans proliferated and mask designs stretched the bounds of imagination. Citizens were asked to stay home for two weeks unless seeking food or medical care. Many office employees were sent home to find a quiet corner that could be turned into a home office. Soon working-from-home-parents were wrestling with their schooling-at-home-children for bandwidth and screen time.

Teachers were sequestered for a week or two to reinvent teaching, making digital chalk so to speak. The Board of Education felt pretty smug that they had ordered digital tablets for every student in last year's budget. The local county commissioners were quickly rewriting history to make certain everyone remembered their support for the tablet budget request that, at the time, had been blamed for a tax increase. Of course, everyone was trying to figure out how teachers and students got connected when not all homes had internet access, and not all parts of the country even had broadband access. Ah, technology.

Through two weeks of quarantine, local nonprofits began to wonder about donations to support clients and staff. Teachers began to worry about those students receiving reduced cost and free meals at school. The hospital staff panicked at the thought of extremely ill and contagious patients filling beds while the normal accidents and emergencies would also demand space.

All in all, those who thought about a redesigned future paled at the thought of restructuring life. And there were those who resisted the redesign, claiming personal freedom, when in fact, being frightened probably explained attitudes better.

xxx

On the first day of no school, Piper went to her school thinking she would get in early and get all sorts of paperwork done, do a walk through and begin a list of maintenance issues that could be addressed while the building was empty. She sighed. Things would be strange for a while. She wanted quiet time to think about educating children online and other concerns she had about the students she cared for. Would they need food, health care, day care, all the things the school seemed to provide? As she pulled onto the Rathborne Elementary School campus she saw several children huddled at the door. She gasped.

Jumping from her car, she was almost knocked down by the enthusiastic students who greeted her. "Mrs. Zubot." Would they ever learn her name? "We thought everyone forgot to come to school today," a bustling fifth grader informed her.

Before she could even ask a question, a car drove up to the entry and three children tumbled out. The car was gone before Piper could act. She turned to the new arrivals. "Why are you here?"

"Mama gots to work," said a lisping third grader. Several other children nodded.

"But school is closed because of this virus." She silently counted noses.

"Who says?" came a challenge. "My mama says some folks can stay home but she gots to be at the grocery store early or lose her job." More nods.

Piper unlocked the door and let everyone in. "Let's go to the cafeteria. You all know how to behave."

"Can we have breakfast?"

And she knew. These were the kids she worried about, those who ate two meals a day at school and carried treats home over the weekend. She smiled and pulled her phone from her pocket. She woke up her son, Jeff, and her retired friend, Sean Hennessey, ordering them to get food and get to school. Before she could even dig some milk and fruit out of the coolers, several more children appeared.

That was how the secret school operated during the first week of quarantine. Don't answer the phones. Don't let the kids on the playground. Find some secret help. Piper went to school every day. And kids appeared. Parents had to work. Many were parents who didn't read a newspaper or listen to news. They just worked to survive. They kept sending their children to school. And Piper took them in. She reasoned that she could keep her operation a secret. After all, everyone was in quarantine. The superintendent had emailed everyone that he was going to enjoy two weeks of quarantine at his cabin in Macon County. He left the Board of Education staff to work out teaching online while he rested. No one would be coming to the schools.

Soon Piper found herself at a 'closed' school with forty-three children and no staff. She called in the troops - her son Jeff and his two friends, Ricky and Ryder, along with her father and mother, and good friend Sean. The team came and provided food, teaching and story time. Forty-three children learned math from an old Coast Guard retiree; reading from a long-time elementary school teacher; science from an old farmer who had everyone growing bean sprouts; and PE and computer operations from three energetic high schoolers. In addition, they formed a choir, had impromptu art lessons, and designed a train layout around the empty cafeteria.

xxx

The quarantine was causing people to do strange things. So Dusty ignored the fact that Sean had borrowed train supplies from the attic. But when the sheriff came into his office, masked, the detective couldn't ignore the order to arrest that troublemaker, Mrs. Zubov.

"Oh, that's right," the wily sheriff had sneered, "She's your sister-in-law or something. Have her close that school or arrest her." He walked out of the office followed by his masked minions.

Dusty was alone in his office. Danny was at a meeting with county staff to develop pandemic protocols for local government operations. Mars was at a meeting with Chamber of Commerce members to help them understand pandemic protocols. Teniquia was at the hospital working with the security and ER staff to develop pandemic protocol enforcement.

He wondered why he was still at the office and not out discussing pandemic protocols with someone. Oh, right, he had to finish up the sheriff's budget for the county manager. Because no matter what, everyone would still be taxed, and county employees would still be paid.

That's why he was the only one available to go out and arrest Piper. Of all the things he would have liked to arrest her for, operating a school for her kids was not it. Dusty knew after listening to Lynn that several parents were leaving their kids at school without regard to any government mandate. He also knew that these were the children who needed all the extras from the system - breakfast, lunch, after school care. Pushing back his chair, he stood, swore, and made his way to his car and Piper's school.

The school looked deserted from the street. He drove slowly around the block and spotted several cars tucked up against the tree line at the edge of the campus. There had been an old trailer there years ago that had provided housing for an old maintenance man. After his death the school board had removed the old dwelling. It was the perfect spot to hide something, like cars for the secret staff.

Parking at the back, Dusty walked to a door and banged loudly. Finally a youngster peeked out of a classroom. Soon several smiling kids were waving at him. Piper's son, Jeff, came to the door. "Yeah?"

Dusty walked in, giving a wave to the kids who returned to their classroom. He turned to the young man. "Where's your mother?"

"Oh, man, she's in trouble, isn't she?" Jeff didn't know whether to panic or grin. The friction between Dusty and Piper was always entertaining when it bubbled over. Jeff nodded his head in the direction of the cafeteria. "She's making sandwiches for lunch. She says if she doesn't feed the kids no one will until they come back to school."

Dusty couldn't argue with that. He knew the living conditions of many of the students. He had arrested many of their relatives. "Someone ratted on her," he explained as the reason for his presence.

Walking into the cafeteria Dusty almost laughed. Sean Hennessey and Bri Llewellyn had an assembly line operating. Slices of bread were sprawled across a table, and the men were adding lettuce, bologna, and a slice of cheese. Ryder Plummer followed, closing each sandwich, slicing it in triangles and placing it on a small dish with a scattering of chips. Several children were already seated at the tables. Glenda Llewellyn was passing out milk cartons, encouraging everyone to sit up straight and be patient.

Piper walked in with a bakery box. She handed it to Dusty. "Each youngster gets two cookies." She walked to the kitchen and returned with plastic gloves. "Put these on, there's a virus going around." Ricky Mitchell was placing plates with sandwiches in front of the seated students. Dusty followed with his cookie box.

Once everyone had been served, he went to find Piper. She was in the library instructing five kids on how to check-out and check-in books. "After lunch," she told the new librarians, "I'll bring in small groups and you help everyone find a book and check them out. I showed you how to do this yesterday. Do you have any questions?"

"Mrs. Zubot?" A hand waved from the check-out desk. "Can we let them take more than one?"

Piper thought. "On Friday they can take two so they can read over the weekend." The youngster nodded.

"Oh, Mrs. Zubot?" called Dusty in as innocent a voice as he could manage. She turned and glared. "Can we have a teacher conference?" He smiled an evil smile.

Piper almost spit fire. She walked up to the tall detective and rasped, "What do you want?"

"The sheriff sent me here to arrest you for violating quarantine." He grinned.

"And what should I do with these kids? Let them huddle at the door until their parents come for them?" She was so angry Dusty was certain there was steam coming from her ears.

She was winding up ready for her second breath when he waved her to silence and pulled her out of the room. In the hall he said, "Someone has complained to the sheriff that you're running this underground school. We'll have to close it down. You can operate until Friday. When the kids go home, you have to tell parents. The sheriff will have a patrol car here on Monday morning chasing everyone away."

She hung her head. When she looked up, Dusty could see tears in her eyes. "Some of them won't be safe at home. They get their meals here and we look after them."

He hugged her. "I know. You can tell them to call you if they have problems and you'll send your friend, Dusty, to help them. Will that do?"

She sniffed. "You'd do that for me?"

He hugged her again. "Nah, I'd do it for them."

She smacked him on the chest. "You are such an ass."

He kissed her on the forehead. "Let's go back to that library. I need something to read."

And that's how Dusty and his team found themselves on student safety patrol.

xxx

Lee wasn't certain how to hold support group without getting together physically. She had heard about something called a Zoom meeting. But she hadn't experienced it yet. She wondered how you shared secrets with everyone around you listening. Technology, she shivered.

Today she had commandeered a small picnic shelter at the river park. Three tables should allow enough space for everyone to do this safe distancing thing. She marveled at the number of new words and phrases that had entered into everyday speech in the last few weeks. She watched Connie arrive. Beth was not far behind.

"Do we have to wear masks?" called Connie, swinging a blue mask by its ear loops.

Lee made a decision. "No, we need to see faces, see smiles. Just stay at a safe distance."

Beth walked into the shelter and took a seat. Connie decided to share her table. "What are you doing here?" Beth asked the new bride.

"I just wanted to be supportive in these strange times. Schools are closed and we all seem to be hunkering down. Our group members need us to stay connected."

Lee thought about that. "You are absolutely right. The pandemic conditions won't help those who need group support." She already knew that nursing home and hospital rules were creating anxiety with her hospice families and patients. She scanned the parking lot. "I guess the others are staying away today." She looked at her two good friends. "We can just support each other. What's new?"

103

Renee Kumor

Beth sighed. "I needed to be in group today. I told my sisters."

"How did that happen? Can we help with anything?" asked Lee.

Beth began her explanation, first talking about meeting with Collie about his rental cabins, and afterward going to her family farm to be alone and decompress after her visit to that cabin with so many terrible memories. Then she described being surprised to see her sisters who had come to the farm to clean it for Patti Ann to use as quarantine space when she comes home from college. "I told them. We cried. We hugged." Beth smiled. "They loved me and I'm stronger." It was a triumphant report. She had come to group to share the good experience with her friends. Connie and Lee cheered.

Something niggled at Lee's memory. "Collie has cabins?"

Beth nodded. "I have to research how his father paid for them. See if he had any obligation to keep them and under what conditions." She shrugged. "He's becoming one of the next generation of farmers in Verona. He wants to do things right."

"Does he rent them?"

Beth looked at Lee. "You looking for a new place?"

Lee smirked. "You don't like my little trailer?" The other women laughed. They had each visited Lee's home. She continued, "I had a conversation with one of my brother's friends who was asking about using empty cabins for homeless housing."

"I've been listening to Piper talk about homeless students and wondering how this pandemic will hurt their ability to learn, since classes will be online for a while." Connie was happy to contribute something to the conversation.

They talked about the changes they were seeing in the community regarding education and even grocery shopping. Lee decided to end the gathering on a high note. She asked,

"What thoughts does the new wife have to offer about changes?"

Connie smiled. "We're together. Doug still goes to work every day. I sort of homeschool the kids and we cook dinner together and we all seem to smile a lot. I don't know how other families are managing but our new family is using this time to grow stronger, just like Beth."

Beth smiled because she hadn't known she was growing stronger until tonight. Group - the magic of friends.

Lee dismissed them. "Next time I hope the others can join us, or maybe we'll try meeting online. But you two have made my day. Strong and happy - that's a goal for all of us." They all smiled, unsure about hugging in the new rules of life. They walked to their cars, waved, and drove off.

Lee sat in her car for a moment. Cabins! She had an excuse to visit Sean. She had information. Maybe she could just drop in for a minute. A minute? Part of her knew that this visit would be longer than a minute.

CHAPTER 13

Heath had heard from the boarding school about release dates. After making their travel arrangements, he had a few days before the kids were let loose. Time to visit the old woman, get things rolling.

Driving onto the grounds of Emily Jacobs' property, Heath noticed a sorry looking truck and a young man raking. Emily was seated at the edge of her yard, waving her arms. Heath knew she was talking. She was always talking, giving directions, spouting orders. What a pain in the ass!

Both Emily and the gardener stopped and watched as the dark SUV pulled into the yard. Climbing out of the car Heath waved as he slipped on a mask, "Hello, Miss Emily." He gave her his sincere eye flutter. At least he hoped it looked sincere. These masks hid a lot. He only hoped it hid his real scheme. "I've been worried about you with all this virus news. Shouldn't you be wearing a mask or something?" His eyebrows threatened the yard man who was also not wearing a mask.

"Heath?" Emily couldn't rise because of her ankle. "Is something wrong?"

"No, ma'am," his eyes showed concern above his mask, "the kids are going to be sent home from school. I thought we could all stay together. I'm worried about you being alone." He worked his eyes, hoping for sincerity. "And I don't think I can handle those kids alone. I thought we could all ride this out together."

Emily had never liked this man. But the idea that she would get to spend time with her great-grandchildren delighted her. She wondered what he was planning. She'd have to wait and see. But for now, anticipating a visit with the children was exciting.

"That sounds like a brilliant idea," she beamed. "When do they arrive?"

"The school will let me know. I thought I should get here as soon as I could and get things ready." He looked at the gardener.

"Heath, this is Juan," Emily introduced the men. "Juan is helping me. I took a fall the other day trying to get my garden ready for spring flowers." She waved at her bound ankle.

"Miss Emily," he chided, "you know you could have asked me to drive up to help. Hilton Head isn't that long a drive." He turned to Juan. "I'm glad she has folks she can call on, Juan." Sincere eye flutter.

The young man nodded. He was uncomfortable being present at what appeared to be a family reunion. "Miss Emily, I will take these clippings to the landfill. Do you need me for more chores?"

"'I'll call you if I do. You tell your mother I'll call her in a few days to schedule house cleaning." Juan nodded, and began to collect the yard waste, throwing it into his truck. Emily turned back to Heath. "Tell me about these plans. Have you had lunch?" He helped her out of her chair and guided her into the house.

"Who was that fellow?" he asked as he slipped off his mask. It had served its purpose. That gardener couldn't identify him.

"Juan?" Emily glanced out the window and watched the old truck pull away. "He helps with chores around here and his mother comes in to clean twice a week. Do I need to schedule her more with the children coming in?"

"Miss Emily." Heath put on his best caring face. "I'm really worried about this virus. Let's cancel your cleaning lady for a few weeks. Me and the kids can handle things. I plan to keep the kids in that old cabin for a few days to make sure they don't have fevers or something that might make you sick."

"What about you?" she asked. She had noticed he removed his mask once he entered the house.

"I'm not worried about me."

"I mean how do I know you won't make me sick?"

Damn, he thought. Quarantine flashed in his mind. "I was out hunting for the last week. I think I was quarantined without knowing it." He smiled triumphantly. "I even took my temperature before I came here today."

That's an out and out lie, she thought. "You're very considerate," she said, reminding herself to stay alert. This man was up to something.

"How is that ankle?"

"It's fine," she said as she wiggled her foot. "See I can move it. It's the bruise on my hip that is sore." She looked embarrassed. "I didn't want to talk about my hip in front of Juan."

"Did you see a doctor?" He couldn't believe his luck. He'd bring Yetta out in a day or two and deal with Emily on Saturday. He'd have a busy few days, the kids arrived Friday. He'd have to settle them at the cabin. Move Yetta here. By Monday this should all be over. He ramped up his sincere smile.

"I'm fine. It was just a fall." She attempted to move to a chair. He was immediately at her side and helped her.

Emily sat at the kitchen table and Heath poured her a glass of water. He checked the refrigerator and the pantry. "Ah, do you mind if I run to the grocery for a few things. I can bring us back some dinner and we can plan for those kids." He gave her his sincere smile.

Emily nodded. "I am looking forward to seeing them and to have them for a long visit."

She pointed to a notepad by her landline phone. "There are a few things I need." She made some additional notes and handed him the list.

"I'll be back soon." He was gone.

She watched his big SUV leave the yard and glanced down at her note pad, still wondering why he had come. Her eyes focused on a reminder. She realized that she had wanted Juan to finish the work on the flower bed at the patio off her bedroom. Thoughts of the spiteful gnome who tripped her passed through her mind. Juan could take care of him.

She placed a call. "Juan," she greeted him, "I have more work for you. Come Saturday. If no one is here, just finish what we started when I fell, till that small garden outside my bedroom, and cart away the yard waste. I'll order some annuals from the nursery for the following week. You can pick them up. Schedule me for the following Saturday to put in the new plantings." He replied. They discussed the time the job involved, and she ended the call saying, "Perfect. Oh, and tell your mother not to come next week. I'll call once my grandchildren arrive. See you Saturday."

xxx

Sean wasn't certain about the new protocols for living in a pandemic. Will had closed the plant for a week or two, while the government, CDC and customers figured things out. Sean had helped Piper at school until the sheriff closed them down. Next he had taken advantage of Will's empty plant to do some intensive maintenance on a few machines. He brought in his new apprentice, Andy, who appreciated picking up the hours. The two of them had cleaned and tinkered away the day. Sean had stopped at Uncle Chicken's on the way home for a Greek salad. His doorbell rang before he could sit down to dinner.

To his surprise, Lee was at the door. He stood back to let her enter. She stood in his house, seeming lost. "Are you sleepwalking again?" he asked. She had come to his home late one night in a sleepwalking trance. It had been just before Christmas. Dr. Rita had diagnosed the action as stress created by her two volunteer positions, hospice nurse and sexual assault victim support. Sean had found a dead body in the back of her truck that evening. No worries. Dusty and Lynn had solved the crime.

"I'm awake." She looked confused, her gray curls peeking out of her jaunty knit cap.

He stared at her, puzzled. "Can I take your coat?"

"I came to give you some information about farm cabins." She didn't demure when he helped her off with her coat.

He kissed her cheek, tossed the coat, flipped off her hat, and pulled her into his arms. She turned her face up to look into his eyes. He kissed her on the lips. "Have you had dinner?"

"No."

"Are you hungry?"

"No." She pulled him in for another kiss. And that was that. Without another word, he led her to his bed.

Afterward as they rested under the sheets Sean sighed. "We just get better."

Lee didn't say anything. Each time they made love she was more confused.

Sean gave her one last squeeze. "I'm hungry." Another kiss. "Did you just come here to use me, or did you have a reason?"

"Cabins!" she gasped and threw herself back on the pillow to stare at the ceiling.

Puzzled at her non-explanation, Sean stretched, climbed out of bed, and found some pajama bottoms and an old sweatshirt. "Come on to the kitchen when you're ready. I'll have dinner on the table."

He was gone and she looked around the room. Climbing from the bed, she looked for her clothing and couldn't seem to find it all. Disgusted with herself, she stumbled to the other bedroom to hunt for some of her clothes. She found clean underwear, one of her old sweaters and a pair of sweatpants. She couldn't believe that she had a stash of clothing at Sean's house. She sniffed. He was keeping her clothes clean. Blushing at what all this left-over clothing meant, she found her way to the kitchen.

"Greek salad, bread and beer?"

"Why not?" She was beyond propriety.

Once dinner was served, Sean asked, "Cabins?"

She nodded and went into her explanation of Collie Maddox's farm cabins. She suggested that Sean approach Beth Seymour, who would be able to help her client evaluate any proposal with regard to Collie's risk. They talked for some time about the idea because both of them were motivated by a sense of community service and community problem solving.

Sean looked out the kitchen window. "It's late." He raised an eyebrow.

She hung her head because she knew he was asking if she was staying the night. "I don't want to risk giving you this virus."

He chuckled. "That horse left the barn about an hour ago."

This man was like an addiction to her. She hoped he never found that out. "I guess I could do some laundry so when I leave in the morning, I'm not wrinkled."

"Sounds reasonable." He picked up the plates and began scraping them so she wouldn't see him smile.

xxx

Heath grocery shopped then stopped by to checked in with Yetta before going back to Emily's. "When you gonna

112

need me?" Yetta asked. She had been enjoying Heath's attention these past weeks.

He rubbed her rear, knowing he hadn't time to do much else. Yetta just wasn't that inspirational. "I'll stay with the old lady for a few nights. I'll get you Friday night, bring you to the house, and introduce you as the nurse I hired." He planned to end her nursing career at the same time Emily drifted off.

"Do you understand what you gotta do?" Yetta was looking forward to Friday night. "Give her that stuff in her tea. She won't taste it, but she'll feel weak. When you say she needs a nurse, she should agree."

He slapped her behind. "Gotta go. She'll get suspicious." He had no idea what was on Emily's mind, but he wanted to get away from Yetta. "See you Friday." He was out the door.

He traveled back to Emily's, delighted at the isolation of her home. Things would be so easy. "I'm back, Miss Emily," he called as he entered the house. "I think I got everything. You still have that sweet tooth? I got a few treats at the bakery."

"I'm in here," she called from the living room. She put aside a book when he found her. "I do like sweets. Thank you for remembering."

He looked around the well-appointed room. "Why don't I make you a cup of tea while I hustle up some dinner? Afterward we'll enjoy a piece of that pecan cake." He noticed a cane. So that's how she gets around, he thought. He planned to take away the cane as Yetta's drugs began to work.

Emily was surprised at his offer of tea. "Thank you, that sounds lovely."

Heath returned to the kitchen, put away the groceries and began the necessary preparation to get a carryout meal on the table that would look somewhat home cooked. While out of Emily's sight, he dashed down to her small office and easily located the file with her annotated will - the file had been moved, but to him nothing looked disturbed. He ruffled through some other files unable to find a new will. She hasn't met with that lawyer yet, he thought with glee. His early January escape to the Bahamas with that sweet chick hadn't caused a problem. The River Bend January snows probably kept Emily at home and at her age she probably forgot about her interest in changing her will. This was too easy.

He walked into the living room. "May I escort you to dinner?" He reached out and helped her to her feet. He wondered if she would have time to enjoy the dessert before she became wobbly with Yetta's elixir.

CHAPTER 14

Things are certainly quiet in lockdown, thought Lynn. She walked around her office checking things. Nothing needed to be done. All face-to-face meetings had been cancelled for the next few weeks. She had just had a tutorial from Kevin, the IT consultant, about the way to handle meetings online. He had helped her organize an account for the Philanthropies. Online meetings would be very efficient. She just hoped that her board and committee members would accept the technology. Although she was having a personal debate about platforms. There were Zoom meetings and Team meetings - she couldn't decide which one made her look thinner. Hmm. Technology was always a challenge.

But there was something else to do. She decided that during these strange times it was her job to stay in touch with her donors. She made a list of those who lived alone and might need assistance. She also made a list of local non-profits whose executive directors might need to talk with someone about funds, client needs, staffing issues and isolation. That list was long. She decided to organize her first online meeting for late afternoon. Following Kevin's instructions, she crafted an email invitation for an executive directors' meeting. Once that was completed, she attacked the list of donors.

By call three she learned that she had to make the calls short to make progress. Everyone was at home and eager for human contact, even just a phone call. She promised everyone that she would be brief but check in regularly. Emily was next on her list.

"Emily, it's me, Lynn. I'm checking in on my favorite people."

"You mean your favorite donors," countered Emily and Lynn laughed.

"I can't fool you." Lynn continued, "I'm checking in to make sure you're okay. You live alone and I worry about you now that we're all in quarantine."

"Thank you for the call, dear," said Emily. "I'm fine and my grandson-in-law has come to help me through lockdown."

Lynn remembered Emily's concerns about the man. "I thought he lived somewhere else?" She was puzzled and must have sounded that way to Emily.

"The children will be sent home from their boarding school, and he has asked me to help him care for them." Emily waited for Lynn to process that information. "As we've seen, this virus is changing the way we do things. And having the children here is something I will enjoy."

"I know you'll enjoy having the children close." Lynn agreed wrapping up the call. "Just let me know if there's anything I can do for you." She would stay in touch just in case that grandson-in-law didn't deliver as he promised.

xxx

Emily hung up the landline phone, again wondering where she had lost her cell phone. "Was that a friend?" asked Heath. She was certain he had been listening to the call.

"Yes, my friend Lynn is checking in on her older friends." Emily gave him a half smile. "She was delighted that I'm not alone and that you've decided to bring the children here." She slumped in her seat and Heath rushed to her side.

"What is it, Miss Emily?"

"I feel so weak. I really am glad you showed up. Do you think I should call my doctor?"

He gave her one of his concerned looks. "I hear those folks are all tied up with these virus patients. The news said hospital beds are at a premium."

"Do you think I have the virus?"

"No." He gave her his medical professional imitation. "You don't have a fever and you don't seem to have any other symptoms they talk about on TV. I think your fall just tired you more than you know."

Emily pulled herself up in the chair. "You may be right. I'm sorry you have to take care of me."

He shrugged, donning his self-sacrificing persona. "The kids will be here to help soon." He was thoughtful a moment. "What if I find us a nurse or CNA to help you, help us, until they get here?"

Emily studied him and thought about the suggestion. Maybe a few days with another person in the house would make her feel more comfortable with Heath. "That sounds like a good idea. I can call my doctor for references."

"No need," he rushed in, "I have to run some errands tomorrow. I can check with the health department or with one of those healthcare provider services."

"Thank you," she said. Her intuition told her he was up to something, but he was so agreeable and eager to help. She'd have to stay alert. She yawned and slumped down again.

He lifted her up and carried her to bed. "Miss Emily, you take a nap while I run out for some dinner." She looked ready to argue. "I won't be long, and I won't let you sleep long, so you won't have trouble getting to sleep tonight."

She nodded and accepted the blanket he pulled over her. She listened as his car left the yard. The next thing she knew he was waking her. "I have dinner." He helped her up, waited as she used the facilities and then helped her to the kitchen for a Chinese carry out meal.

XXX

Lynn stared at her computer screen. All the agency reps were arrayed in tiny boxes. She had introduced the meeting by telling everyone that life was strange and the Philanthropies was here to assist in any way. Two dozen heads nodded. Twenty-four professionals looked like trapped feral animals. She checked the notes she had prepared. "I have

117

some questions. Let me put them out and you think about them. Then I'll go alphabetically for your responses. Okay?" Feral heads nodded. "What do you need in the area of client support? Do you have plans with regard to funding needs? Can your current cash position, savings and anticipated grant income support you for an extended period of time?"

She called on the first rep and began to take notes. The conclusions were not surprising. No agency had funds to sustain services and staffing long term. Basic client needs would be most at risk. Food and shelter were high on everyone's list. The next biggest challenge was fundraising - how to do it in lockdown, when to do it and how to tell the story of need for funds?

As the discussion came to an end, Bertram Luft of the Hunger Alliance added, "I hear talk that the federal government may be making funds available for all sorts of entities to keep people in their jobs. They say it may come in the form of loans and some portion of the loan may not need to be repaid. They haven't spelled it all out yet. But it sounds promising."

With that encouraging information, Lynn said, "The Philanthropies will look at helping with your immediate needs. And we'll try to keep abreast of any federal programs." She looked at her tired, weary friends. "As long as we work together we'll survive." No one looked as though they believed what she said.

xxx

Lynn had conducted her first Zoom meeting from her office. She wasn't comfortable working technology alone, but Kevin's IT office was just across the parking lot from the Philanthropies in case she needed help. Once the meeting concluded she made some notes and went through the mail that was piling up. She and Nelda each tried to get into to the office daily to manage all the things you never considered when working from home. In Lynn's opinion those things were what mattered most - office supplies. She couldn't believe how hard it was to find a working pen at the house, or something to write on besides a discarded carryout menu.

Her office door jiggled. She peeked around the wall to the entry foyer. Yolanda Valeri was trying to break in. "I see your car, Lynn. Let me in," she demanded.

Lynn slipped on her mask per Philanthropies protocols and unlocked the door. Once Yolanda was inside, she locked it again.

The woman smirked, "Take off that mask, I have business. Besides your husband works with my son, so we probably already share the same germs." She marched into the conference room.

Lynn was reminded again how much she hated it when people marched in. Something had Yolanda in a snit. "Coffee?"

"I thought you kept some wine here."

Lynn dragged out a bottle, grateful that the decorating committee for the Valentine's dance had sent over a few bottles in thanks. Lynn didn't want to think about how much of her stash they drank as they created decorations. She poured a good portion in a paper cup and stared at her guest.

"I can't go to the orphanage this year," complained Yolanda. "I can't get into South Africa, or into anywhere. And they told me I might not get back into this country if I leave." She scowled after attacking the paper cup.

Lynn worried about the State Department. Yolanda was not a pretty sight when she was angry. "You can Zoom. Kevin can show you." Her guest gave her another scowl. "I just did it. It's easy."

"I can't visit those kids," Yolanda screeched. "I love them. And I want to see Mason and Riva. She's pregnant. They're so excited."

Yolanda had met Mason Donovan a few years ago when he came to town to close his father's estate. They had become good friends and Mason had helped Teniquia and Jasmine Fuller organize their Black History Forums. While he was in River Bend his good friend Riva was arrested in Durban, South Africa for demanding support for her orphanage. Mason had rushed back to help her in her pursuit of fairness and funding for those mixed-race children. He stayed and married her, welcoming Yolanda to the celebration and to work with the orphans. Yolanda had been going to visit each year since, coming back to River Bend to organize funding opportunities for local River Bendians to support Mason and Riva's children.

Lynn was sympathetic. She knew how important those children were to her friend. "It's what it is, Yolanda. No one is going to be going anywhere until this is under control." Yolanda scowled again. Lynn tried a diversion. "How's Mr. Donovan's grant project coming?"

Mason's father had given Yolanda $500,000 to address nonprofit community need in River Bend. Yolanda had worked diligently to award his funds in the spirit he had intended. The largest grant was a three-year investment to help several local agencies develop a program or create a new agency or something to help clients learn financial management and protect themselves from financial exploitation. The group had found a promising organization in another state and had been attempting to organize a local program using that agency as a model.

Yolanda threw herself back against her chair. "You know our first guy died. Thanks for the contact in Des Moines. She sent us to another fellow." The local committee had used some of the funding to hire a facilitator familiar with their project goals. Rueful grin. "And this virus has him trapped in Peoria or someplace."

"Trapped?"

"He's got some family issues because of the virus that he's attending to. And he already has us zooming."

"So you're on top of things. It'll keep you busy while everyone sorts this virus out."

"I want to go to Durban."

"Sorry."

Lynn didn't understand any Italian, but she was certain Yolanda was swearing.

CHAPTER 15

Meg, the oldest of Emily's great-grandchildren, didn't like it one bit. There was no reason for her mother's husband, though he must be the widowed husband now, to take them to the old cabin in the forest. She watched trees, and more trees, flash by the windows. The idea of staying with their great-grandmother had delighted the kids. But in his next breath, Heath had explained the cabin interlude and asked for their phones. He said they would have no signal at the cabin, and he would keep them at Emily's place for their eventual arrival.

Maybe he was telling the truth and maybe not. He was saying it again in answer to little Amy's question. "Your grandmother sprained her ankle when she took a tumble in her garden. It was easier to bring you kids here than to move her. But we decided that you kids need some quarantine. You know this virus is attacking old folks. So we thought you should go to the cabin for a few days. She thinks I should get you back to the house next Saturday if no one has a fever. You think you kids could handle being at that cabin alone?" He adjusted his face mask.

"Alone?" The thirteen-year-old worried about being responsible for the other two kids.

Heath's eyes looked at Meg over his mask. "Yeah, I don't want to get sick either. Your grandmother and I have been quarantined together and I want to keep her safe. She's really excited about all of us staying together through this virus thing."

Meg looked at her siblings. They were as puzzled as she. And it was hard to read faces because Heath had insisted they be masked also. "We can survive if there's food and stuff."

He laughed through his mask. "I got it filled with food and I brought in a generator so you have electricity. I repaired that plumbing your father added. You kids will be all set for a great camping experience.

Meg listened to his line of bull and cast a glance at her brother. He wiggled his eyes in what she thought was the same unease she felt. Cody, her eleven-year-old brother, seemed to be indicating that he didn't believe anything Heath was saying either. Last summer Heath had kept them from Gram for two months by enrolling them in a wilderness camp, even Amy who, at eight, was the youngest camper enrolled. And he had only allowed a very controlled Christmas holiday. Eight weeks at a wilderness camp had taught them a lot. Meg suspected this cabin quarantine couldn't be any more challenging than the camp. They'd just have to keep their wits about them.

Arriving at the cabin, Meg was overwhelmed with memories of her parents. It was the same familiar place. They had enjoyed many happy times here as a family. Two artists who had been wrapped up in their creativity had allowed three children to explore uninhibited. Maybe this would be fun.

"Why are there bars on those windows?" asked Amy. Meg and Cody glanced at one another.

"I was worried someone would take your mother's things," replied the man. "She's got some beautiful artwork in her studio and there's been some vandalism lately."

"Somebody took her art?" asked Cody. Heath handed him their packs. Meg grabbed a bag of food.

"Nah, they tried but didn't get anything." Good old Heath ignored the easily accessible lean-to that inadequately housed some old riding toys and grading equipment.

Meg asked, "Why didn't the vandals take that stuff?" nodding toward the lean-to.

Heath looked at the shed. "I brought the equipment up here to fix the septic. It's mostly recent stuff. I used it to do some work on the drain field."

She suspected Heath was lying, but she didn't know anything about drain fields. He was up to something, she was certain. "Won't the vandals come back?"

He stared at her over his mask. "I got everything secured and I'll take the ditcher back to town in a few days." He didn't like explaining his actions.

"How long are we going to live here?" asked Cody. Heath was at the end of his charm. The kids could sense his change in attitude.

"I told you," the man quit trying to be patient, "five or six days. But I'll be here every day or so with food and to check the generator. I think there's enough propane."

They walked into the former artist's studio, a converted and expanded cabin, and the children ran to check the remains of their mother's work. "Did you take some things?" Meg asked.

"I took out her tools. I didn't want you kids to hurt yourselves. And I got rid of the stuff the vandals broke."

"But you fixed the bathroom?" asked Cody as he placed their packs down.

"I made this place as comfortable as I could. I thought you might like to spend time out here and feel close to your mother. It'll be just like old times." He pointed out the bag of food and a microwave and refrigerator next to the small bathroom with its chipped fiberglass shower stall. "I even got new mattresses for the bunks. This virus thing just makes this cabin useful to quarantine you right now. And in the future we can use it as a fun getaway spot." The older children tried not to snort at his reference to a 'fun' getaway spot. They knew Heath. His getaway spot was a casino or golf course, no kids allowed.

"Now I've got an appointment. You all have fun." He was out the door. The kids stood staring as they heard a heavy latch fall into place. Meg and Cody nodded to one another as they removed their masks.

"I think. . ." began the boy but Meg put her finger to her lips. He nodded.

Little Amy asked, "Can we play with Mom's art supplies?"

"Sure, go ahead," said her sister, "Just don't break anything." As Amy became distracted the two older children did a preliminary search of the large room.

"I don't see any cameras or listening things," whispered Cody.

"I think he wants us here to scare us," whispered his sister. "Things have been strange since Mom died. He's been Mr. Perfect with his fake smiles and fake interest in us. Except for Christmas with Gram, he's kept us away at boarding school, then at camp and now he's locked us in here." They looked at Amy playing with some bits of charcoal and a sketch pad. She, of all of them, had her mother's artistic talent.

Cody unpacked the grocery bag - white bread and peanut butter? Meg opened the refrigerator and found an opened package of lunch meat and several cans of off-brand soft drinks. Good old Heath! Two kids with serious brown eyes stared around the somber cabin while their young sister got lost in sketching.

xxx

Surviving intensive lockdown like the entire country, Lynn looked around her dining room table or as it was now called, her home office. She and Nelda had managed to operate the Philanthropies from their homes with a few quick trips to the real office for notes or files or masked meetings. So far it wasn't difficult. But Lynn looked over her calendar. How was she going to handle a board meeting? Kevin, the IT consultant, had helped her organize the online meeting with the local nonprofits, but board members? "Same idea," he had

126

assured her. She hoped that her board members were as tech savvy as the nonprofit workers.

When Dusty heard the plan, he had commented, "Do you think I can convince local criminals to just zoom in to their arrest? Maybe even let me zoom to the robbery or whatever. None of us will have to leave home." Of course, he didn't hear Lynn's response because he got a text from the sheriff demanding something. Dusty swore and left the house.

Today she was following Kevin's instructions and sending online meeting invites for the first ever virtual Philanthropies board meeting. Fortunately Penny, the new board chair, was tech savvy. She had reassured Lynn that it all would be easy.

The meeting was a week away, so Lynn got her new constant accessory, a face mask, and decided to grocery shop. Jason had called to say that his college had finally determined their response to this virus. Everyone was to finish any assignments and the semester would be ending. He expected to return to River Bend sometime next week. She nodded to herself, Jason = food, a simple equation.

At the store she found it difficult to concentrate on shopping. Her mask kept slipping under her nose or up to her eyes. The distraction was enough to make her forget items. She finally stopped by the Vidalia onions and tapped a grocery list into her phone memo app, trying to remember all the things she had forgotten during her recent binge shopping.

After filling her cart she gave a quick call to her stepmother. Jim's partner, Robert O'Hara, had been taken to the hospital and was not doing well. "Marianna," Lynn said, "I'm at the grocery. Do you need anything?"

"Thank you for calling," came the reply. "We have what we need. But we have learned that Robert is now in ICU."

Lynn gasped. She had just met with him a few weeks ago. "Does his family need anything?"

"Nothing right now," said Marianna. "You know the hospital restrictions don't allow his wife and children to visit. Millie is at her wits end."

"I've heard that visiting restrictions are in place for nursing homes and the retirement center as well."

"Yes, dear," sighed the older woman. "Your father and I are still trying to figure out how to deal with this."

"I understand," sighed Lynn. "So is everyone else. Just call if you need anything."

"Thank you, dear."

Lynn ended the call, checked her list one more time and got in a check-out line. As she waited, she thought about all the changes that had come after only a few short weeks in lockdown. She wondered what life would look like by summer.

xxx

After leaving the children in the cabin, Heath rushed back to the city and picked up Yetta. He had spent two days, secretly drugging Emily to create a dizziness, and convincing her she needed help. He was ready to introduce Yetta to her patient, or as he thought to himself, her victim.

"Miss Emily," announced Heath as he walked into the kitchen, "I've brought that nurse we talked about. I told her you seem to limp more and more." He had been gone most of the day moving the kids to the cabin, getting them food, making them think he cared. Now he was back at the house, ready to deal with the old woman. This would be a busy weekend.

Emily couldn't argue with him. She was finding it difficult to move. Her bruise was fading but she couldn't seem to stand or walk without swaying. She had misplaced her cane. And she always felt lightheaded. She was beginning to worry. "Thank you, Heath. I think I might need a little help. I would like assistance bathing." She gave him a sheepish grin. "It's been a few days. I've been too embarrassed to mention it. I

128

was worried I'd start to smell." Heath gave her an unguarded smirk as he removed his face mask and Emily had a flash of panic. He's up to something, she thought. But what?

When the nurse walked in Heath said, "Miss Emily, this is Yetta. She's going to help you bathe and anything else you need." Yetta looked very professional in her protective gear and face mask.

It was all going according to plan, Heath thought. The drugs were keeping Emily dizzy and unbalanced. He wanted her dead by tomorrow. Yetta had assured him that his plan would work. Tonight she would get Emily ready for bed and slip her the lethal dose. As Yetta had explained, "This works slow so she just fades away. In the morning we might get a low heart rate, but by lunch she'll be dead."

"Yetta?" asked Emily, "do I know you?" It was hard to recognize anyone during these masked days.

"No, sweetie," replied the nurse, slipping on a clear plastic face shield as an extra precaution. "I'm from Portage. I'm a Masterson."

Emily had lived in the area long enough to be wary of a person named Masterson. She smiled, hiding her dismay. "Yetta, I'd like help with a shower and then I think I'd like to sleep." Emily decided that she would not eat anything this lady gave her. In fact, all her instincts were screaming 'stay alert!' What was Heath up to? If he was planning to harm her, were her grandchildren also in danger?

Heath left the women to the business of bathing. "You are very kind to help, Yetta," said Emily as she was assisted into the bathroom. "I'd like a quick shower and some clean clothing. You'll find underwear and nighties in that bureau."

Yetta nodded. "I see you have a bench in this shower." They both worked at getting Emily ready for bathing.

Emily nodded. "I live alone. I try to be practical." She sat on the shower bench as Yetta brought the water up and asked Emily to approve the temperature. "This gear and gloves," chattered Yetta. "I can't feel anything." Once Emily was settled with the flexible shower hose in her hand, Yetta went to get clothing. A curious woman, she also found several lovely pieces of jewelry that she put aside as things she would take tomorrow on her final check of her patient.

Returning to the bathroom, Yetta helped get Emily ready for bed. "I feel so much better thank you. I'd like to sleep now."

Yetta said, "Yes, ma'am. I'll just get you something to help you rest and to relieve any pain you might feel."

Emily didn't argue, but she vowed to stay alert. Yetta handed Emily a glass of water and three pills. Emily accidentally spilled the water. Yetta smirked to herself. She had been a nurse far too long to trust her patients. Emily was another patient trying something. Yetta quickly got a fresh glass of water but took a moment to add a few grams of sleeping potion just in case her patient was extremely clever. Slipping the fatal dose later to a groggy patient would be very easy. She always felt like the evil queen in *Sleeping Beauty* or some other fairy tale. She had role models that spoke to her. "You still have those pills?" Emily held out her hand to display the medication. "We'll take them one at a time." Yetta stood over the old woman and foiled her attempt to get rid of the medication. Once Emily had finished the water and taken the pills, Yetta said, "Now you sleep, sweetie." She gave her best impression of a caring nurse, turned out the lights, and closed the door.

Immediately, Emily tumbled from the bed, swayed toward the bureau, and grabbed her hairbrush. Thinking only of her great-grandchildren, she put the brush handle into her mouth and pushed until she felt herself begin to vomit. Evidence, she thought, and pulled open a bureau drawer. She lost all her stomach contents on her sweaters. Satisfied, but more lightheaded than she had been earlier, she crept slowly back into bed. Once she pulled the blanket to her chin, she had no other thoughts.

xxx

Dusty walked into the kitchen and growled, "For having to stay socially distant and even trying to work from home that sheriff keeps finding reasons for me to be everywhere that the virus could find me." Lynn looked up. She had been staring into space trying to organize a menu for dinner with all the groceries she had purchased. Dusty flipped an Uncle Chicken carryout bag on the table. "Our friend, Dave, has ramped up his carryout lanes. He even has an app for ordering online." Lynn looked at the bulging bag. "He even has a carryout menu beginning next week for Pedro's. He's some businessman." Lynn had helped Dave organize his wedding on New Year's Eve. That was after Dusty had tried to arrest him for murder. "Will and Piper and Jeff are coming over." As Dusty spoke they heard the front door open.

"I got the beer," called Will.

Piper flopped in a chair. "I'm so worried about my students and their parents now that school was closed until further notice." To everyone's surprise, she walked over and hugged Dusty. "I gave them all a card with your contact info. Remember, you promised to look after them."

"I will. I told the unit they would have extra duty keeping track of your kids."

"What's this all about?" asked Lynn, returning to consciousness now that she didn't have to cook.

"The sheriff closed down my school," explained Piper, "and Dusty said he would allow my kids to call him if they needed help. What's for dinner?"

Will and Lynn looked at Dusty, waiting for an explanation. He shrugged. "I brought some dawgs and wraps."

131

Will rolled his eyes. "Not what's for dinner? But why are you looking out for her kids?"

Dusty shrugged again. "Piper was worried about them. I had to help her or arrest her. It was a hard choice."

Piper pulled food out of the bag. "He's such a pain in the ass." Turning to Jeff, she asked, "Dawg or wrap?" She emptied the bag and lined the food up on the table. "Sean's going to drive by with lunches for the kids. No one seems to have considered all the fallout from this lockdown."

Four adults stared at the wrapped food, lost in thoughts of the new reality. Lynn finally nodded her head. "That's what I've heard from the agencies. Everyone is reorganizing service delivery and stitching a different kind of safety net." Paper crinkled. They all looked for the sound.

Jeff glanced up as he prepared to bite a dawg. "What?"

"The world is falling apart, and you're eating?" asked Will.

"Someone's got to keep their head and be ready for whatever happens."

Four adults looked at the hungry, and thoughtful, teen. "You're right," said Dusty. "We'll all keep working and figure this out as we go." With that everyone grabbed some food and talked about the future.

CHAPTER 16

Today is the day, thought Heath as he opened his eyes to a glorious Saturday morning. He almost felt like dancing, his wealth was so close. The first step should be completed soon. When he awoke Yetta, she was reluctant to leave the warm bed. They had sampled at lot of the old lady's alcohol last night. Yetta much more than Heath. He had wanted her asleep, not eager for sex. "Come on," he tugged at the blanket, "Get up and check the old lady. Let me know what's up. I gotta check on those kids today."

"Sure, sweetie, then we can talk about our arrangement." She sat up and blinked. "Can I shower first?"

"Why don't you check her first then we'll see about a shower." He leered.

She threw on the wrinkled protective cover over her nightgown, adjusted the used face mask, and shuffled out of the room and down the hallway. Walking into the dimly lit bedroom, she could tell that the old lady hadn't moved at all through the night, flat on her back like a corpse. Yawning, Yetta recalled that she had set aside a few pieces of jewelry, pieces a dead lady wouldn't miss. She cast one more glance at the body in the bed, determined it didn't seem to be breathing, then shuffled toward the dresser. She picked up the pieces she had set aide and did a long, searching investigation through the remaining items in the decorative box. What the hell, she thought, and shoved all she could into a velvet pouch she found in the top drawer.

Heath was waiting for her in the kitchen. She brushed against him in a suggestive manner as she slipped off her mask. "She's done for. Now what about you and me take that shower?" She turned her back on him as she slipped off the protective cover.

He put an arm around her waist, pulled her back against his chest, rested his other hand at her throat, whispered, "All set," and twisted her neck until she went limp. He let her slip to the floor, checked for a pulse and found her cache of jewelry. Swearing softly, he piled the small mountain of valuables on the kitchen counter and smiled slyly to himself - robbery! He would take the gems with him. When he returned from checking on the children at the cabin, he would find two dead women, call the police, and suggest robbery. He wondered if the police would want to talk to the kids to verify his story. Nah, he thought, he was overthinking this. He wouldn't mention the kids because the police might want to question them.

Stick with the plan. Robbery just made it easier to get rid of the bodies. The police would take care of that. The kids would be dead by Sunday morning, and he would be rich by Monday. Then he had another idea. He'd stop at an ATM in River Bend to show he had not been home at the time of the robbery. The receipt always had a date and time stamp. He checked his watch. He better move so timing was on his side.

Grabbing his jacket, the jewelry and his keys, he was on the road within minutes planning to return in a few hours. Keeping his speed contained, he gave an impression of a tourist as he took a bend in the road and noticed an old truck coming toward him. It was that guy Juan's truck. This was getting better and better. Not only would he have his ATM receipt alibi, but he could place Juan in the neighborhood. Juan and missing jewelry and two dead women. Heath smirked to himself. This was too easy. But who was he to argue with fate?

xxx

The big SUV sauntered past Juan, intimidating his sorry truck. He was trying to encourage the tired truck to move, to have a little pride. He needed a new ride. He needed a better job. He needed everything that everyone else had to make life enjoyable. He had nothing but this old crate - and his mother.

But he had dreams. He had learned his lesson after those months in prison. He wanted a clean life. And he knew it would take hard work. Not the easy illegal methods his old friends touted, but hard every day work like his mother and the other maids did. That was his resolve - work, save, and get an education. He might be old by the time it happened, but he wouldn't go to prison again. He shivered. He had to keep reminding himself of these goals. Last night one of the old friends tried to draw him back into trouble. Juan snorted, how dumb do they think I am?

Juan came around the bend into view of Miss Emily's house. It looked really quiet. That SUV he had just passed, that was the car the man, her relative, drove. Maybe he was running an errand or something. Juan pulled up to the house and decided to begin work and not bother the old lady. He remembered how sore and wobbly she had been the other day. He carried his yard tools back to her secluded patio.

xxx

Emily's eyelids felt heavy. They didn't want to open. Her arms and legs felt as though they were weighed down with rocks. But she had to get to the bathroom. Maybe that nurse Heath hired could help. She listened. No one seemed to be awake. She glanced at her clock - nine-thirty. Was she alone in the house? Her old bladder couldn't wait for help. Staggering, she inched her way into the bathroom, relieved herself, gripped the sink to wash her hands and face. Gasp, her face! She was pale, her hair a mess. Staggering back into the bedroom, she noticed her empty jewelry box. Had Heath stolen her things? He *was* up to something! He had robbed her. She suspected that those drugs had been intended to kill

135

her - a deep sleep into death. Her husband had written that scenario into one of his plots years ago. Then she gasped, her grandchildren. Was he going to hurt them? The more she thought the more she convinced herself that the children were in danger.

She stopped. There was a sound. Was it outside her bedroom window? Was she in danger? She peeked behind the drapery. Juan! Then she remembered, if this was Saturday, she had asked him to finish the work on her bedroom patio. She pulled the curtains back. The motion caught his attention. She waved him over to the sliding glass door and signaled for him to open it. As he pulled the screen aside and grasped the door handle, she gave a furtive look behind her. It was too quiet. Something was wrong.

"*Si?*" he asked as he slid the door open a few inches.

Emily put her finger to her lips, indicating no sound. She gestured him in and whispered, "Help me." He was puzzled and concerned. "Get my robe and slippers. Quietly!" He did as directed and helped her into her clothing because she was very unsure of herself, holding on to the bed post. "Now, get me out of here." She gestured to the sliding door. "Quietly," she hissed.

Juan didn't like this at all. He had a police record. He was just getting back on his feet with his mother's help. Emily pulled him close. "We're in danger here. I'll explain. Get me to your truck." He was like a statue. Emily didn't notice. She was in escape mode and had one more thought. "Juan, get my bag." She pointed to a green designer bag in the corner on the floor. He grasped the bag and placed it in her outstretched hand. "Let's go." She clutched his arm with her free hand. He could feel her tension and see the anxiety in her eyes.

"*Si.*" Although every instinct told him this was trouble, he did as instructed, helping her onto the patio, closing the patio door and almost carrying her to his truck, wondering what sort of hell she was dragging him into.

Emily scanned the yard. "No car?"

He shook his head. "Only your car. No one else was here when I arrived. I saw that man's car on the road." He assisted her into the truck.

"Take me away quickly." Emily clutched her bag and sank down in the truck's passenger seat.

She was so frightened that Juan asked no more questions but got them out of the yard and onto the road toward River Bend before he finally prodded her, "Where?"

"Let me think." She peered out the truck window and wondered if she was overreacting as she tried to recall all of Heath's actions. He brought that nurse in and Emily was certain they had drugged her. She remembered retching up the pills last night. In fact, now that she remembered, she realized that was why her throat was sore this morning. She thought she vomited in a trash can or some place so the medication should be available for testing.

She frowned to herself. She felt like she was living through some murder mystery plot, one of those spine-tingling thrillers she enjoyed so much. But her intuition was on alert. She was suspicious and she was doing necessary things like escaping from some unknown terror with the help of her gardener. Her gardener, right! He wanted to know the plan. "Take me to your mother. I need to think." Maybe she should start reading more romance fiction, those spin-tinglers caused a person to be paranoid. Maybe.

"*Si.*" Juan looked at his passenger as he got closer to his mother's place. "Will my mother be safe?" A good question based on the old woman's behavior.

Emily took a deep breath. She had to trust someone, even if it was this young man. "I think someone tried to harm me," her voice getting stronger as she spoke. "I think he tried to poison me. I threw up the medication because I was suspicious." She drank water from a bottle he handed her. "It's a long story, but I think I need to hide, and we need to talk to the police. I think my grandchildren are in danger, too."

Juan paled. "The police will think I did this. I got a record."

"Nonsense, we'll talk to my friend Lynn Powers."

"Ah, Miss Lynn." Juan looked at the lady with relief. "She's my friend, too." He thought over everything Emily had said. "If you are in danger, I don't want the neighbors to see you. We'll drive into the backyard, and I will take you in the kitchen door. No one will see you and we can call Miss Lynn as soon as we explain to Mama." Juan didn't even want to think about what his mother would say.

"I like the way you think," smiled the woman. "I may still be in danger and a threat to anyone I'm with."

xxx

Saturday morning Jody answered her door. It sounded as though someone were just leaning on the bell. "Noah?"

"I noticed that your shop is closed so I'm checking on you."

"Everyone's shop is closed. We're all contagious and quarantined, remember?" She pulled him in.

"I'm exhausted. Viruses should be for young people."

"Are you sick?" She followed him into her kitchen.

"No, but many of my patients are. I have to wear all that gear just to tend them." He flopped in a chair at the table and pulled the crossword puzzle toward him. "I'm seldom at my office so I haven't checked on you. How are you feeling? Do you need anything?"

She smiled at him. "I'm open - running my business on the internet through email and texts. Folks working from home seem to need a lot of office supplies. But I may have to let two of my people go if this lasts long. There's just not

138

enough work." She placed a cup of tea in front of him as she asked, "Scrambled or over easy?"

"Scrambled." He never took his eyes off the puzzle as he diligently penciled in letters.

The rest of the morning they spent quietly enjoying a shared breakfast and talking about the changes driven by the pandemic. As she stood at the sink wiping up after breakfast, Noah took her hand. "I've missed seeing you." He pulled her into an embrace. "I was worried you might be the next patient I saw on a respirator." He nuzzled her ear. "We old folks have to be careful."

"Is this careful?" she asked as she placed her arms at his waist. "You could be giving me this disease."

"No, I'm careful." He sighed into her ear leaning his head on her shoulder. "I'm also old. My mind has plenty of ideas about you, but my body hasn't had enough sleep." He pulled his head back to look at her making certain she understood his desire and his fatigue.

Jody laughed at him and gave him a kiss on the cheek. "We could rest and watch a movie. I know what you mean about tired. I also think we're under a lot of stress, times being what they are."

"Snuggle it is." They tuned the big screen TV to a movie channel and soon Noah was asleep, his head in Jody's lap and an old throw keeping him warm.

She looked down at the tired, endearing face and pushed the curls back from his forehead. She had to admit when he visited, she felt calm and relaxed, the old worries of the business and retirement faded away. He was good for her mental health.

xxx

Juan knew that his mother was easy to rile, but he hoped she would listen to his story and to the old woman before she yelled or fainted. Pulling behind his mother's place, he helped

139

the woman out of the truck and almost had to carry her into the house.

"Mama," he called, "we have a guest." He seated the woman on a chair at the kitchen table.

Lucia rushed into the room, patting her hair. She stopped as she caught sight of the frail woman sitting at the table dressed in a bathrobe gripping her purse in her lap. "Miss Emily?"

"I'm sorry to intrude, Lucia," said Emily, "but your son has offered to help me contact my friend, Lynn Powers."

"Miss Lynn?" Lucia watched as Juan gave the woman a cup of tea he had heated in the microwave. Then, he set a plate of cookies in front of her.

"Thank you, dear," said the woman as she removed the tea bag and placed it on a small saucer Juan had set on the table. She then reached for a cookie, tasted it, and smiled, "Did you make these?" she asked Lucia.

Juan's mother nodded. "I bake because my son likes to eat. And I bake and sell to my friends. They like the familiar things for celebrations." Lucia's recipes brought back the flavors and memories for many of her friends of their homes before they crossed the border.

"These are delicious," remarked Emily as she dribbled crumbs onto her robe. She drank tea and ate another cookie while Lucia stared at her and Juan. "These are Mexican cookies?"

Lucia smiled. "My cookies are from all of Central America. My friends have told me that I have baked as they remember the flavors." She took another cookie sheet from the oven. "I use only the best ingredients. Everyone says my cookies taste as they remember their mamas'."

As the ladies appeared ready to launch into a world baking discussion, Juan cleared his throat and said, "Miss Emily would like to contact Miss Lynn. What is our plan?"

"I like your suggestion. We need a plan. She's probably at home," said the older woman as she watched Lucia fill another cookie sheet with small mounds of dough, "but I don't have my cell. Heath took it from me."

The more he heard the more Juan became uneasy about this man's odd behavior. "Maybe I should call," suggested Juan, "We will ask her to visit and not say you are here."

Lucia was ready to burst with curiosity. "What is going on?" she finally demanded.

Emily said, "Let me explain. I think my grandson-in-law tried to kill me." Lucia stumbled into a kitchen chair. The old woman continued, "I didn't take my medicine when his girlfriend gave it to me. I mean I took them but vomited. Juan came to work in my garden and helped me get away. I don't know where Heath is, or his girlfriend. But he was planning to meet my great-grandchildren at the airport one day soon and take them to our cabin in the forest. I think the children are in danger and I have to talk to Lynn." She sipped her tea and went on almost to herself. "I think he's trying to get control of my money." Emily thought for a moment about all she suspected. "We have to get to Lynn and her husband."

"Her husband?" asked Juan.

"Of course." Emily rolled her eyes. "He's a bigshot detective." Juan felt his knees wobble. He recalled meeting the man the day he helped Lynn with her garden.

Lucia had made herself a cup of tea and pulled in closer to the table. "How can we help?"

The two women talked through several options and finally decided on the direct, or almost direct, approach. Juan worried about how much more trouble he would be in.

"Miss Lynn," Lucia sobbed into the phone initiating phase one of the plan, "I found something I think my son stole. Please come to my home and bring your husband." She sobbed again and then gave Lynn directions to her home. She ended the call.

They all looked at one another. Emily patted Juan's arm. "Don't worry. I'll see that nothing happens to you."

Juan could only see another jail sentence in his future.

CHAPTER 17

"Dusty, I don't want you to get carried away," instructed Lynn as she settled into Dusty's SUV. "I don't want a shoot-out or anything. Lucia said her son was ready to confess."

Dusty looked at her and rolled his eyes. "I'm only with you because you tempted me with a stop at the bakery on the way home."

"I made you French toast for breakfast. How can you be hungry?"

He nodded his head. "I'm not hungry now, but I suspect after this wild goose chase of yours I'll need some biscotti."

She laughed. "Lucia sounded so frightened. I like her son. You met him when he helped me mulch and plant my garden."

"That's the guy?" Dusty barely remembered the young man who had been covered in leaves and twigs after a day working for Lynn. He had been grateful Juan had been her garden slave that day. She nodded and frowned through the windshield as they pulled up in front of the small house.

Lucia was at the door before they even knocked. She almost pulled them into the dark living room. As Lynn's eyes became adjusted, she gasped, "Emily!"

Juan was sitting in a chair in the corner. Emily was stretched out on the couch her back braced by a pillow with a blanket across her legs.

"Did anyone follow you?" she asked in a whisper.

"Follow us?" Dusty should have known that this would turn into one of Lynn's dramas.

Juan jumped up and got chairs from the kitchen as Dusty scanned the room. His detective instincts were buzzing on alert - nothing was as it seemed. "This better be good," he warned Lynn.

She opened her mouth to protest, but Emily cleared her throat. "We have a story to tell you, detective, and we need help." With that she and Juan related their story. Then she said, wrapping up, "And I think my great-grandchildren are in danger, if not already . . . I can't even say it." She pulled the blanket to her eyes. "He told me he was picking them up at the airport and would keep them at our old cabin for a few days in quarantine."

"Old cabin? Is this place close by?" asked Dusty. "Could we get to them easily?"

"We own a small parcel where my granddaughter, Alicia, kept her art studio. It's right beside the state forest. Near the head waters of the James River. I can't give you good directions because I didn't go there often."

Dusty asked several questions and was soon on his phone talking to his staff. All his listeners understood was that the other detectives were to do some research that was to be quiet, and they were to move fast. He broke from his conversation to ask, "Ms. Jacobs, where do you want us to take you?" Lucia and the older woman exchanged glances.

"I can stay here," she replied, and Lucia nodded.

He looked around the small house. "I'll have someone come and stay with you." He issued more instructions into his phone. Ending his conversation, he said to Lynn, "You stay here, too." He explained his plan further, "I'm meeting my staff at the office to search flight schedules for the kids and tax maps for the property. Once we get things organized, Tee will come here to provide security. We'll try to locate this fellow, his girlfriend and the children." He turned to Emily. "Do you remember the girlfriend's name?"

"Yetta Masterson." Emily shrugged. "When she said she was a Masterson, I became very nervous."

Dusty then asked, "Can we go look at your place, do a walk through?"

"Certainly." She thought a moment. "If the house is locked, the patio door to my bedroom should be open. We didn't lock that door when Juan helped me escape."

He attacked his phone again giving more instructions. He turned to Lynn, "Tee will be here as soon as she can. You keep things calm." He kissed her cheek, acknowledged the others and was out the door.

Dusty called almost immediately after leaving. "Tell Ms. Jacobs, her grandchildren arrived at the airport yesterday. We'll be checking with airport security for video." Lynn explained the call to everyone at the house.

"I want you with him when they go to the cabin," Emily said to Lynn after Dusty's call. "If Heath has left them at the cabin, those children will be so frightened." She wiped her eyes. "I'm so glad I made you and Penny trust managers. Take my new will to Mr. O'Hara's office before you do anything else. Here I'll sign it and you two women witness it." She pulled the papers from her designer bag and signed the documents. "Once I sprained my ankle, I never got back into town to give it to him." She signed the paper and wiped her tears.

After Lynn and Lucia had also signed, Lynn said, "I don't have a car."

"Juan, he will take you," said Lucia.

"I can't leave you two alone," argued Lynn.

"We'll be fine. Lucia needs help baking. We have plenty to do." Emily sounded like her problems were almost solved.

Lynn thought for a moment. She really did want to find those children. She was their almost guardian after all. She knew no one would find Emily at this tiny little house on a quiet street. "Just don't tell the security officer where we went. You can say that we went to buy more groceries, or

145

something." The ladies nodded, conspiracy gleaming in their eyes. Lynn and Juan were soon in his truck.

"Where are we going?" he asked as he pulled on to the main road.

"We'll give this will to my father. His partner, Mr. O'Hara is in the hospital." She thought a moment. "Then we'll go to my place and use my computer to search the county tax records looking for this cabin." She glanced at Juan. "You're dressed to hike. I'll get ready, too." He was in his sturdy yard maintenance clothing.

He looked at her with startled eyes. "Your husband, he might -

"Don't worry. Just a little hike. You heard Ms. Jacobs. She wants a woman's touch so the kids aren't frightened."

Juan had misgivings, but he knew she wouldn't listen. There was that prison stretch looming in his future, again.

XXX

Dusty got back to the office, happy to see that his staff had assembled, even though it was a Saturday. "Thanks for coming in," he said, "Lynn's friend is really concerned."

Mars was showing everyone some photo on his phone. By the murmurs of the other two, Dusty knew it was a picture of one of Mars' stepchildren being cute. He cleared his throat, "I said thanks for coming in." Three startled faces looked at him.

"I've confirmed those kids arrived at the airport," said Danny Valeri. He smelled of sugar, which meant he had been helping at the bakery this morning. "We just have to locate them and get them to their grandmother. We can put her mind at ease and be home for dinner." He brushed his hands together and Dusty saw flour erupt in little clouds.

Tee said, "My kids are at the park with Lonzo. I was only going to relax by myself today." She sniffed at the chief. "It's not like I'm ever alone anymore." Holding down a job was a challenge for a mom with three young children suddenly at home all day.

Dusty smirked. "Just get over to that house and we'll find those kids. You heard Danny, you'll be home by dinner."

Danny and Mars laughed. Before Dusty could say more, everyone's cellphone rang as well as the phones on their desks. Mars caught the call. He listened, grunted, nodded. Turning to everyone he said, "Samson found Yetta Masterson dead at Mrs. Jacobs' house. He's got the ME and everyone on the way." Samson Teaberry was the officer Dusty had dispatched to search Emily's house.

"Cause of death?"

"He says she's laying on the kitchen floor with her head at a weird angle." The other detectives nodded.

Dusty reset his attitude. He wouldn't be calming a grandmother at dinner, this was murder. "This is more serious than I thought," he grumbled. "Tell Samson he's to manage the scene, we'll be there as soon as we can." Mars relayed the instructions. Dusty continued, "Let me tell you about Mrs. Jacobs and why it's now really important we find the kids and that cabin." After he finished the explanation, he gave more instructions. "Mars and Danny, find that property and get ready for a little hike. Tee, get over to Mrs. Jacobs. Keep her at that house. I left Lynn there with her. I'll have patrol cars keeping watch on the neighborhood. Don't say anything about Yetta yet. I don't want Lynn to get ideas."

Tee asked, "Where is Mrs. Jacobs?"

"At her cleaning lady's house. It's really a good place to keep her until we know more." He turned to Danny and Mars. "You both work on locating that cabin. Get our gear together. We'll hike in this afternoon. I'm going out to check on the murder site." He was out the door. The other detectives followed orders - find the cabin, pack gear, and protect Mrs. Jacobs.

XXX

"What do we do?" Cody asked. Heath had just left the cabin. He had stopped in with a late lunch or early dinner. He had told them it was their choice when to eat.

"Why can't we go outside?" whined Amy as she threw herself on the small cot with its thin foam mattress. When Heath left, she had run to the door hoping to get out before it closed.

"Because we're locked in," said Cody.

"Are we prisoners?"

"Yes." Meg sat beside her on the cot.

Amy started to cry - again. "I don't want to be a prisoner. I want Mommy. I want my dolls. I want to go home." Meg stroked her hair.

"We'll get you home. Please don't cry." Her brother sat on her other side on the cot and hugged Amy as he stared over her head at Meg. She nodded.

Heath Dawson, their mother's second husband and now her widower, said he would return by tomorrow morning with a great breakfast. Meg glanced at the greasy fries and nondescript sandwiches he had abandoned on the table. She had no intention of being in the cabin when he returned.

"He wants Mom's money," Meg whispered to her brother. "It's got to be about money. I wonder if he wants us dead to get our money, too."

"Do we have a lot of money?" asked Cody.

Meg shrugged. "I don't know. I don't think Mom ever sold her artwork, but we had food and stuff. And we go to a boarding school."

"Maybe when our dad died, she got money," Cody speculated. "Or maybe Grandma has money. She lives in a nice house."

"It doesn't make any difference," Meg replied, "He wants to get rid of us." She gave her brother a hard stare. "We have to escape into the forest."

"We can take some food and blankets." Cody was making plans.

"This isn't some kid movie," she told her brother, "This is just get out of here alive. We get into the forest and walk until we find help. It should only take a day. We just escape and walk downhill. We're in the mountains. Down will be that town."

He frowned at her. "OK, but we take some food, and water."

"Clothes," gasped Meg. They had traveled from South Carolina in their shorts, bringing along minimum clothing. "It will be cold in the forest. We better put on two or three shirts."

Searching through their clothing and collecting supplies, they began to plan their escape.

xxx

What a bright, sunny day, thought Heath. It was hard not to appreciate things when life was going according to plan. He had his ATM receipt and for good measure had a gasoline receipt from Portage dated minutes after he left the cabin in the forest. The kids were set. He'd get back to the cabin on Monday and find it had burned down. His sorrow, his grief. He laughed; he'd earn an Academy Award after this weekend. Now it was time to find the bodies at Miss Emily's and prepare his story of robbery and murder, with the lawn guy as the prime suspect.

Coming around the last bend he caught sight of Emily's house and an unmistakable blue flashing light. Police, already? He slowed, spied at least two other vehicles and decided to keep on going. Around two more curves he found a small church yard and parked. He had to think. Maybe someone had visited and found the bodies or had become suspicious when the old lady didn't answer her phone. That damned yard guy! Heath calmed himself. These were things he couldn't control, but he could adapt.

He decided to return to Yetta's place in River Bend. It was a great hideaway. He could stash the jewelry, give the police time to do their paperwork at Emily's, then show up at the house later today. He had a paper trail of the last several hours - the ATM, gasoline receipt. He was good. With everyone staying indoors and wearing masks outside, he'd never be recognized. He'd be a good citizen and mask up for health. Yeah. He laughed out loud. Fate again. That virus was helping him at every opportunity.

Until . . . He took the turn onto Yetta's street and saw a police car in front with an officer knocking at the door. Damn small towns. If they found Yetta's body already that means they probably knew her and knew where she lived. Not like a big city where it would take time to ID, then locate someone. He kept going. His instincts were screaming, "Stay out of sight. Go into hiding." He needed to do some deep thinking. But where? Looking down a cross street he saw the answer.

He drove directly into the hospital parking deck and found a dark corner. Time to think, to adjust. He ran through all his actions for the last few weeks. They would find his prints at Yetta's and at Emily's. They could track him to Hilton Head. They could track his credit card use. And he had a bag of Emily's jewelry in his car. Damn.

He decided he needed a story that would explain all the evidence. He snapped his fingers! He would say Yetta thought he had symptoms of that virus. He would profess concern that he would give the virus to Emily and the kids, so he went into self-quarantine. Eager to protect the kids and Emily, he could say he hired Yetta to tend the old lady and hired a friend of Yetta's to stay with the kids. He'd just have to stay out of sight for a week or two. His wealth would wait. No one else would be alive to claim it by tomorrow morning. Since the cabin would be destroyed soon, the police wouldn't know that the kids were alone. He could say he left them with a nanny. If they didn't find her remains in the explosion, he could suggest that maybe she had run an errand. He rubbed his eyes. This was getting too complex. But there was no one to disprove his alibi. And the payoff would be worth it.

His new plan, or as he thought of it, his great escape, began to take shape. First, his car. The big, black SUV with South Carolina plates might draw attention. He decided to help himself to a new license tag. He selected one of the cars that had backed into a parking slot. He backed his car into a slot, slipped out quietly, and removed his tag, switched it for a new tag and left the parking deck. He decided to head west and look for a deserted house or cabin in the western counties. He knew that several Hilton Head friends maintained places in western North Carolina. He was certain he'd find something. Fate was on his side, he reminded himself. He'd lay low, or as folks said these days, self-quarantine. He loved this virus.

xxx

Teniquia knocked at the door of the tiny cottage in the quiet old neighborhood. She had come in a patrol car. She knew the neighbors were watching through their curtains. She wanted to make certain everyone knew the police were calling on Lucia. After a quick knock, she walked into the small living room and swooned at the aroma coming from the kitchen as she closed the door.

Walking through the house Tee found the two women working in the small kitchen, one clearly the maid. But the other? She squinted. "Mrs. Jacobs?"

"Yes, dear." The woman was wearing an old house dress and apron over her small, thin body while she transferred cookies from a baking sheet to a cooling rack.

The officer introduced herself then took a quick tour of the house, even checking out the backyard. "Where's Lynn?"

"She went to get us some supplies," replied Emily. "We have this baking to do. Lucia is, er, baking for her cousin's wedding."

"We're in a pandemic," replied the suspicious officer. "Where's Lynn?" The detective took a cookie from the cooling rack and swayed at its rich sweetness. "My mother needs this recipe."

"Wait until you try these." Emily opened a plastic container and offered the officer another cookie. "But you have to have some tea and then you can sample this cake. It's coming out of the oven in about fifteen minutes."

Teniquia heated some water in the microwave and took a tea bag from the box Lucia handed her. Then she sat to wait for the cake. But she didn't forget to ask, "Where's Lynn?"

The two women looked at her. Finally, Mrs. Jacobs said, "She went to help find my great-grandchildren."

Teniquia rubbed her brow feeling a Lynn headache coming on. She ate a few more cookies and decided that she would forget she knew anything. Lynn couldn't possibly find them in the forest anyway. It took Mars and Danny awhile to find the property location. And she had helped them collect the night vision goggles and the camping gear and some food and water. Lynn wouldn't be that prepared. She'd probably go off in her heels and a swishy skirt thinking this cabin was under some neon sign blinking, "Lost kids here!" Yeah, Tee didn't have anything to worry about. Lynn wouldn't run into the chief.

The women said nothing and kept baking. There was a knock at the front door. Tee pulled her weapon and gave the two ladies a scowl, signaling that they stay hidden in the kitchen. She glanced out the window. Another patrol car? She opened the door and replaced her weapon in its holster. Sherri Steiner, a young patrol officer stood out front.

Tee waited for her to enter but Sherri whispered, "Outside." Tee stepped out, closed the door, and waited. Sherri took a breath, "I'm to replace you. Dusty wants you back at the office. You're to take the lead on the body they found at Mrs. Jacobs' place, and he wants you in the office in case he and the guys need anything. They're leaving for the forest."

"Samson, too?"

"No, he's doing stakeout at Mrs. Jacobs' house in case the guy comes back." Sherri was newly sworn, having recently completed her training. She glowed with excitement.

The detective blew out her breath. This was turning into a Saturday that was going to make up for the last boring week of quarantine. "Only Yetta's body, right?"

Sherri shrugged. "She was the only one at Mrs. Jacobs'."

"Come inside," offered Tee, "It's time we told these ladies what's happening." Once inside she called, "Ladies, could you come here?" When Lucia and Emily had taken seats as the detective indicated, she began, "This is Officer Steiner. She's come with some news." Tee had decided it was time they knew about the murder. "Yetta Masterson's body has been found in Mrs. Jacobs' house."

The expected gasps came, then Emily took a breath and explained to Lucia, "She was the nurse that Heath brought to help me last night. She's the one who gave me the drugs to put me to sleep."

Tee pulled out her notebook and began asking questions and making notes. "How do you know it was Yetta Masterson?"

"She told me her name." Emily shook her head. "When I heard the name Masterson, I knew I should be cautious. That's why I spit up those pills."

"How long was she at your place?"

"Heath brought her by yesterday and told me she would help me bathe and things because I couldn't seem to recover from a sprained ankle." She gasped. "Do you think he was drugging me?"

The detective shrugged. "We'll test you to see what's in your system. Who's your doctor?"

"Doc Noah."

"Do you mind if I ask him to come over and check you and draw some blood?"

"Maybe that would be wise." Emily watched police drama. She understood these things.

"I have to get to the office and organize the investigation. Officer Steiner will be staying here with both of you. Any questions?"

"What about the children?" Emily was now worried about the youngsters' safety.

"When I left the office to come here, the chief was planning on hiking into the property this afternoon. That's why I'm running the investigation. He's going to get the children and expects me to get the murder investigation organized." She raised her eyebrows silently asking if there were more questions. There were none. She stepped to the door with Sherri and whispered a few instructions, waved good-by and was gone.

Sherri turned to her charges. "What's that great smell?"

And two frightened ladies relaxed a bit and dragged the new cookie tester into the kitchen.

CHAPTER 18

A phone rang, jolting Noah out of his nap. Jody woke with a start; she must have dozed off, too. The movie had ended, and the internet streaming service was waiting for the next command. As she watched, he threw off the covering and stumbled to his feet. He reached into his pocket and soon had the intruding phone in his hand.

"Yes?" After listening for a long minute he asked, "Tee, please repeat that. . . . Poison? . . . . Tests?" He listened some more. "Where is she?" More conversation. "She wouldn't be safe in the hospital. This damned virus." He looked around the room and saw a desk. He made a motion indicating that he wanted to write. Jody dashed to the desk and found paper and pencil. He looked at her. "Take this down." He proceeded to relay the information coming from the caller. "I'll get right over there."

When he ended the call Jody was staring at him, the pencil poised for more direction. "This sounds serious."

"Come with me." He straightened his clothing. "It seems Detective LaMont wants me to draw some blood from Emily Jacobs. They think she was poisoned but survived. She's hiding out with her cleaning lady." He took the notes from her and scanned them. "You write beautifully." He kissed her cheek.

"If I hadn't heard your conversation, I would think you were making this up."

"These are really strange times." He escorted her to his car.

xxx

Stumbling through the county online tax maps finally paid off. "Look, it's on forestry road 1345, and amazingly has an address. I bet we can find it on GPS." Lynn grabbed a Post-it from the desk drawer and jotted the address and the road designation.

"I don't have GPS in my truck," said Juan getting a funny feeling.

"That's OK," said Lynn, "We'll ask at the visitor's center, then use my phone. Isn't technology great!" She grabbed her bag and towed him out to his truck handing him two backpacks when they dashed through the kitchen. "It's a state forest. There's a visitor center. We'll ask them. And my phone has a map and GPS." Before pulling the door shut, she instructed the dog, "Watch the house."

"We're going to ask the visitor center people to show us where some guy may be hiding some kids or even killing them?" Juan felt himself being sucked back into prison through no fault of his own. This woman was crazy.

"No, we'll ask for a map of good hiking trails to the headwaters." She shook her head. "Juan, you have to be flexible." She belted herself into the seat as Juan revved the engine.

"Why are you so flexible?" he asked as he drove his old truck out toward the countryside.

"Because my husband doesn't like me interfering with his investigations and I have to work around him."

"Now we are making your husband angry?" The young man wanted to cry. How was he ever going to get ahead, find a path to a good job, when he was teamed up with a crazy woman who had no conscience.

"Stop!" Lynn shouted and almost stopped Juan's heart. "We need some food and water." When they had stopped in The Heights to allow Lynn to dress for hiking, they had thrown empty backpacks into Juan's truck. "We'll need water and some snacks when we find the kids." Juan pulled into a small gas mart.

Finally they were on the road into the forest supplied with drinks, snacks and the map Lynn was wrestling with that they had gotten from the visitor center. The center was closed for quarantine, but the helpful rangers had left brochures and maps beside the locked doors. And Juan had another lesson in flexibility as he followed her directions.

xxx

"Doctor Noah," a cheery Sherri Steiner greeted the callers.

"Little Sherri," grinned Noah, "all dressed up and dangerous." He looked over the petite patrolman decked out in her official gear.

"Don't be condescending, Noah," Jody spoke like a general.

"Mrs. Donlin?" continued the officer as she stepped aside.

To Sherri, Jody said, "I haven't seen you for months. Congratulations on your new job."

"Yes, ma'am." Sherri blushed. She had once dated Jody's youngest son. By this time Emily and Lucia had drifted into the living room. Sherri straightened to her five-foot height, and the police officer took charge. "Doctor Noah and Mrs. Donlin, this is our hostess, Lucia - and you know Mrs. Jacobs. I've sent for a patrolman and one of our crime techs to collect the blood sample. We will be taking it to the ME, following all chain of custody protocols as we do in collecting evidence for a murder case."

Jody gasped. Noah said, "I am prepared for that task, but then Jody and I want an explanation. Murder?" "Don't be so pompous, Noah," said Emily as she settled on the sofa and rolled up her sleeve. "Someone tried to murder me. Get the job done and we'll tell you everything." She gave the doctor a curious glance. "And we expect an explanation as to why Jody is with you."

"What smells so delicious?" asked Jody as a distraction.

"We'll share it with you," promised Sherri, "once this job is done." Noah wiggled his nose, appreciating the aroma, and got to work.

"And we'll still expect an explanation," Emily reminded Noah as he took her arm, looking for a vein as Sherri's crime techs knocked at the door.

xxx

It was late afternoon and the sky was darkening when Lynn and Juan finally got to the trail indicated on the map that followed the tumbling waterway up to the headwaters. It was a three-mile hike, but was well marked, according to the map. They pulled into the trees, hiding the truck as best they could. Once parked, Lynn climbed into the truck bed and began to organize their equipment. "We'll have to walk fast to get close enough before dark."

"Why are we hiking in?" Juan asked. "We can drive to this cabin."

"We have to sneak in," explained Lynn. "The son-in-law could be holding the kids hostage or something."

"Miss Lynn, I can go in myself," offered Juan, "You stay and wait for me to return with the children." He didn't know what he would do in a hostage situation, but he was certain Lynn would be a liability.

"We'll go together." She spoke in a voice that said there would be no more discussion.

Juan kept his silence. He figured, if she was like his mother, after the first mile she'd be ready to make camp. He took the backpacks she handed him and helped her out of the truck then helped her pack the food and water, then helped her adjust her own pack.

After studying the map for several minutes, she said, "I don't think we'll need any camping gear." The backpack with water and snacks was already heavy enough for her. They agreed on the direction and plunged into the forest.

xxx

"I don't like the looks of that place," Mars said as Dusty's SUV bounced over the forest road. "We should just go in the front way." He stared at the satellite photo of the property.

"We don't have a warrant," growled Dusty. "We'll go in the back way, follow that trail on your map and cross over at the top of the ridge."

"Park at the turnout where the trail crosses the road," Mars told Danny. "We should be able to get to the ridge in an hour."

Dusty growled again. He didn't want to race three miles up hill.

When they pulled into the area, Danny remarked, "Someone's already here. Most be some early-season campers." They all looked at an old truck tucked deep in the trees and thought nothing more of it.

Pulling the SUV off the road, the men got out and collected their gear for the hike to the ridge. Danny distributed water and power bars. Mars handed out the night vision equipment and the radios. Dusty made certain his boots were tied and his pack fit snuggly without impeding his ability to reach his weapon. He hated hiking when he was armed. It meant River Bend was getting more and more like a big city.

They started out with the sun behind them, painting all the new leaves with a golden edge, sort of like kissing everything good night. The wildlife in the forest was bedding down for the night among the new growth and fresh scents while the nocturnal creatures were just beginning to stir. The officers had no time to enjoy it.

Mars pulled up. "There's someone ahead of us." "Maybe the folks from that truck," suggested Danny.

159

"Mars," said Dusty, "you go ahead and do some recon. I don't want to scare someone or run into that son-in-law." Mars handed his pack to Danny and melted into the underbrush. Dusty and Danny continued to move forward but at a slower pace.

Within minutes, they heard Mars call, "Chief" in a voice that made Dusty growl. He and Danny rushed to meet Mars. And there they found Lynn and Juan.

Dusty swore.

"Hi, honey," Lynn greeted her husband.

"Don't honey me." Then he scowled at Juan. The young man tried to melt into the ground.

"Don't be mad at Juan," said Lynn, "We came because Emily asked us to be here when you got the children because they would need help."

"How did you find this place?" Dusty asked. He knew how hard it had been for his team to locate the hiking trail and cabin.

Lynn shrugged, "I asked around."

"Chief, we're losing daylight." Mars interrupted another string of oaths from Dusty.

The detective nodded. "Keep up," he told Lynn. And the troop took off toward the ridge.

xxx

"Can we get out through the roof?" Meg had initially asked. Heath had the door locked and all the windows barred. But there were small windows in the roof gable on either side of the fireplace chimney. After a lot of thought and theory, they had worked out a plan to climb into the rafters and push out a small window in the gable.

They stripped the beds and tore the sheets, tying the wide strips into a long rope. Cody climbed along the rock face of the fireplace, taking their improvised sheet rope. The girls held their breath as they watched. He worked his way to the

160

window on the left because the rock work seemed to offer a small ledge under the sill to help him balance. Cody had tied the sheet rope around his waist saying, "If it's not long enough you can just add more strips." He had been correct. The girls added three more lengths.

Once at the small ledge he tried the window. "It doesn't open," he shouted down.

"Can you break it? Or kick it out?" suggested Meg. As she spoke, she scanned the cabin for some sort of implement.

"Get a rock," said Amy trying to be helpful. The older kids shared a nod.

"Good idea." Cody wiggled some of the rocks along the chimney face. One came out in his hand. He didn't know if it was big enough, but he'd try.

"Wrap it in a bit of the sheet," said Meg. "I don't want you getting cut."

Cody gave that some thought. "I have an idea." He pulled more sheet rope up the wall. He wrapped some around his hand for protection, then held the larger end of the rock and shoved the jagged, pointed end into the glass. It took several tries because he had to find leverage by grasping a ceiling beam with his other hand. But finally, there was a crack. Having another idea, he dropped the rock and grasped the beam with both hands. Next, he swung his feet into the crack. He had no control as his feet went through the window. Struggling back to balance on the sill, he cut the backs of his legs.

The girls saw the blood and Amy started to cry. Meg said, "Does it hurt much?"

"Yes," he said as he cleared the jagged pieces of glass to make the window opening safe for the girls to use. "But we can get out." Untying the sheet strip from his waist, he wiped the blood with the end of the rope, then tied it to the beam. "Send

161

up Amy. The sooner we get out the sooner you can clean my leg." Meg nodded.

She pulled her sister into position. "It's a good thing Heath sent us to that wilderness camp. Remember how we rappelled?" she asked Amy.

"Sort of." The little girl took a deep, frightened breath as she stared at the knotted rope in the rafters. It was red with her brother's blood.

"Just pretend you're walking up the wall." Meg was trying to ignore the bloody rope.

"Okay." The little girl began her ascent with her siblings encouraging her at every step.

Cody had cleared the glass shards from the sill so Amy could kneel in position. Once she balanced beside him up in the rafters, he said, "I want you to walk down the outside of the cabin just like you walked up, okay?" It was getting dark.

Amy sniffled. He helped her twist into position on the small rock ledge. When she seemed secure, he tossed the sheet rope out the window. "This is the tricky part," he said as he instructed Amy to squat on the sill beside him. Once she did, he had her take the rope, still tied to the beam. As she held the rope, he encouraged her to stand on the empty window frame and lean out backwards.

"I'll fall," she whimpered.

"No, you won't; you have to get down there so I can pull the rope back up for Meg."

"I'll be all alone in the dark."

"So move fast. She'll be there in a few minutes after I pull the rope up and I'll be sitting here the whole time." He could hear her sniffle as they stared into the dark forest. He helped her lean back and get her feet out of the window. She moved into the darkening night. He waited and heard no thud. She didn't fall. Yet.

Finally she whispered, loudly, "I'm here."

"Don't move." He pulled the rope back up and dropped it down to Meg as he said, "Remember to turn out the lights in case Heath is watching. He'll think we're asleep."

XXX

When the searchers arrived at the stream crossing, a rock path at the foot of a small waterfall, they had just enough daylight to guide them across and climb to a good promontory to look over the property. Mars whispered down to the team. "The cabin has a light on." He studied the scene with his binoculars. "I'm looking at the front door. I can see movement in the cabin." He slid down to the group. "I can see a path emerging from the back of the cabin coming this way and the forest road close to the front door. We can work our way to the edge of the trees."

"It's almost seven now," said Dusty, "Let's contact the squad coming in at the front and let them know we're here. They should be in position at that privacy gate for the property." They all nodded. The other patrol would be blocking the forest road to prevent anyone entering or leaving the property. "Mars, get back up there and watch." Was Heath Dawson with the children? Were they safe?

XXX

When Meg reached the ledge, Cody began to pull up the sheet rope. "Why's this so heavy?"

"It's Amy's backpack. I put some water in it and some stuff to clean your cuts that I found in Mom's cupboard." They got the pack up and, remembering Amy was under the window, whispered, "Move over so this doesn't hit you."

They lower the rope down the outside of the cabin. Meg moved to the sill, then to the window frame, leaned back and disappeared into the night. A whisper came back to Cody, and he leaned out of the window and soon stood beside his sisters.

"Let me see your legs," said Meg.

"It's too dark," argued her brother.

163

"Let me just wipe them with some water and wrap them with these extra strips I brought." Wilderness first aid, another gift of wilderness camp!

He agreed because his legs felt slimy. He was correct it was too dark to see, but Meg dribbled water onto the back of his legs, wiped them dry, applied some ointment, and then wrapped his shins in torn sheeting strips. She stood up. "All done."

xxx

Dusty pulled the rest of the group together. "When we go in, you and Juan stay here and wait." Lynn nodded. "If we bring out any kids, you be prepared to give them something to drink and calm them down." Juan nodded because he was now officially part of the rescue team.

"Chief," Mars called down from his vantage point, "something's strange. All the lights went out in the cabin."

"Maybe they're going to sleep."

They all craned their necks looking up at Mars as he adjusted his sophisticated equipment. "Shit. I can't see anything moving through the windows."

"Are the children in there alone?" asked Lynn.

"Or maybe he drugged them?" asked Danny. "How smart are these kids?"

"I don't see any movement," called Mars. "There's no vehicle to suggest he's there."

"Let's get closer," said Dusty to the team. Mars slid down from his spot and joined the scramble up the rocks along the stream bank to find the path to the cabin.

xxx

"Let's get out of here," Meg whispered once she finished wrapping Cody's wounds. "Keep low in case Heath's out there somewhere watching. Let's follow our plan and go to the river."

"What plan?" asked the little girl.

164

"This is a prisoner escape," Cody told his sister. "We don't want the guards to see us." He grabbed her hand and followed Meg.

The older children knew the geography well. They had spent many summers at the cabin with their parents and had been allowed a lot of freedom to explore. As the oldest, Meg took charge and led them toward the rushing water. "We can cross the rocks at that little waterfall and follow the trail. I think we should do as much walking as we can tonight and hide in the daylight if we haven't found help."

"I'm scared," whimpered Amy.

"I know, but prisoners have to be tough," said her brother. "We'll be at Grandmother's by dinner tomorrow and we'll tell her about our adventure."

"We're going to Grandmother's?" Amy liked that idea. "Will she hide us from Heath?"

"Yes," said her sister, "She'll probably get the police after him."

"Goody." Amy couldn't clap her hands because her brother and sister each held onto one as they walked into the dark forest away from the cabin prison.

And then the world exploded!

xxx

"Was that a bomb?" gasped Lynn as Mars and Danny raced ahead. They could hear debris returning to earth as pieces of cabin crashed into the surrounding trees.

Dusty said, "Stay here." He dropped his pack and clutched his side arm. "Juan, stay close to her."

"*Si.*"

xxx

The kids were thrown to the ground by the impact of the explosion. The trees caught most of the debris that had become airborne. "He meant us to be in there," whispered Meg. "Let's keep moving. He might be close, watching." The

165

three kids tripped and stumbled in the dark over the trail that in daylight they could run without hesitation.

"Wait," whimpered Amy, "you're going too fast. Can't we hide until morning?"

"He might be following us," Meg whispered as she tugged at her sister.

"We have to move in case he's out there. We promise, Amy, we'll be at Grandmother's to sleep tomorrow." Cody held Amy's other hand, urging her to follow Meg.

"I'm thirsty," she cried.

"You can drink as soon as we cross the river."

Two watchers kept the threesome insight. Once the children were close enough, Danny stepped out of the forest cover. He held a small light over his head and said, "Don't be afraid, we're the police."

Amy screamed, but her brother stepped forward. "How do we know you're not lying?"

"Good question," said Danny as he used his free hand to pull his ID from his pocket. "Can you read it in this light?"

"I can read it," said the older girl. She studied it as she held it close to Danny's lamp. "You're from River Bend. Do you know our grandmother?"

"She sent us to find you."

"He locked us in the cabin," groused the boy. "He tried to kill us."

"That's all right, young fellow, we're here now," Danny patted the young boy's shoulder.

"Can we see Grandmother tonight?" asked Amy.

"Yes. I'm going to call my friends to join us, and we'll help you get down to our cars." With that, Danny whistled as Mars and Dusty came out of the darkness with Lynn and Juan stumbling behind.

"Are you kids all right?" Lynn was on her knees in front of the little girl.

"Do you know my grandmother?" she asked.

"Yes, and she's going to be so happy." Lynn hugged her then hugged the other two children.

After assuring themselves that the children were well, Dusty got on his radio. Concluding his discussion, he gathered the group together. "Because our people were so close, they let the fire burn and are telling the fire responders that three bodies were in the explosion. We're taking the kids to a safe house and Tee is bringing their grandmother. We've decided that we're going to let this story play out."

"What safe house?" asked Lynn.

"Ours. We'll rotate patrolmen in and out." He turned to Juan, "Will you and your mother be okay?"

"*Si*, our neighbors will watch out for us."

As they collected their gear Amy began to cry, "I'm tired." She plopped on the ground, crying, and pulling her t-shirt hem to her eyes.

"I'll carry you," Juan said. "You ride on my back like on a horse. Maybe your brother can carry my pack."

They began the three-mile trek back to the cars.

xxx

It was a tiring, slow hike from the head waters in the dark to the cars parked in the forest. Juan had carried the youngest child the entire distance. Danny had assisted the young boy and Mars had guided the older sister. Dusty, of course, had to look after Lynn who was as tired as the kids.

Through most of the return he had been on the phone or radio with everyone coordinating public response to the explosion in the forest and to the dead body at Emily's. As the carpark came into sight he sighed, certain that he had all bases covered. According to his plan, Tee and Emily would arrive at the house in The Heights where Lonzo would be ready to check out the kids without an ambulance. Dusty wanted this rescue under everyone's radar. A patrol car was parked at the entry to the neighborhood. And another car was sitting at Will's house. As Dusty had explained, "If anyone asks, Piper slugged Will and it's just a domestic thing."

When Dusty had called them to get them in sync with the domestic disturbance story, Piper had screeched at the implications of bad publicity, but Will had sworn, "She is a mean one. I fear for my life sometimes." To which Dusty heard her swat him. But he ignored the violent sounds, focusing on the children's safety.

They finally arrived at The Heights with Juan and his tired truck following Dusty's SUV. And the party began.

Dusty pulled Juan aside, thanked him for his help and asked him to keep quiet about the events in the forest. He slapped Juan on the back and said, "Return to your mother and tell her all is well. Don't tell anyone else."

"*Sí*," said the young man, too tired to say much more.

Lynn rushed to hug him before he got into his truck. "Tell your mother we'll call if you two can help." She and Dusty watched the truck leave the yard, the truck lights finding Piper and Will as they dashed across the street to catch up on the news.

Once the kids were in the house and reunited with their great-grandmother, Dusty started to organize the program. Lonzo checked the kids for ticks and cuts, cleaning Cody's legs and praising his sister for the fine job of first aid. Emily was settled at the kitchen table with a cup of tea watching the youngsters receive care. Lynn, with the help of nosy Will and Piper, got the bedrooms ready for overnight guests.

As Piper complained when she barged in, pushing Mars out of her way, "If I'm going to be known as a violent spouse, you owe me an explanation."

To which Mars, large and quick, moved aside and said, "Yes, ma'am."

After making the beds, Lynn and Piper readied a snack for the kids then marched them through quick showers, and into bed. Or as Lynn observed, "I think they fell asleep in the shower."

With the three children tucked in, they returned to the kitchen as Dusty finished his assignments. His staff yawned as he outlined tomorrow's work. "We're in the office at 8." Three detectives yawned again. "We'll get this murder organized and start investigating the explosion. Tee, you'll organize security here." She nodded as she leaned against her husband.

Dusty sort of waved a dismissal. "All of you get out of here." The tired staff straggled out the door.

Dusty looked at Piper and Will. "Thanks for your help. These kids had a rough time these last few days."

Will threw an arm around Piper, who seemed to be asleep on her feet. "Call if we can help." And the tired couple walked home.

"Miss Emily," said Lynn, "let me help you up to bed."

"Thank you, dear." She stood and hugged Lynn then hugged Dusty. "Thank you both. Now what?"

Dusty hugged her back as he said, "You and the kids are staying here until it's safe for you to return to your place. We'll have security set up. This virus will keep things quiet." He yawned. "We'll figure the specifics out tomorrow."

The three of them tromped up the stairs. After checking the children and showing Emily her room, Lynn and Dusty sought the privacy of their room. "What a day," he moaned as he slipped off his boots and pulled off his sweatshirt.

Lynn sat in a chair to pull off her socks. She had shed her boots somewhere in the kitchen. "I can't believe all that we did from the time we got Emily's phone call."

"Can you work from home for the next week?" he asked. "I'll have security, but I think Mrs. Jacobs and the kids will need some personal looking after."

She nodded as she walked into the bathroom to wash up for bed. "I'll be here. How long will they be our guests?"

He joined her washing up. "I have no idea. That fellow who tried to murder all of them is out there some place."

Lynn shivered at the thought. She climbed into bed and snuggled close to Dusty. "I know you'll keep them safe."

He kissed her forehead. It had been a long day.

CHAPTER 19

It was convenient to have a witness staying at the house. Dusty invited Emily to go into the office with him after breakfast with a nod to Lynn that she watch the kids. He hustled Emily into his car. "I'll make this quick," he promised her. "The kids will probably sleep late."

Escorting his witness, both appropriately masked, into the office, he cleared his throat and masks appeared on the detectives. "I want us to interview Mrs. Jacobs and get her back to the kids. Tee, you take her back and interview the kids." With those basic instructions, the team began their investigation.

Emily sat at a desk and answered questions as Danny put information on the white board and the others made notes at their desks. She told them about her granddaughter and the marriage to Heath. She described Alicia's illness and explained how funds were distributed through the trust. After questions about inheritance, she explained her reorganization of the trust and her new will.

"Does this fellow know about your will?"

"I don't know if he even knows about my old will," Emily replied, "He doesn't know about the new one because I just signed it Saturday and gave it to Lynn to give to her father."

Mars, the most financially savvy detective, said, "Let me get this straight. In Alicia's will, Dawson became guardian of the kids, and he would inherit from the kids if they all predeceased him." Emily nodded. Mars rubbed his eyes and continued, "In your old will, after your death, the kids got control of their funds at age of majority. And if they predeceased Dawson, after your death, he would get control of all the money." She nodded again. "Then you reorganized the trust to be managed by your niece, Babs, along with Penny and Lynn. And your new will?"

Emily sighed. "I can't change the guardianship, so Heath still controls their lives. And I can't change Alicia's will regarding inheritance if the kids predecease him. So I gave all my money to the trust and the managers will control it. I've taken him out of any relationship to the trust by dissolving any reference to Alicia and her spouse inheriting management." She hung her head as tears rolled down her cheeks. "He just doesn't know about all these changes."

The unit thought about this information. Finally, Dusty said, "The kids and you are safe. When we find him, we'll make certain he knows the new plan. In the meantime, we're going to investigate Yetta's murder and bring him in as our suspect."

Wrapping up the interview he assigned tasks, "Danny, get this information organized. Mars, go out to the farm and inform the Mastersons about Yetta's death. Tee, take Miss Emily home and interview those kids."

The hunt was on.

xxx

Lynn was cleaning the remains of Dusty's pancakes and Emily's tea and toast when she heard the tentative sounds of three children approaching the kitchen. "Miss Lynn?" Meg was the designated scout. "Is Gram awake? What do we do now?" Amy and Cody stood behind her at the doorway.

Lynn smiled. "We have some breakfast. How about pancakes, eggs, bacon?"

"Yes." And Lynn knew by their enthusiasm that they wanted it all.

She gestured them to the table, and she sat. They did, too, with a certain wariness. "I think you and your grandmother will be staying here for a few days. My husband wants to make sure you're safe. We don't know where Mr. Dawson is but we don't think he can find you here." The kids stared at her, silent. "We have some rules to keep you and Emily safe." They nodded. "You can play around the house, but you may not leave the neighborhood. There will be a patrol car always on the street. We may have other officers in the house if Dusty thinks it's necessary." They stared as if hypnotized. "Right now, I'm going to call Dr. Robin to come look at those cuts and check you all out. And while we wait for her, you're all going to help me get breakfast."

"We get to cook?" Meg thought that sounded adventuresome.

Lynn reached out and caressed her cheek. "Since you'll be living here, you have to learn to help cook and clean. You'll have to help me make your grandmother comfortable." They nodded their agreement. "Do you have any questions?"

"We don't have clothes," replied Meg. Lynn had found Jason's old t-shirts and jogging shorts for them all to wear last night. She had their dirty clothes already in the washer this morning.

"What about school?" asked Cody.

"Can I play with the dog?" Lynn's dog Chips had been nosing Amy while she sat at the table.

"Good questions. The dog would love to become your friend." Amy grinned. "When your grandmother returns, we'll talk about clothes and things. The clothes you were wearing yesterday are in the dryer right now. And let me make some phone calls to answer your other question."

Lynn made two quick calls. Soon Piper and her son Jeff were in the kitchen helping with breakfast. A few minutes later, Dr. Robin arrived for medical checkups along with her son Ryder who thought he might find breakfast somewhere. Within minutes the kitchen was filled with laughter, teasing and a lot of food.

After breakfast Jeff and Ryder took the kids out to explore, as Lynn put it, the limits of their world. Dr. Robin,

Piper and Lynn settled down to talk. "They're all fine. Cody's legs will heal without scars. Lonzo did a good job last night." Dr. Robin sipped her coffee.

Piper slouched over her coffee. "I'll have to discuss schooling with Emily. The boarding school may go online, or they can transfer to our system and be ready to return to classes here if they'll be staying with her."

Lynn shrugged. "I have no idea. It'll all depend on when they're safe."

"Keep an ear out for any trauma," suggested Dr. Robin. Lynn gaped, puzzled. The pediatrician said, "You may hear some nightmares. Or they may exhibit some anxieties. If they run and play and bicker like regular siblings, they're probably okay."

The women heard the dog bark and children giggle and squeal as the older boys explained the intricacies of backyard basketball. Lynn poured more coffee and they settled in to listen to regular siblings at play.

xxx

Dusty had directed Mars to visit Ms. Masterson after Emily's interview. They had managed to withhold the name of the victim until family could be notified. To some degree this quarantine was helping keep information under control.

Mars drove out to the old Masterson farm, a place with a long and colorful history. He could see the remains of the old burned-out trailer because the spring foliage was just beginning to dance on the tree limbs. He shivered as he remembered that scary night, racing out to save Shonda and her young son, Cooper. They had been threatened by Shonda's crazy ex. Law enforcement arrived a minute too late. Granny Masterson had shot and killed the man as he tried to beat Shonda and throw her into the blazing inferno of the trailer.

Life was now great for Shonda. She and Cooper were protected by the Masterson family and Shonda was now in a long-term relationship with the Masterson chief IT geek, Darwin. Mars had to smile. Who would have thought any woman would have found anything to love in Darwin, a skinny, acned nerd, and sometime criminal? But Shonda had seen something, and Darwin had grown into her affection becoming a serious, successful, almost clean-cut looking, businessman.

Getting closer to the old farmhouse he noticed Granny Masterson standing on the porch, dressed in her usual housedress and work boots. One never presumed with Granny, as he recalled from a previous visit years ago when she ran him off her property swinging a broom. He climbed from the car and nodded. She nodded in return then turned and walked into the house. He adjusted his face mask per protocol and followed.

Mars had a ticklish relationship with the Masterson family. On the one hand, he was a silent partner in River Dog Brewery, owned in part by Zeke Masterson. On the other hand, as a member of the River Bend First Bank board of directors, he knew that Granny Masterson was wealthy. And on that same hand, because his uncle, Hutch Dunn, was her attorney, he knew that Granny, under a corporate name, owned a lot of property in the county. And finally, as a law enforcement officer, he knew Masterson family history, including the reasons behind the murders of two of her grandchildren a few years ago. Those two had dabbled in vice and murder until someone meaner and more deadly caught up with them.

Darwin had been party to their crimes but had not been close enough to their schemes to interest police. And he seemed to have turned a corner since Shonda and the brewers joined his life.

Inside the quiet, clean house, the old woman wearing no mask, asked, "What you want, law man?"

Mars knew the old lady was sharp. He would be straight forward. "Yetta was found murdered yesterday." He watched the old woman. She wasn't surprised.

"I read somebody died at some house. She was a fool."

"We searched her place. I think she rented it from you. We searched for any information that might lead us to her killer."

"I know you didn't need no warrant." She looked directly at him. "Did you take any of her things?"

"No, ma'am. We just looked for evidence that the person we suspect of her murder had been at her place."

"It was some man." She didn't ask.

Mars understood by her comment that she knew Yetta well. "Yes, ma'am."

She stared at Mars and asked, "When can I clean out my rental?"

No sentiment here, he thought. "We need to know who claims the body and where should it be sent. With times being what they are, there may not be funerals and things." He pulled at the mask which felt as though it were climbing into his nostrils. "You can clean out the house any time. The team has finished with it."

"I'll tell my attorney to just have her cremated. Not much family left." She nodded and seemed to shrink. Waving him to take a chair, she sat opposite. "Our Eddie," she waved at Mars' face mask, "got that there virus. Our Nikki," Eddie's wife, "quit her hospital work to tend him."

Mars pulled his mask off. This wasn't protocol. This was personal. "Can I help?"

"You maybe could stop at the brewery. They could say what they need. They want me to stay away because of my age."

"Ma'am, they're just worried about you."

"I told them boys I would wait two weeks and then I was helping."

"I understand. I'll go see them now." He stood. "Before I go, can I do anything for you?"

"You tell Darwin about Yetta. He'll help me clean the rental."

Mars nodded and returned to his car.

xxx

Emily removed her mask as she got out of the car. She smiled at Tee. "I know Dusty sent you because you have a way with youngsters. I'll call them." She looked around the yard. "I hope they're awake." But the kids had seen her arrive in a patrol car and appeared as if by magic.

"Gram," Amy asked in awe. "Did you ride in that police car?"

"How else could she get here?" Cody wanted to demonstrate his investigative ability for the detective. Then he showed Tee the backs of his legs. "Remember when your husband bandaged my legs?"

"I sure do," Tee replied. "We were happy you didn't need stitches. Are you healing?"

"Dr. Robin came to see me this morning. Her son plays basketball. She says I'm fine."

Meg joined them. "His name is Ryder." In just one day she had met so many cute teenage boys in The Heights she was having a hard time managing all her instant crushes.

"Children," said Emily, "my friend, Tee, wants to talk with you about the cabin." They turned their attention to the detective.

"I would like to talk with each one of you separately." Because they were standing in the yard, she removed her mask. She looked at Amy. "How about you first, young lady? We can sit at that picnic table on the patio." Amy was so excited to be first; she spun around, grinned in triumph at her

177

siblings and raced to the table. Tee turned to the older children. "Stay close so you'll know when it's your turn." They nodded and ran to claim seats on the kitchen porch. They could watch and snack at the same time.

xxx

"We can't figure it out. How'd he get sick so quick? We just heard about this bug." Zeke Masterson, one of the brewers, was angry at someone, or something.

"When did he get sick?" Mars asked interested in more information about master brewer, Eddie Erhardt.

"It was like Zeke said, we were told to quarantine and soon he couldn't breathe," declared Kane Solomon, another brewer. The two men were explaining to Mars that the third brewer, Eddie Erhardt, a paraplegic, had contracted the virus. "Nikki is caring for him. We run errands for her. She keeps telling us to follow what the CDC says."

"How can we operate like this?" Zeke challenged the air. "We can't open. We can't serve. We have bills.

The three men were sitting in the empty brewery. No masks. Plenty of angst. "Everyone is in the same boat," counseled Mars. "This place will survive." He had read some of the information being sent to banks. "I think the governor will ease some restrictions so you can do a limited business. And you might think about serving outdoors when summer is here."

Kane looked around the bar and out into the street. "You think we could be street vendors?"

"No," replied Mars, "I think you can put your tables outside and let your customers eat and drink outdoors, with the food trucks coming as usual."

Zeke slapped the table. "That don't mean anything. Our brewmaster is sick. We don't have a supply for more than . . .," he thought, "Hell, I don't know how much longer we can operate."

"We'll figure it out," said Kane. He looked at Zeke. "At least I know your pretty bride will figure it out."

Zeke grinned. He had been married only a few weeks to Barbara, the brewery CFO. "She is working the books hard."

Mars looked around. "Where's Darwin?" Kane waved a beckoning gesture. Mars knew that meant Darwin was on the CCTV cameras and had been called.

He appeared almost instantly. "Hey, Mars."

Mars stood. "I came to tell you and Zeke that the dead body we had yesterday was Yetta. We searched her house and we're finished with it." He turned to Darwin. "Granny wants you to help her clean it out."

Darwin nodded. "I'll go see her." He knew why Granny wanted him to help. They had some secret banking to work out.

xxx

"This guy locked them in the cabin." Tee threw her mask across her desk. By tacit agreement they kept the office door closed and themselves unmasked. "There were bars on the windows. These kids climbed up the rock fireplace and used sheets to make a rope to rappel down."

"Did they have a reason to be suspicious?" asked Danny.

She shrugged. "They didn't trust him. The older girl, Meg, said she thought he wanted their money. In her opinion, he kept them out of his hair by keeping them at a boarding school and at wilderness camps all summer. She thought he used their mother's money to live high without them noticing."

Danny studied the ceiling as if it had giant puzzle pieces to move around. "Boarding school, summer camps, and he was living the good life. That must be some money he got for all of them to live so well."

"Mrs. Jacobs said she made sure there was enough money for the kids to be cared for and for him to spend a lot

179

on himself," said Tee. "She said she also paid for the greater part of school expenses so the bills he received were smaller than they should have been, giving him more money to spend on himself."

Dusty shook his head. "She's a smart lady. She knew what sort of creep he was. Her daughter's will making him guardian almost tied her hands."

Tee nodded. "She's smart, all right. That's why she and those kids survived this attempt." They all agreed.

Mars walked into the office waving a report in his hand. "The fire inspector says the propane tank exploded. He says there may have been a bomb, but they need a few more days to finish going through the ashes to find the evidence." He flipped the pages. "He says these tanks are pretty safe. So I think he suspects something funny. They just have to find something in the debris."

"Danny," said Dusty, "check Dawson's credit cards and see if he bought anything that would suggest making an explosive."

"Mars," added the chief, "you get those airport tapes that show him with the kids. I want him to know we have a record of him in town when Yetta was murdered. He may try to tell us he was somewhere else."

Masked or not the unit began organizing the case evidence for the DA to prepare and file charges.

CHAPTER 20

Piper walked into Lynn's kitchen, sniffing the aromas. "How can you cook for so many people?"

"I'm not," she replied, "Emily is a fair hand at cooking. She and the girls are making something."

Piper slumped in a seat. "Doyle is staying at school. He was hired to maintain some labs. He said the school has put a few students up in a dorm to do jobs like take care of labs and help with all the technology since everyone is taking online classes." She sighed. "I worry about him being all alone."

"He'll be fine. He'll ride this out in quarantine with other students as smart as him. What about Brice?" He was Piper's oldest son and had been working on Broadway in the chorus of a popular musical.

"He's coming home. He says the writing is on the wall. He says he doesn't have enough time in the union to get the few jobs that are available. He says he'll help his grandfather with the vineyard." She shrugged. "I can't get my mind around what's happening."

Lynn had never seen the tiny principal so befuddled. "What do you mean?"

"School online for some maybe for the rest of the year." Tears came to her eyes. "Do you know how many of my students rely on receiving meals at school? Breakfast and lunch. Then the Episcopal church packs up bookbags with weekend snacks for them." She shuddered a sob. "What will happen to them?" She hadn't recovered from the ire of the superintendent. He had lost it when he learned she had been running an underground school.   Lynn sat at the table and took her hand. "You're not the only one concerned about kids and the elderly who rely on all sorts of community support. There's a group of folks getting together to make plans. We're meeting on this Zoom thingy tomorrow morning. Do you want to join us?"

Piper gave her a soft smile. "Every time I complain about life, you give me an opportunity to make things better." She stopped talking and tried to contain her tears. "Nothing ever gets better."

Lynn rushed to her side to hug her best friend. "You have to keep trying. We have to keep trying. And if we didn't try, things could be much worse. Look at what the Sharing Shelter program has done for your students. Look what River Bend Reads has done for literacy. Look at how the domestic violence shelter has changed and protected lives. Maybe not all lives, but, Piper, we, our community, we've done some really good things and made a difference."

"Hi, Mom." Jason came into the kitchen carrying his usual laundry bag. He looked at the two women in tears. "Has something happened to Gramps?" With the virus elder health was on everyone's radar.

Lynn stood. "No, honey, we were just thinking about all the work we have to do in these strange times. I guess school sent you home."

"Yeah," he nodded, "we start online in a week after they get organized."

As he spoke three children tumbled into the kitchen. "We saw some big kid come in here," announced Cody, eager to meet the big kid. Lynn laughed.

"Kids, this is my son, Jason. He's home from college." She turned to her son. "These are Emily Jacobs' grandchildren, Meg, Cody and Amy. They're staying with us."

"Because someone's trying to kill us," boasted Cody. He knew how to get a big kid's attention.

Jason was impressed. "No kidding! How?"

"He tried to blow us up," explained Amy, "but we escaped."

"Why don't you all have a snack and tell Jason all about your escape," Lynn suggested as she pulled Piper into the living room. They bumped into Emily.

"I heard you talking. May I help?" Emily took Piper's hand. "You're as sweet and caring as your mother. I can't leave this house, but I bet I could give Lynn some money to help out."

Lynn thought about the older woman's offer. She gave her friends a slow smile. "Do you know that if a few more of our regular donors were given the opportunity, we might create a fund to keep doors open and services getting to those in need." She was already making a mental list of people she would call after the morning meeting when she learned the extent of what was needed. She knew that there would be a demand for services at the same time as there would not be opportunities to raise money.

They heard laughter from the kitchen. Piper wiped her eyes. She nodded toward the happy sounds. "I think I need some of that." They all agreed and moved into the kitchen to share snacks and joy. Because the kids loved retelling their daring escape!

xxx

While Dusty had a murder, attempted murder and explosion demanding his attention, the sheriff had other distractions demanding his attention: why hadn't Dusty arrested Piper for violation of the governor's quarantine mandates? And the new question: shouldn't he arrest the former sheriff for trying to escape from the retirement community?

In the middle of a murder investigation, Dusty had to deal with virus insanity. Covid was taking its toll on everyone and challenging assumptions regarding personal freedom. Nowhere did this challenge inspire more protests than from the elder residents of the local residential retirement community that had put rigorous restrictions in place. Residents were asked to stay in their cottages or apartments. Meals were delivered. No visiting with neighbors. No visits from family and friends. The campus was closed. And former Sheriff Bergy Bergman, a resident, had had enough!

The current sheriff, always looking to make life miserable for Dusty, saw the former sheriff's antics as a gift. Bergy was encouraging Dusty to run for sheriff in the next election. So, when the governor's mandate - stay masked, stay home, and stay out of trouble - was being flaunted by Bergy, the current sheriff chuckled. Bergy made it so easy.

"Yeh?" Dusty answered his phone.

"That friend of yours is trying to escape from the retirement home," drawled the sheriff. "You gotta follow the mandates and arrest him." Click.

Dusty stared at his phone. He looked around the empty office. He sent out an alert. "Bergy on the run." And left his office.

Before he even got to the back property line of the retirement community - because how else would Bergy leave unseen? - he got a call from Mars. "I got him."

"Where?"

"He got some of his old deputies to meet him on the back side of the property, near the greenway. I think he planned on using the greenway to get to his old house. They couldn't get him and his wheelchair over the fence."

Dusty swore. "Keep him on the grounds and threaten those deputies."

Dusty arrived at the scene just as Mars dragged the last of the aging deputies back over the security fence. The retirement community management had locked the gate that allowed access to the greenway. Bergy was in his chair on the other side swearing at his friends. "He's just a boy, you guys can take him on." Three old deputies looked at young, healthy

Mars. They looked back at Bergy. "Hell," growled the old man at the old deputies, "in the old days you fellas were tougher."

"In the old days they had no sense," snapped Dusty as he joined the group. He lowered his voice. "Bergy, settle down. Sheriff Dunwoody heard about this and suggested you should be arrested for violating the governor's orders. He's not kidding."

"It's my freedom, my rights," sputtered Bergy, pulling a mask from his wheelchair pouch and throwing it to the ground. That was the cry of so many citizens, unwilling to heed the concerns and directives of the healthcare community.

"You and everyone else," snarled Dusty. "What if your freedom makes Thel really sick?" She was Bergy's wife of fifty years. "What if these good friends of yours come down with this virus because they tried to help you? What if you get so sick you never see those grandkids when Janet brings them back from Japan?" Bergy had a daughter who lived with her Navy husband and two children in Japan. The old man finally began to look subdued. Dusty nodded. "Think about your freedom and how it might take freedom away from everyone close to you when they get sick."

As they spoke, the current sheriff walked along the greenway toward the gathering. Dusty and Mars raised masks as per requirements. "Well, well," snipped the sheriff, "Life a challenge, Bergy?"

"No, sir," replied Bergy, comfortable on his side of the fence, "I just called some friends together to let them know that it was our duty to work with our community to help out. I asked Dusty and my friends to help collect more books and board games and puzzles for my friends here in the community. And they asked me to do some fund raising for food and things for the older folks in James County who might need extra help during these times." Bergy gave the man a sly look. "We didn't want anyone to know about our charity work. I hope you'll keep our secret." Bergy looked at everyone on the other side of the fence. "You all take care. I'll let you know when I need you again." He spun his electric wheelchair around and putt-putted away along the path back to his cottage.

XXX

Sean Hennessey had enjoyed his first Christmas holiday in years - Dusty's trains, invitations to dinners and brunches and parties. He was in the social whirl of River Bend. He had enjoyed every minute. Well, not every minute. He was mystified by Lee Stahlmeier. She had spent several evenings with him during the winter - very adult evenings. She was an old friend from high school, and he had enjoyed all their time together. Until she pulled away and she couldn't explain to him why.

It had been a week since her last visit just as this quarantine thing was getting started. She had concocted some excuse about cabins for homeless families. He had passed the information on to Lynn and attempted a follow-up with Lee. He called regularly and left messages. And now everyone was quarantined. She lived in that little trailer on her brother's farm. She wasn't all alone; she was surrounded by family, and she was a nurse. If anyone got sick out her way, she was probably tending them.

He sighed. Pursuing Lee would have to wait. This quarantine was a busy time. Mrs. Zubov was so concerned about her students that she had had Sean teaching until she was closed down. Now she had him driving around town checking on homebound tykes to see that they had their tablets up and working. He was also helping two of the neighborhood churches amplify wireless signals so that the neighborhood kids could do schoolwork while lingering in the parking lot or social distancing inside the church gathering spaces.

The tiny principal also worried about the youngsters getting food and eating properly. On Fridays Sean drove the neighborhoods, handing out bookbags with weekend snacks. The school board was organizing a meal delivery service for the district and the churches were ramping up their bookbag food supply chain. But as Piper had explained, it would take time to get it all organized. So Sean drove around town checking on kids and handing out lunches. He didn't understand how he could be so busy when everyone was supposed to stay home. He barely had time to keep up with his job at Will Zubov's factory. But Will knew he was helping Piper. That man would make all sorts of allowances to keep his pretty wife happy.

On one of his delivery routes, he passed by the home of Meyer Levine, an old friend of his father. Sean shrugged to himself, might as well check on him. Meyer had a checkered past in River Bend, having masqueraded as an attorney, when he had actually spent his entire career as a court stenographer. He was the person who had found Sean after his father's death, allowing Sean to inherit the millions his father had won in the state lottery. No matter what, Sean owed Meyer.

He drove up to the house and Meyer waved from his porch. "I'm fine," croaked the old man. "My daughter keeps checking on me."

Sean raised his mask. "I just wanted to make sure you're okay. Need anything?"

Meyer, always the opportunist, replied, "She doesn't bring me any beer." He hesitated, "Or any of that Thai food from that brewery." Sean and Meyer had visited River Dog Brewery a time or two.

"I'll see what I can do. Does tomorrow work?"

"I'll be here."

With that Sean waved and returned to his car. A visit to Meyer always lifted his spirits.

xxx

The house was getting crowded. Even with Jason bunking in at Piper's, Lynn was always bumping into someone. What pandemic? She couldn't find a spot to herself. Emily and the children had taken over. Lucia and Juan came in frequently to help. They helped cook and clean and worked in her garden. Dinner was always prepared those days Lucia came to help.

Lynn had to smile. Jason always came over, sniffed to decide if her house or Piper's smelled better for dinner. He also came over daily to help the kids with homework. Although the boarding school felt confident they would soon be bringing students back, everyone was reluctant to send the children away with Dawson still unaccounted for. After much discussion with Emily and canvassing the kids for their thoughts, Piper got them all transferred to River Bend schools.

The three children were enjoying themselves. Although contact with others was restricted, they played across Lynn and Piper's property, even helping Bri Llewellyn with the vineyard. Meg was developing a gigantic crush on Piper's youngest son, Jeff, who was trying very hard to be kind, but distant. Cody had mastered the art of driving the golf cart Bri had fashioned as his vineyard transport. The youngest, Amy, and her devoted companion, Chips the dog, roamed the property discovering bugs and flowers and small animals and bird nests.

Emily watched her great-grandchildren and rejoiced every day at the bizarre circumstances that brought them to this place and time. She was sitting in the living room thinking about life and thinking about the future she should plan for her small family. There was a knock at the door. She had been

188

in this house long enough to know that no one knocked. It must be a stranger at the door. She panicked. Could Heath have found them? Would he knock?

Lynn came into the entry hall and opened the door. "Abe," she greeted someone.

The man mumbled something Emily couldn't hear. He must be masked, she thought. She heard Lynn gasp, then say, "I'm so sorry. That was so quick. She only seemed to be ill a few days before she went to the hospital." More mumbles. "Let us know if we can help you with anything." Final mumbles and Lynn closed the door.

"Is something wrong, dear?" asked Emily.

"Mrs. Cohen next door died of this virus," explained Lynn. "She went to the hospital three days ago. Her son just stopped to tell me. He didn't want to get close. He feels he's contagious."

"Abe Cohen?"

Lynn came and sat in the living room. "Yes, do you know him?"

"I think he may have known my daughter during one of her quieter visits to River Bend. He was a nice young man." Emily smiled. "I guess he's not that young now."

"He's still a nice man," Lynn said. "He and his wife have been living with his mother for a few months. During that winter storm a tree fell through the roof of their house. They have been living next door while their house is being repaired." Lynn stared out the window a moment. "I think he'll be happy that he was able to spend these last months with his mother. I know she enjoyed the company. She had lived alone for many years. I wonder what they'll do with the house?"

And just like that Emily knew what she wanted for her small family's future. She'd call her attorney tomorrow and get him on it.

CHAPTER 21

Emily thought about Mrs. Cohen's death. These days no one gathered for a service, so she was content sitting on Lynn's kitchen porch considering death and the family's sorrow. She remembered Abe Cohen as a young man. Of course, the real life middle aged, gray-haired fellow barely resembled that memory. She reached down to pet the dog who liked to assist her in her afternoon porch meditations. "What do you think?" she asked him, "Should we have Robert's office check this out?" Chips yawned his approval.

Reaching for her cell phone, she called the law office and identified herself. "I'm sorry Ms. Jacobs, Mr. O'Hara is still in the hospital. Can Mr. Hoefler help you?"

Jim was soon on the line. "Emily, how's my daughter treating you? Do you need anything?"

"First tell me how Robert is doing," she requested.

"He's on a ventilator and his wife and family are very concerned." Jim's voice told Emily that he was also concerned about his longtime friend and partner. He sighed into the phone. "Can I help you with something? We have your will in your files and have received the survey of that property where the cabin used to be."

"Jim, make arrangements to clean the property and gift it to the forest folks. I don't want the children there again."

"I understand. Anything else?"

"I've been thinking," she began, "that I should move closer to town now that I have children to raise. It may be too soon, but I'd like you to talk to Abe Cohen about his mother's house. Since I've made Lynn one of the children's trust managers, I thought we should live close. Does that make sense?"

Jim sighed. Time for reality. "Emily, you have no say about the children. Legally, that Dawson fellow is still their legal guardian."

"He tried to kill them," her screech reminded Jim.

"I know," he conceded, "but we have to go through the proper channels." He thought a moment. "I want you to hire H. Lawrence Grayson as the kids' attorney. He just worked a child protection case because a mother put her child at risk. Maybe he can do the same thing for your kids and get you named as their guardian or something."

"How long will that take?" she asked. "I don't want Heath near my grandchildren again."

"Call Herbie Grayson," Jim encouraged his client. "And let's think about reducing the trust money that rolls into his account each month. You're taking care of the kids. He doesn't need that money."

Emily chuckled. "I like the way you think."

"And I like the way you think," Jim replied. "Moving those three kids into The Heights would liven the neighborhood. Let me investigate the Cohen house for you. I don't know if the layout would suit you. But you could always remodel."

After more discussion they ended the call. Emily and Jim had developed a plan to help the children. As a realist, she felt comfortable with his support for her ideas and began to plan the next phase of her life, the best phase - raising her great-grandchildren. All she needed was to talk with that Grayson fellow.

xxx

Once the Mastersons had been advised of Yetta's death, Granny and Darwin had gone to the rental. They had two goals: clean out Yetta's shit and get that laptop. The shit part was easy. Yetta was a slob. Granny stuffed everything into black trash bags and piled them in the back of Darwin's truck to toss into the landfill.

The laptop was another story. It had belonged to one of Yetta's former, as in dead, boyfriends. The guy had been killed running from the police. Granny and Darwin had learned that the information on the laptop revealed several offshore banking accounts. Using electronic transfers through his offshore accounts, the man had been sending Yetta money every month so that she would maintain a safe house for him. The house had been safe; he had died escaping from police.

After his death Yetta had called Darwin, the Masterson family IT consultant. She had explained that she received money from some funds and, though the man was dead, she would really like to continue receiving the money. During an afternoon of cyber investigation, Darwin had located the various accounts worth several millions, gave Yetta a small raise, and moved most of the funds to an offshore account that he controlled.

He confided his findings to Granny who, as everyone knew, was the family financial mastermind. She advised Darwin to keep the funds under his control and offshore. She knew from experience that a family always needed an untraceable source of income at various times. Even though, as the leader of the Masterson family, she did not tolerate renewed criminal activity, she was not against using criminal funds to help the family with legitimate need. Time would tell.

As Darwin tossed the last bag of trash into his truck, Granny said, "I'll call them Amelia's Maids to do a good clean. This here virus might slow things down a bit." She patted the house key in her dress pocket. "Let's get this here computer to my place and see what we got."

Soon the two of them sat in her kitchen. "Well?"

Darwin had opened the laptop and had been assessing the cyber history. "She never used this," he said. Click. Click.

"She must have tried a few times right after that guy died. But no more."

"What does that mean?"

"It means she was stupid." Darwin had never liked cousin Yetta - a weak, lazy woman. "It works out for us. The laptop left no signal to be followed. If anyone was watching for any trace, they should be bored by now."

Granny thought. She was the family thinker. Because of her, Zeke and Darwin, the last direct descendants to the original Masterson criminal clan, would inherit her, unknown to them, wealth. She wanted to protect them. They had moved the family from lowlife crooks and panderers to respectable businessmen and loving family men. Granny wiped her eyes. Her grandsons were caring men in solid relationships, good with children, loyal to their friends - all the traits that had never, in generations past, been exhibited by any Masterson man. She wanted to protect them and help them. The plan began to form.

"We don't know what this here virus is going to do to the brewery or our lives," said Granny, coming out of her deep thoughts. "I'm Yetta's kin. I'll get control of her bank account. Keep that monthly money coming. We'll deposit it in the brewery account." Darwin waited because he respected Granny's cunning. "We'll tell Zeke that you and he are her heirs, and that money is from some annuity." Darwin blinked. He didn't know that Granny even knew what an annuity was. He nodded. "We'll use the money to help carry the brewery until we understand what's happening."

"It's not much," he pointed out. "I could increase it."

"We don't need to increase it yet. I reckon you don't want us looking into those accounts."

He nodded. "Each time we do, we leave a trail. We just don't know who else had access to the old accounts. We sort of left footprints when we moved the money. Even though I moved the money carefully, I worry someone could be out there looking for my signal. If things get too bad for the brewery, I'll risk it to increase the money." He shrugged. She understood.

"I got me some other accounts," she said. "Let me know if the brewery needs more."

"Yes, ma'am."

"Any more word on our Eddie?"

"No, ma'am. Zeke says it doesn't sound good." He closed the computer and passed it across the table to Granny. She carried it into her bedroom.

When she returned, she said, "We got us a plan." Virus or not, her grandsons' business would survive.

xxx

"How good are you at talking to kids?" H. Lawrence leaned against a doorframe and drawled through his face mask. His sister-in-law looked up from her computer.

"What kids?" Beth adjusted her face mask.

"Emily Jacobs wants us to challenge the guardianship of her great-grandchildren." Beth was puzzled and he explained. "It seems this guy, their guardian, left them locked in a cabin in the forest and it blew up. They managed to escape by making a rope of torn bedsheets."

"You're making this up." Her eyes seemed to roll across the top of her mask.

"Swear to god." He raised his right hand. "I just spoke with Emily and talked with Mars because he and Dusty's crew rescued the kids." He grinned. "So how good are you at interviewing kids?"

"Where are they?"

"Hiding out with Dusty and Lynn."

xxx

Beth arrived at Lynn's front door, masked and ready. Jason answered the door. "Beth?" he squinted. "That is you?" She nodded. "You look different."

"I'm masked."

"No, besides."

"I've lost some weight." She liked saying that.

"Oh, I thought you had a new hairdo."

She thought about whacking him on the head with her iPad. Instead, "That, too."

He grinned. "I knew it was something. What do you want?"

"I came to interview your houseguests." Is this kid really a college junior, she asked herself?

"No one's supposed to know they're here. Some guy is trying to kill them."

She rolled her eyes at him. "Mrs. Jacobs called our office and wants us to be their attorney."

"I thought Gramps was her attorney."

"The kids." Beth was losing patience with this pre-law student. "She wants us to represent the kids against their guardian."

"Oh, right, the guy who's trying to kill them."

She glared at him over her mask.

"Beth," Lynn greeted the young attorney. "We're all locked down. Why don't you go to the backyard and you can talk to the kids at the picnic table?" Lynn glanced over her shoulder. "We're really trying to keep Emily healthy." Beth nodded.

Once settled at the table Beth removed her mask, set up her recorder, opened her notepad and waved. She wanted the kids to feel comfortable. She'd stay the magic six feet away. The children dashed out carrying drinks and snacks.

They aligned themselves across the picnic table in age and size. The eldest and tallest said, "I'm Meg. Grandma said to cooperate with you because you're going to -

"- get rid of that scumbag," finished the boy. He grinned, "I'm Cody."

"And I'm Amy," said the youngest. "I'm an artist like our mama. And he *is* a scumbag."

Beth liked cooperative witnesses. She smiled at them. "Your grandmother is correct. Our plan is to present your story to Child Protective Services and then go before a judge to have him removed as your guardian. I'll need all the information about staying at that cabin." She gave them her most serious lawyer look. "I don't want exaggeration or lies. I just want the truth." Three children nodded solemnly.

After the interview Beth returned to her office and entered all the information into the children's file. H. Lawrence came into her office, adjusting his mask. "Is this true?" He waved his iPad having scanned her notes in the office cloud.

"I told them not to exaggerate," she replied. "And I confirmed with Danny and Mars. This is what happened. We're just waiting for a report from the fire marshal."

"What do we know about this guy?"

She shrugged. "Dusty's folks say he has no priors. He gets his money from the trust funds Mrs. Jacobs transfers to his account every month."

"When will we be ready for court?" H. Lawrence loved to go into court holding all the cards.

"Give Dusty some time to find this guy. When they do, I'll get on a sympathetic judge's calendar."

Beth thought about children and how life sometimes worked against them. And how sometimes they found adults willing to keep them safe. She smiled to herself, keeping children safe was good for the soul. She could feel her soul eager to challenge the scumbag.

CHAPTER 22

Damn, she knows her business, he thought. Eddie Erhardt let his eyes roam around his sick room from his hospital bed examining all the equipment needed to tend him on a daily basis. As a paraplegic with a skilled nurse for a wife, he had managed very well. He had managed business success, marriage and now, he thought, he was managing death. For two weeks his wife had thrown off the scrubs and the PPE to make certain that he felt her touch, her caress and her kisses. But nothing was making him better.

"Promise me, Nikki." He whispered and coughed. He gently squeezed her hand. "Promise me."

She felt the gentle squeeze and knew that was all the strength he had. Tears ran down her cheeks. "I promise." She returned his gentle touch. "No hospital. DNR."

"Love you. . . more than . . legs," he whispered. Was that a chuckle at his favorite way of declaring his love and devotion? Or was he trying to find a breath? "Love you. . .more . . .than life."

Her head popped up. She scanned his face. He was looking at her. He knew. She knew. It was time. She moved to his bed, cradled him in her arms and felt his life ebb. She thought about the first time she had met him - his battered, bleeding, unconscious body. Stabilizing him, the flight to evac, the months in Germany. Images reeled through her mind like a movie. The Death and Life of Eddie Erhardt. He had told her once that he was dead until he felt her touch at that field hospital tent. "You called me back, babe."

She understood because that's how she had felt. When she touched him, she sizzled. She hadn't understood that first touch, but all the touches during all his months of care, the sizzle never stopped. She had followed him from hospital to hospital to finally Portage and the brewery. He had joked, "I knew I had to do something desperate for you to notice me." He often told her that when she was working with the bed equipment to get him into his wheelchair.

In return she had many replies, but his favorite was, "I'm doing this to increase my bust size."

His humor never failed. His love grew each day. He never once forgot to kiss her good night, thank her for being his wife and whisper his devotion to her. His death so early in their marriage wasn't a real surprise. Both of them anticipated that they would be blessed to have five years. As he always said, "Anything after that is just gravy."

But they hadn't even had two years. Nikki finally settled Eddie's body on the bed, straightened the sheets, and placed some calls. She had kept friends and family informed. His family would suffer at the news because they had been restricted from coming to his side. Nikki had orchestrated a few online chats. But his deterioration had been so rapid, the last week he had been unable to sit up or speak clearly.

Kane, one of the brewery partners walked into the room. "I've come to help. What do we do?"

"You shouldn't be in here," Nikki told her friend.

"And you shouldn't be alone." He wasn't taking her medical advice. He waited for an answer to his question.

She got up and gave him a hug. "Thank you. The hospital has protocols for body removal. I'll call it in." She watched as Kane stepped to Eddie's body, took a Native American tribal talisman from around his neck and twined it through Eddie's fingers.

Zeke, the other brewery partner, came into the room. She opened her mouth. "Don't tell me to go away," he said as he walked up to Eddie's body, took a medal from his pocket, and pinned it to Eddie's bedclothes. Both men turned to Nikki. "We've said goodbye," said Zeke, "we're ready to help."

Nikki hugged him. "I've said goodbye, too. Let's get him ready.

When the ambulance arrived to remove the body, Eddie was outfitted in his Marine dress uniform, ready to answer the call.

xxx

Heath had spent two weeks in a posh cabin in Cashiers. Some fool had left a window unlatched. Searching through the house he found that the owners were from Florida, elderly and probably hadn't been to the elegant, though dated, place for a year or two. He smirked. Some people had so much money, they spent and never enjoyed. Apparently the owners paid someone to clean it monthly and to tend the secluded yard.

It had been easy to don his mask and to inform some good old country fellow that he knew the owners, had their permission to stay during this quarantine. Heath made certain he gave the man a generous tip and settled into his comfortable quarantine.

But it was time to return to River Bend and claim his money after demonstrating his grief of the bitter loss of his stepchildren and their great-grandmother. He had seen a story on the River Bend Chronicle's website reporting a fire in a cabin in the forest. The story suggested that the fire marshal would be checking the ashes for remains and notify family if necessary. The story seemed to die after two days with a hint that no more information would be available until family had been found and notified. The story of Yetta's murder and Emily's death got even less play. All the newspaper had reported indicated that there had been unattended covid deaths and families would be notified. No mystery, no interest.

Two weeks in a fancy cabin in the forest. He had never been so bored. It was a good thing he had cable and internet. It was now time to go collect his money. Hot-diggity!

Back in River Bend he did a quick pass by Emily's house. No one there. Pieces of police tape, tattered and torn, waved at him as he passed the property entrance. Next he drove by Yetta's place. It had a 'For Rent' sign. He made his way to the Moorings Inn, a low priced, barebones motel. He could stay under everyone's radar here and probably find some entertainment. It had been a long, lonely stay in that cabin.

Once settled in the motel, using the name of the cabin owner and paying cash, he went out to buy a few things. This evening he would cruise for some entertainment.

xxx

Lynn was beyond grateful that many of their favorite family carryouts maintained operations during quarantine. When Emily or Lucia had run out of cooking ideas, or life had been extremely demanding, she always found a carryout menu and did a quick online order. "Jason, Kew at the Happy Dragon will have our food ready in thirty minutes." She slipped her phone into her pocket.

Cody turned to Jason. "Can I ride shotgun?"

"Me, too," echoed Meg."

"I want to go, too," cried Amy.

Jason rolled his eyes. He had never had siblings. Now he had three kids under foot daily. Was this what having siblings meant? They shadowed him, asked questions. Amy always wanted to hold his hand. The dog even liked her better. And there they were, three eager, adoring kids. What else could he say? "Cody has shotgun. You girls buckle up in the back. Have masks in case we need them." The kids shouted joyfully and raced to Jason's sorry old Jeep. He grabbed Lynn's credit card and followed his temporary siblings out the door.

Thirty minutes until the Chinese carryout was ready posed no challenge in a small town. The challenge was the errands added to the food pick-up chore. Emily had books to be dropped off at the library, Lynn wanted Jason to pick up a file at her office that she left on her desk, and Dusty had ordered some dessert. There would be a stop at the bakery for another curbside food pick-up.

The kids chattered about life in The Heights, marveled that the world looked the same even though everyone was quarantined, asked a thousand questions and marveled at Jason's brilliance. He drifted into the library parking lot, swayed into the drop-off lane behind several other readers, and allowed Amy to hang out the back window and drop the books in the return slot. Checking his watch, he knew he still had plenty of time, so he went to the bakery, waited his turn, then pulled into the curbside pick-up space. Umberto came out in a mask with two big bakery boxes. After handing the boxes through the back window to Amy and Meg, he took his phone from his pocket, slid the credit card through a tiny attachment, waved Jason out of the spot and directed the next customer into the space.

Back in the car Meg moaned, "This smells delicious. What is it?"

Jason darted through traffic toward the highway to Happy Dragon and Lynn's office before he answered. "I think I smell biscotti, something chocolate and fresh bread." The kids all groaned in longing. "Dusty gets carried away when it comes to food." The kids eagerly agreed with Dusty.

"That's him!" shouted Cody. Riding shotgun had responsibilities.

"That's who?" Jason hated to have passengers yell while he was driving and thinking about other things.

"Heath!"

"Heath?" came a questioning echo from the back.

"Who's Heath?" the driver wanted to know.

"The guy who tried to kill us," stated Meg who always, in Jason's opinion, kept her head. "Dusty's been looking for him." They watched a masked man walking toward the liquor store.

"How do you know it's him?" Jason had learned a few things with a detective for a stepfather.

"He's wearing the same shirt he wore when he got us at the airport," replied Cody. "And he walks like himself." Not surprising, that was a statement Jason understood.

"Put on your masks," ordered Jason as he pulled the Jeep to the curb at the quiet side street leading to the highway. Grabbing his cell, he snapped a photo and asked, "Do you know which is his car?" He gestured toward the cars along the street. Cody scanned the area while Meg helped Amy with her mask.

"That black SUV looks like his," said Cody as he unbuckled and looked out the rear of the car. Jason snapped a photo of the SUV. He texted Dusty and forwarded the photos along with their location.

Over his shoulder, he said to the girls, "Sit down low. See if you find some hats or things to use as a disguise."

"Disguise!" There was awe in Amy's voice. Could life get any better?

Meg found two baseball caps and a floppy wide brimmed hat. Jason slapped the brimmed hat on Cody saying, "He's the most visible. You girls put on the caps to hide your hair." His phone pinged. He read Dusty's reply. "Dusty says to just watch. He'll send a car."

They all squirmed low in their seats feeling special in their new role as official police stake-outers. The store had a brisk business, but Heath soon came out with his purchases. He scanned the area as he climbed into his car. Everyone sat lower in the Jeep. "There's Danny," hissed Jason.

"Who?"

"One of the detectives. He's driving that bakery truck." Jason almost laughed. Danny had probably been helping

Umberto get out curbside orders when he got Dusty's alert. The bakery truck pulled beside Jason's window.

"Go home," Danny said, as he slipped down his mask. "Mars is out on the highway and Sherri is behind me." Danny had known Jason long enough that he understood that the youngster, like his mother, wanted to know details. Jason nodded. Danny pulled away.

"Can't we watch them shoot him?" asked Meg.

"I think they're going to follow him out some place and then shoot him," replied Cody.

"They aren't going to shoot him until they talk to him," explained Jason because he was the criminal procedure expert in the car.

"I would shoot him," offered Amy.

"We'll go get our order at Happy Dragon," said Jason trying to distract his bloodthirsty passengers. "Dusty will tell us what happened when we get home."

Three kids murmured agreement because the bakery aromas were intoxicating.

xxx

Danny cruised behind the black SUV. "That's the tag on the car," he argued with the dispatcher. "It's a black SUV."

The dispatcher's voice echoed in the bread truck. "It should be attached to a metallic gray Kia sedan."

"He must have switched plates. No wonder no one spotted him." Danny relayed the information to his team. After some chatter, they had a plan.

Sherri was elected to pull the suspect over. With a quick pop from the blue lights, Heath hustled to the roadside. Sherri pulled up her face mask and after checking the license tag, proceeded to chat with the driver. "Sir," she offered her very professional voice because who could do anything else with clothe over her face. Charm was out. "We've been asked to pull over the car with this tag. Is this your car, sir?"

Renee Kumor

Heath made certain his mask was in place. "Ma'am, I've been in quarantine in Cashiers. Could someone have switched plates?"

Sherri nodded noncommittally. "I see. Could you step out of the car, please. It's very difficult to deal with you while I'm wearing my required mask." She smiled but who knew?

He climbed out of his car as Mars drove up in another patrol car and slipped on his mask. He walked up to stand beside Sherri as she scanned Heath's credentials. She turned to Mars. "This is Heath Dawson. His driver's license says he's from South Carolina, but his tag is from North Carolina."

Heath shook his head in sadness. "I bet someone switched tags without me noticing. I've been in self-quarantine. I wanted to visit my grandmother and not get her sick."

"Does your grandmother have a name, sir?" asked Mars.

"Emily Jacobs."

"Oh," exclaimed Sherri, sounding as innocent as her mask allowed. "She was my Sunday school teacher. Is she very sick? Is it this virus? Are you coming to take care of her?"

Heath adjusted his mask and slumped in concern. "She's elderly, you know. I'm worried about her, and I wanted to be with her to make sure she survives this lockdown." He was really confused. Shouldn't Emily be dead? Shouldn't they be saying they had been looking for her relatives? Did something go wrong? He had a funny feeling.

Mars nodded. "It's terrible. Folks not being able to see kin." Heath nodded in agreement. "Why don't you get in my car, sir? I can get in touch with the local patrol and ease your concerns."

"Well," Heath waffled, "I don't want to take advantage. I know others are just as concerned about relatives."

"It wasn't an offer of help," explained Mars as another patrol car blocked the road. "It was an order. We've been looking for you. Ms. Jacobs is in protective custody, along with the children. And we want to talk with you." He grabbed Heath's arm and handcuffed him as another officer joined the group. Mars assisted Heath into his patrol car. "We have a few questions for you, sir." He slammed the door. He had known Ms. Jacobs a long time. The virus was bad enough for older folks, they didn't need half-assed relatives trying to murder them!

CHAPTER 23

Noah ran his hands across Jody's shoulders and down her naked back. His skilled hands didn't caress so much as examine. "You're very healthy. You could firm up those muscles though with some weights or working on some gym machines." He kissed her shoulder.

Jody snuggled in his arms. "Are you going to charge Medicare for this examination and opinion?"

"No, I just thought that while I had you close, I'd kill two birds with one stone so to speak." He ran his hand further down her back and caressed her rear. "I think this is a very practical arrangement. You don't take up time in my office and I can make you blueberry pancakes before we get to work."

"You're just here to reduce visits to your office and eat breakfast?"

"I said I was doing the cooking," he reminded her.

"Is that all this is Noah - we play doctor and share meals now and then?" Jody asked as she propped up on one elbow.

He sighed and she felt his breath tickle her neck. "I don't know what this is. Do you need an answer today?"

She kissed his jaw. "I don't know if I want an answer. I enjoy your . . . er . . . company."

"I've been giving us a lot of thought," he said as he pulled her tighter. "May I share some of them?"

"Please do." She gathered the blankets around them and settled in his arms to listen.

"I think there are several options," he began, "but I guess, I need you to weigh in on them. First, I think one of my sons would like to buy your business."

"What? When did that happen?"

"Do you object?"

"No. Which son?"

"Clint. He lost his job in this shutdown because his employer just closed the office. It was quite a shock. Now he's talking about taking more control of his life, working for himself. I suggested that your business might be available. He did some research and wants to talk with you about it."

"When were you going to tell me this?"

"Today. He's been closing out his life in Fort Wayne, you know, preparing to sell his house, getting his wife and kids ready to relocate. He got an offer yesterday. They're going to move in with me if the sale goes through and you two work out a deal."

"Isn't that risky? He might not like the work or have the money I need for a sale."

"He'll have the money because I'll help him. And he knows this is what he wants, to raise his kids here and his wife can get a job as a nurse anywhere."

"You'll help him?"

"I want you to be a free woman so we can travel and start a new life."

"A new life?"

"I was thinking we can sell my house to my son and your house to someone, and we can get a different place - our own place and enjoy the rest of our lives together."

"That sounds like a proposal, Noah." She shifted under the sheets, uncertain whether to pull away or snuggle closer.

"It does, doesn't it? It didn't start out that way in my head." He stared at the ceiling seeming to marvel at the situation.

"So, it's a random thought and you're surprised it sounds like a proposal?"

"No, maybe it's a good idea that finally became a great idea. We should give it some thought." He gave her a tentative glance, before finding wrinkles in the blanket that should be straightened.

She was silent a moment. "I don't want you to always be examining me when we're in bed together. That makes me think I don't have your attention."

"I'm not examining you, Jody, I'm loving you."

She gasped. "Was that you speaking without thinking again?"

He gave an exaggerated sigh. "Yes. It seems I do quite well when I let my mouth go free range." He pulled her in for a long kiss. "I think I have my answer to us. Does it match your ideas in any way?"

"I think it's better than the ideas I had."

"What ideas were those?"

"I thought you would retire, and I would hire you to work for me since you're in the store every day and I could travel and leave you in charge." She laughed when he pinched her rear. "But you have a better idea. How about breakfast? I want to call Michelle and talk with her about the selling price of my business."

"How about if we spend a little more time in bed and I'll buy you a bagel at the coffee shop."

She threw her arms around him. "Great idea since we both still have day jobs."

xxx

Dusty walked into the new virus prescribed interrogation room. One of the big conference rooms. There was a conference table but only four chairs spaced out. A masked guard stood inside the door.

Heath had been demanding a lawyer since he was placed in the back of the patrol car last night. Dusty threw a file on the table. "Your attorney phoned. He just left Asheville and says traffic is light. He'll be here in about an hour. We can put you back in a cell or you can stay here if you don't cause trouble."

211

"I can be quiet." Heath wasn't in the mood to argue or show attitude. "I'd like something to drink."

Dusty nodded to the patrol officer at the door. He stepped out and soon returned with a bottle of water. "I can't speak with you until your attorney arrives. Tell the guard if you need anything else." He nodded to the suspect and left the room.

Tee and Mrs. Jacobs were in the security room watching CCTV of the conference room. Dusty stepped into the room and raised an eyebrow. That was all he could do with a mask on. But Emily understood. "That's him. The last time I saw him was that Friday he brought Yetta to my house. Will the children have to see him?"

Dusty tugged at his mask and shrugged. "We don't need them to see him. We already have their story about the cabin. It will depend on the DA as to whether the kids have a role at any trial."

They talked for a bit more and then Tee drove Emily back to The Heights. The detective said as they arrived, "Mrs. Jacobs, I'm not going to talk with the kids now. I interviewed them when we brought them out of the forest. The DA will tell us if we need more interviews."

xxx

Piper came into Lynn's house in a huff. She glanced around, no Lynn. "Can I help?" Emily was snug on the living room sofa reading.

"Is Lynn in the kitchen?" Piper looked like her pants were on fire.

"She ran to her office for something," replied Emily. "Are you sure I can't help?"

Piper threw up her hands. "I'm trying to keep everyone at a distance. Trying to keep my parents healthy. Trying to mask when necessary." She stopped and turned bright red. She was not wearing a mask.

Emily laughed. "Piper, I see you every day. If you had a disease, I would have it by now." She sat up. "What is your problem?"

With a huff, Piper plopped on a chair. "My son arrives tomorrow, and he needs a place to quarantine. He thought he would stay with us or his grandparents." Her eyes flared. "He's been living in New York City. He's probably filled with viruseses."

"I don't think that's a word."

"You know what I mean." She got up and paced. "Maybe he can stay in the barn for two weeks." Pace. Fret. "No, everyone uses it. He would infect us all, including the dog."

Emily enjoyed all the activity in Lynn's house and took a minute to wonder why she thought living in her secluded country house was so charming. "I have a suggestion."

Piper looked at her with raised eyebrows.

"He can stay out at my place. I don't like it empty. They cleaned out the body and Amelia's Maids disinfected everything. But I don't like it being empty."

The tiny principal returned to the cushiony chair. After some thought she said, "That would work. He can cook for himself and do some chores for you."

Emily smiled. "He won't have wild parties, will he?"

Piper sat back and thought. "No, he's a quiet fellow. I don't think he has many friends left here in town. He's been gone since high school with college and his job."

"What does he do?" Emily shook her head. "Or what did he do before life changed?"

"Marianna helped him get an audition for a chorus on Broadway. I think he was pleased to be working at even small parts in an exciting industry." She hung her head. "Now he'll lose all that experience and contacts."

"He's young. Life will work out for him as it will for all these other youngsters caught in the beginning of careers."

You're very optimistic, Emily."

"No, I'm very old. And I can tell you life never stops; it just veers into new directions." She sighed, pulled her book back into her lap. "And we adjust even when we think we won't."

The two women sat quietly thinking about veering life until one of the children came into the house bringing yet another change of direction. "Grandma?" came a plaintive cry, "The big kids won't let me help."

Emily smiled at Piper then turned to little Amy. "Just the person I need. I was just telling Miss Piper that the big kids aren't as clever as you."

"Really?" came the hopeful, shy voice. And life veered.

xxx

Lynn sat at the mask-free zone in her yard with Beth Seymour. "Did you explain the Sharing Shelter program to your client?"

Beth nodded. "Your program pays more than he charges in rent."

"Does that mean we'll get a better deal?"

"No, that means he'll rent to you at your rates. With that extra income he's willing to repair the septic system and do some repairs on roofs and things."

Lynn frowned. "We're not made of money."

Beth, always her client's advocate, replied, "He's not made of money either. But he is willing to hire some of the renters and pay a fair wage. It won't be full time work, but it will give your folks a little income and maybe an opportunity to get on their feet and move on to something more permanent."

"Some of them already work. Will he make it a condition of renting?"

"No. He's just willing to help folks who want to work and don't have jobs." Beth shuffled some papers. "He expects you or those ministers or the school people to police the area and handle any troublemakers. He says he's not going to get involved."

Lynn understood that. During the short life of the shelter program, they had run into a few troublemakers, malingerers, and outright crooks. But the pastors and the school resource officers had handled things so far. She had learned some hard lessons in her early years of charity work. Not everyone appreciated kindness and charity. Some folks seemed to think it their due, and some were very skilled at gaming the system. The entire nonprofit human service community had established some guidelines and community wide responses to troublesome people. She hoped James County was getting a reputation for steely-kindness - she wasn't sure how to explain it, but it was a term the pastors used when talking about how you know when you've helped enough and when you give someone the boot.

"Have we got a deal?" asked Beth. "He won't throw any current renters out, but as a cabin becomes vacant, he'll let your committee know."

Lynn nodded. "The committee has a list and can assign a family within a day."

Beth tapped a message into her phone. She read the immediate reply. "Collie says he agrees. He'd like a contract."

"We have the one I gave you. We use it for the churches."

Beth texted again. "Deal. He'll start repairing the septic field this afternoon."

xxx

Dusty watched the well-dressed, high-priced Asheville attorney smirk as he entered the interrogation room. He was scornfully masked - in Dusty's opinion that was an attitude some folks had when required to mask in a given situation when they believed this virus thing was a hoax.

215

"Do I really need this, officer?" the attorney challenged tugging at the mask.

"Yes, unless you want to be the person we charge with spreading the virus in the jail."

"My client won't be in your hell-hole after today," sneered the attorney. "I'd like some privacy with my client." Dusty nodded and left the room.

In the hallway he met Mars who asked, "How was the perp's lawyer?"

Dusty shrugged. "It's a good thing Herbie has made us immune to pompous asses." Mars chuckled. Dusty continued, "He thinks he's going to spring Dawson. See if the DA wants to go with a first appearance hearing this afternoon."

"I'm sure he's ready if there's a judge on site." Mars trotted down the corridor to start the legal process.

After a respectful length of time Dusty knocked at the interview room door. Opening it, he advised the attorney, "We're setting up a first appearance. May I conduct a preliminary interview?" The attorney nodded. With that Dusty ushered in the officer to stand at the door while he sat at the table to begin.

Dusty asked his questions, and the attorney advised his client to remain silent. It was an old game, but Dusty didn't mind. It was giving the DA time to set up the hearing. A quick rap on the door and Mars announced, "The judge is ready."

The hearing only took a few minutes for the DA to layout the evidence for suspicion of murder, attempted murder, and arson. The defense attorney argued for bail. It was denied. Dawson was led back to his cell.

Outside the courtroom Dusty asked the pricey attorney, "So, you think you can get him off?"

Another sneer. "Who the hell cares? He paid my fees and as long as he continues, I'll represent him." He sized up Dusty. "You've been around long enough. That's how things go." He spun on his heel and left the courthouse with his arrogant stride.

CHAPTER 24

Lynn stared into her computer screen. Lockdown, shutdown lowdown was her objective. She wanted to stay in touch with all the local nonprofits so that the Philanthropies would be able to assist the community. Part of her plan was to speak individually with several directors and this afternoon she was zooming with Audrey Decker of Exceptional Children. Audrey was the executive director of a program serving developmentally delayed individuals. Her concern today was for the adult residents of her group homes. She sobbed, "How do I keep them safe when they have difficulty understanding shutdown? We had our first resident taken to the hospital last evening."

Lynn could see her digital tears. "Audrey, how can we help?"

"Just listening to me helps." She dried her eyes and became the professional director. "My staff is working hard to observe the CDC protocols as well as keeping our residents calm while tutoring them on the importance of hand washing and distancing and other basics. We're investing in several larger TVs and some handheld gaming devices that are geared to youngsters. We think our residents will like them." She was distracted for a moment as someone came into her office. Lynn watched as Audrey spoke with one of her staff members.

Returning back to the screen Audrey said, "Sorry. Another little crisis. We're trying to figure how to keep everyone healthy and allow visits with their families." She sighed into Lynn's home office also known as the dining room. "We're making this up as we go along."

Lynn nodded. "Everyone is. We can give you a grant to purchase those electronics if that helps."

Audrey gave Lynn a digital smile. "That would be perfect. Less budget juggling. The health department has sent over masks and some other gear. Our biggest concern is that our residents are at a greater health risk for this virus than other folks. First because of the group living conditions and second because they have several physical health problems already."

"I understand," said Lynn. "Just keep me up to date." Audrey nodded and Lynn prepared for her next director conference as Audrey disappeared from the screen. In a few minutes Salley Connelly appeared. She was director of the domestic violence shelter and Lynn's sister-in-law.

Salley waved and her lips moved. Lynn said, "You're on mute."

Salley rolled her eyes. "I'll get the hang of this soon. How are you?"

Lynn shrugged. "Just checking in with you directors. I just spoke with Audrey. Managing a group home is challenging. That made me wonder about your concerns for the shelter."

"Hand sanitizer and masks are the new black. Our clients understand the health risks and want our protection, so they cooperate. The shelter is much safer than their other options." Salley went on to describe the shelter health protocols. Concluding, "I bet that's more than you wanted to know."

"You're correct. But check in with Audrey. Some of your policies may work for her."

Salley agreed and Lynn ended her work day staring at a blank computer screen and marveling at how everyone was adjusting to the new reality. It was bumpy but she was encouraged by the thoughtful, adaptable professionals in the nonprofit world.

xxx

It had taken Tee several weeks, slowed down by the national response to the pandemic to finally find someone in Des Moines who would talk with her about a twenty-year old murder. One day an email popped up with an invitation to phone. She checked the name on the email, Rose Marie Jaeger. The detective shrugged thinking this was probably a good time to call because crime was slow under a virus.

Not much to do. The only criminal on the unit's radar was being held without bail - that Heath guy. Plenty of folks around town were sick. She paused a moment thinking about the folks who had succumbed to the virus. Some fine community leaders and a few not so fine people but fortunately, her mother and close relatives were still healthy. And they should be! They only saw each other. Tee had taken as many precautions as she could to keep her family safe. Lonzo, as an EMT, was having a more difficult time with prevention. He used his protective gear and stripped almost naked before entering the house after his shift. But he hadn't seen his father and cousins since quarantine and only saw Tee and the kids regularly.

One last look around the quiet office - she placed a call. "Rose Marie Jaeger? This is Detective Teniquia LaMont from River Bend, North Carolina."

There was a sharp in-take of breath at the end of the phone connection. "Yes, ma'am. This is Officer Jaeger."

"I received your email response to an inquiry I made a few months ago."

"Yes, ma'am." Then a cautious silence from Des Moines.

Tee said, "Did you reply in response to my inquiry?" She didn't know what she had expected from this contact, but tension and reserve had not been on her list.

Rose Marie slowly replied. "Yes, ma'am. I did contact you about your inquiry. I'm new to my job and I've been assigned to review some cold cases. This one caught my attention."

"Why-" Tee had a question ready, but the officer interrupted.

"Mr. Halstead may be my father." The voice came over Tee's cell as a whisper. The questions tumbled out. "Do you know him? Is he alive? Can I meet him?"

Realizing that this had just gotten very personal, Tee asked, "May I call you Rose Marie? And you can call me Tee."

"Yes, ma'am, I mean, Tee." She sighed. "It's a long story. Sort of as long as my life."

"I've got time." Tee pulled out her notebook and held her pen ready.

"Mr. Halstead was a drug user. He was a professor and met my mother when they both were doing drugs. Mother got pregnant and her family, my grandparents, took her back home and took care of her. Over time she met and married a marvelous man, Max Jaeger. He is the only father I know. They had other children and we had a great small town farm life. They were always honest with me about my origins. As mother used to say, "This is a small town, and everyone knew why I came back.'"

Tee laughed. "River Bend is a small town, too. So I understand."

"They didn't know about the murder or how Mr. Halstead might be involved. Our town was far enough away from Des Moines that we never heard the news. I guess Mother returned home before the murder." Silence. Tee thought the young woman was gathering her thoughts. "I always knew his name. Once I learned the internet, I even did a search. He had just disappeared."

"Let me fill in from there," offered Tee. "Bill, as we call him, was beaten up at some point and left for dead. A very caring man, a hobo in fact, found him along the train line near

Chicago and took care of him until he healed. The two men spent about twenty years together homeless and moving from place to place. The caring hobo, Wayne, died of cancer and asked Bill to look after his family." Here Tee chuckled. "Wayne's daughter is a police officer in Huntington, Indiana." Rose Marie gasped and chuckled, too. Tee continued, "I had occasion to meet Bill when he helped us find a lost child. He said he was from Huntington and wanted to return to his family. We helped him reunite, but his police officer daughter soon got suspicious."

"He didn't harm anyone?"

"No, he slipped right into Wayne's family, and everyone loves him. Wayne's wife suspected first but wanted Wanda to have a father after all these years. Bill finally admitted who he was, but by that time he was embedded in the family and had committed to being daycare for Wanda's new baby."

"Baby?"

"Wanda and her husband had a baby last October and Bill is the nanny. He lives with Wayne's wife, Nora, and we think there's a romance blossoming. He's doing some work writing for Nora's employer, a healthcare facility, and he's working on a book about his hobo years. And he bakes bread and pies for everyone."

"He sounds so different than what I have imagined over these years."

"Did he know you existed?"

"I don't think so," Rose Marie replied. "Mother says she never told him. Those of her friends who knew, probably never told him."

"He is a very sweet man," replied Tee. "I suspect he wasn't as nice when he was younger and a druggie."

"Mother says he was smart and handsome," she chuckled again, "and persuasive." Rose Marie was silent for a moment. "Can I meet him?" It was a whispered request.

Tee sighed into the phone. "I haven't even told Wanda that I've continued to look into Bill's past. Let me talk to her and I'll get back to you. Wanda's family has grown attached to this man. We'll be raising some challenging issues and old stories."

"I understand," replied Rose Marie, "Please see what you can do. I would like to meet him."

"But what about the cold case?" The detective was curious. "I know you want to meet him, but will we upset his new life?" Tee wanted to protect Bill and his new family.

Rose Marie was silent for a moment. "I don't want to disrupt his new life either."

"Why was he a person of interest in your cold case?" asked Tee.

"I don't know the particulars of this case. I just opened the file. Let me do some quiet investigating. Don't worry. You'll hear from me again." With the promise of further discussions, Rose Marie ended the call. Tee slumped against her desk. She'd wait a few days and call Wanda. She checked her watch. Time to take that report to HR for security time sheets at Dusty's place before packing it in for the day.

XXX

Lynn staggered into the kitchen, arms filled with files. Cody and Meg followed her with grocery bags. "Put the food away."

Cody looked at her. "But this is your house."

"You eat here?" He nodded. "Then you can put food away. I know you know where it all goes." She had had a tiring day and these kids were no longer guests.

Jason stumbled into the house with more groceries. "Mom, did you buy more of those chips? Someone ate the rest." He squinted at the two younger kids.

"I think it was Emily," said Lynn. "She's a real junk food junkie."

"Grandma?" Meg was shocked.

"Yes, she is," agreed Cody. "I saw her sneak the last donut yesterday."

Amy came into the kitchen at the end of that admission. "Yes, and she ate those cheddar cheese thingies."

"Groceries," cooed Emily as she entered the kitchen.

Lynn gave her a squinty-eyed look. "I've just learned that you're the one eating everything in sight."

Emily blushed. "I admit it. You buy such interesting things. I have to try them all." Her eyes traveled to the grocery bags. "What did you get today?"

The kids began to sing out the food. "Frozen pizza puffs. Blueberries."

"Crunchy peanut butter."

"Bran cereal?" Lynn looked at Emily. "I thought you told me to buy that."

"I did, dear," blushed the food junkie. "With all my sampling of these new foods, my body demands a little help to recover."

Lynn flopped into a chair laughing as all the kids stowed the groceries.

xxx

Dusty walked into the office and pulled off his mask. Only a few weeks and this was already old. He slumped into the sagging, but comfortable, chair behind his desk. Sighed. Almost time to go home. And realized he wasn't alone. "Mars?"

"Ugh?" Mars came out of his trance and stared at Dusty.

The chief had enough experience with his unit that he knew some important issue had Mars' attention. "Can I help?" Because he also knew that only a personal problem could command all of the young detective's intense attention.

"We're having a baby." Mars' voice bordered on despair.

Dusty knew that Mars and his wife Trina had planned on a baby to quickly join the family that already included Trina's two small children. "Is something wrong with Trina's health?"

Mars looked at Dusty. "This virus. How can we have a baby with everyone sick? Will the hospital let us in? What if she gets sick before the baby is born? What if -

Dusty raised his hands in a calming gesture. "There are a lot of what ifs," he began, "but maybe we'll have a cure before the baby gets here. When is it due?"

"Around Thanksgiving."

"See, plenty of time."

Mars didn't look assuaged. "I think I have to resign."

"What?"

"I can afford to give up my job. That way I can be with her and the kids and not bring any germs home."

"Have you talked this over with Trina?"

"No. She's too busy being excited about the baby. She says it will make our family whole. And it will be my first baby and my mother is excited and trying to figure out how to get out of London." When Mars married Trina, she had been widowed for a few years and had two small children. They had planned for this third child or as Mars called it, his first, to come along quickly after their marriage. "I was going to tell her we should wait until after this virus and she told me last night that I was too late and now what do we do?"

Dusty sat up and studied the perplexed young man. "I don't want you to resign. I'll work with you anyway that makes you comfortable. The whole unit will do what we can for you." Dusty stood and walked over to Mars and perched on the edge of his desk. "I want you to believe all will work out because I know you don't want to upset Trina and cause her to regret this child."

Mars gasped. "No, I, we, want it. But so much is different than it would be if things were normal."

"This is now normal," sighed Dusty and he stood. "Just remember, the unit will work with you."

Tee rushed into the office removing her mask. "Mars," she greeted her colleague with a grin, "I just got a text from Trina. Congratulations!"

She was followed by Danny who walked in, pulled off his mask and grinned. He held up his phone. "My wife just heard from Trina! Great news!"

Dusty looked back at Mars. "I told you. The unit will work with you."

Mars nodded, looked thoughtfully at his friends and, finally, grinned.

CHAPTER 25

"What do you mean murderer?"

"Calm down, Wanda." Tee gripped her cell hard enough to probably crack it. "You only heard one thing and I've told you a lot, like he has a daughter and stuff." Tee repeated all the information from her conversation with Rose Marie.

"We have to solve this murder," barked Wanda. "Bill didn't kill anyone. He's my baby's grandpa-nanny!"

"It's a cold case. Read my lips," she enunciated over the phone.

"I don't care. His daughter will help us. She doesn't want her father to be a murderer either." Wanda gasped. "What would Mother say? She'll say the same as me, I'm sure. We have to solve this case." Wanda's insistent fury raced through the phone.

Tee rolled her eyes to no one in her empty office. "Rose Marie said she'd do some quiet investigating. She probably only has time to work this case on the side." Dusty walked into the office and gave her the eye. "I gotta go, Wanda. I'll talk to you later."

He slipped off his mandatory mask as he entered the office and closed the door. "Trouble?"

"Remember that hobo, Bill?" Dusty nodded. "His story just got more interesting, and more complex." She explained all she had learned.

Dusty shook his head. "We do get ourselves into fixes."

"What should I do?" Tee was struggling with that nexus where crimes and friendship intersect.

"Let the officer in Des Moines look into it. She's invested in a good outcome."

Tee nodded. She thought Dusty was correct. Rose Marie didn't want to hang a murder on her father. "Did you want me?"

"Yeah," he waved her to the door. "That protective service hearing is this morning. I want you there to guard the kids. They know you."

"Yes, sir." She sent a quick email to Wanda promising to call later and dashed for the court.

xxx

Once Heath had been arrested, Emily's legal team worked fast to stop the automatic deposits to his account. Beth also learned that all his credit cards were assigned to him by the trust. She hurried to terminate the accounts. He had demanded an attorney at the time of his arrest, paying the fees with the current funds in his personal checking account. He had been well represented at an initial hearing and a plea of 'Not Guilty' to the charges that had been filed. Bail had been denied and he was now spending time in the James County jail.

Last Friday he had been served with a notice to appear at a custody hearing. The notice informed him that Child Protective Services was initiating action to terminate his guardianship of the children. Heath smirked at the challenge and faxed copies of the notice to his attorney in Asheville. The reply told him that this case would involve additional time and fees. Heath authorized the funds to be taken from his account. He walked back to his cell, confident that this was just a blip on the road to regaining his freedom and access to his monthly funds.

However, at the protective service hearing he was heard to shout, "I have no money?" at the bailiff who had delivered the news. Heath's attorney had sent a message to the jail that the second payment had been denied. No cash, no defense. He had gotten all the legal advice he had paid for. The firm wished him well.

The day of the protective service hearing, Heath was almost dragged into court. He was masked but still managed to give off his surly attitude. He planned to let the judge know that Emily had robbed him and that he was not getting the defense he was due as a wealthy innocent citizen.

A small, rumpled man sat at the defense table. He turned to Heath who was shoved into a chair. "I'm the public defender. Although this isn't a trial, I can give you advice because my office will be handling your criminal case when it comes to trial."

"Fuck you," growled Heath and turned to face the bench.

xxx

H. Lawrence Grayson accompanied Beth Seymour into court. He had heard rumors of the volatility of this Heath person. When he heard Dawson respond to the public defender at the defense table, he prepared for a great courtroom drama. Judge Dunn didn't put up with any shit, especially from assholes. He grinned behind his mask. Beth wouldn't need his support. They took their seats in front of Judge Dunn, a jurist well-known as a child advocate, and not so well-known as a good friend of Emily Jacobs. She gaveled the courtroom to order.

The social worker for Child Protective Services was called by the department attorney. The social worker reported on her interview with the children. The fire marshal was called to give his report on the fire analysis of the cabin.

"Do you have evidence to charge Mr. Dawson with arson?"

The fire marshal replied, "Yes. We were able to find parts of the explosive device and timer. The DA is preparing the case."

Teniquia was called and asked to report on charges pending against Mr. Dawson for this incident. "The DA has worked with our evidence to bring charges of arson and attempted murder of the three children. Bail was denied at his first appearance."

Judge Dunn turned to Heath, "Mr. Dawson, this is not a trial, but a hearing to determine if you should be removed as the children's guardian. Any charges filed against you will be presented at a more formal criminal trial. Have you anything to say at this time?"

He stood. "Judge, I've done my best for those kids. I promised their mother I would look out for them just as though they were mine." He tried to look sincere over his face mask. "I put those children in that cabin to make sure they were healthy and wouldn't make their grandmother sick from this virus. I was only going to keep them there about a week. I had it stocked with food and warm blankets and I planned to visit them daily." Another sincere wiggle of his eyebrows. He sat down.

The judge said, "Thank you, Mr. Dawson." She then turned to Beth. "Ms. Seymour. I understand you are council for the children. I would like to enter their testimony into the record of this hearing." Beth nodded and walked to a side door where, as the bailiff opened it, she motioned the children to come into the courtroom. She indicated that the kids should stand before the judge as Tee stood beside the bailiff.

For the record the judge asked the youngsters to state their names. Once that was completed, she explained, "I have heard testimony from the investigators in this case and from Mr. Dawson. I would like to ask each of you some questions." Three heads nodded. "Can you describe the conditions of the cabin when you arrived?"

Meg began, "He met us at the airport and told us we had to stay at the cabin to protect our grandmother from the virus.

He said there was food and he brought in new mattresses and fixed the toilet."

"He gave us a loaf of white bread and peanut butter," added Cody.

"And no jelly," complained Amy in a heartbroken cry.

Meg scowled over her mask at her siblings to be quiet, then continued, "He left us with some drinks and snacks and told us he would be back the next day. We looked around for cameras and recorders because we didn't trust him."

"And he locked us in," cried Amy. "I couldn't play outside."

Meg took a deep breath and continued, "He came back the next day with food."

"Cold hamburgers and greasy fries," complained Cody. "That's when we started to plan our escape."

"Escape?" asked the judge in an innocent voice.

The kids then entertained her and everyone else in the courtroom with their escape story, going into detail about ripping sheets and rappelling down the side of the cabin. The listeners hung on the children's every word as they told of Cody cutting his shins on the glass shards. And they finally got to the end, as breathless, Meg said, "We were all outside. I cleaned the blood off Cody's legs, and we walked into the dark forest."

At that remark, Beth was certain everyone in the courtroom thought of Dorothy walking through the forest with the Lion, the Tin Man and Scarecrow. Oh, my.

"That's when the cabin blew," concluded Cody.

"It knocked us down and I cried," added Amy. All those evil monkeys from the wicked witch getting closer.

"And we ran into the police who said our grandmother sent them to rescue us." Dorothy and Toto were saved! Everyone in the courtroom sighed in relief.

The judge looked over her mask at the children and then at Heath. "It is the decision of this court to support the recommendation of the Child Protective Service worker and dissolve the guardianship by Mr. Dawson of these three children. He placed them in jeopardy with no adult supervision. We are making no determination as to his guilt or innocence on the criminal charges pending, only on the facts as presented with regard to the children's safety and protection." She gazed around the room. "It is the decision of the court that guardianship of the children should go to their great-grandmother as recommended by the social worker in charge of this investigation." The gavel came down. The judge stood and left the room.

The bailiff took Heath by the arm and returned him to jail, but not before he shouted, "This is a railroad job. I'm their guardian. I want my money returned. I'll get even with that old bag." The door closed on his shouting.

Armed and in her uniform Teniquia took over the role as the children's guard. She moved them through the courtroom, behind the bench to the judge's chambers. Beth and H. Lawrence followed. Inside the room, Emily was seated on a small sofa waiting. The kids screeched their surprise and joy to see her. "You kids were great," said the judge, praising them and handing around cookies. Masks slipped down and the kids ate cookies and drank milk while the adults wrapped things up.

"I don't think you'll hear from him again," said the judge. "The DA has a great case for the arson and for that Masterson woman's murder." She then turned to Beth, "Well, Ms. Seymour, your reputation as a legal defender just keeps growing." Beth had had several high-profile courtroom wins since she joined H. Lawrence's firm.

"I knew she would be a good addition to my team," boasted H. Lawrence.

"Can it, Herbie," growled the judge. "You're lucky she's staying with you and not opening her own practice." She then turned to Tee. "Officer will you return the children and Emily to their home?"

"Yes, your honor." A lot of happy people left the judge's chambers.

xxx

"Robert died last night," Jim told his daughter.

"Oh, Dad, I'm sorry. How is Millie?" Lynn felt a tear trickle down her cheek.

"She's got her kids here. She says when this virus passes, she'll do something as a memorial." Jim sighed into the phone. "I wasn't taking this thing seriously until now. I think I'll organize the office for more working from home." He sighed again. "Marianna and I agree that we should stay as isolated as possible."

"I understand, Dad. Let me know what you need. Jason and I can run errands."

Jim chuckled. "Maybe I can use Jason at the office. It'll give him some law office experience."

"What can he do?"

"Run errands. Get papers to me. Take filings to the courthouse. The office staff will use him too." Jim thought a moment, then asked, "Is Emily still with you?" When Lynn said yes, he asked, "May I speak with her?"

"Yes, Jim," came Emily's voice on the line.

"Emily, Robert died last night." He waited as she gasped and expressed her sorrow. "The reason I wanted to talk to you is that I want you to move your business to another lawyer."

"What?"

"These are strange times, Emily. With my partner dead, I'll be cleaning out his files. Securing his share of the business for Millie's retirement funds. I think you need a younger group. Those kids are going to last longer than me."

"Who do you recommend?"

"Don't be coy," he chided. "I sent you to Grayson once and I'll do it again. He'll look out for you and get the real guardianship set up."

Emily sniffed. "What do you mean real?"

"Listen, old girl. You better get things lined up for their future. This virus can grab you the way it did Robert." Jim gave his client realistic direction. "Who do you have in mind for their guardianship in the future?"

She let out a breath into the phone. "You're right. I'll call this afternoon."

xxx

The world was quarantined. Living alone meant isolation. Beth Seymour had had a great day in court for her young clients. But most of the time she was working from her tiny apartment. She could go into the office, which just happened to be the floor below her tiny apartment. But just like her apartment, her office was empty. Her brother-in-law and boss, H. Lawrence Grayson had initially sent everyone home for two weeks. He then developed a staggered plan of attendance and suggested Beth could work from upstairs in her tiny apartment. Soon life had become phone calls, email, and online meetings. But not much in person-to-person contact.

It was group meeting night, but no group! This lockdown and virus had eliminated a lot of contact. And Beth missed personal contact. She missed talking with her group members. She missed hugs and smiles and tears. She missed the support and friendship. She even missed Lee pushing them for more honesty in the discussions. These last few months she had lost weight, finally talked with her sisters about her trauma, and was beginning to feel human - to laugh and hug and tease. And now - no hugging, no face to face gathering. Beth was lost.

Group meetings gave her strength. Now what - no meetings. No support. She could hear food calling.

On the other hand, she thought she heard a quiet voice, the voice she thought of as her realistic self. It was suggesting something. Beth sat still and listened. And the voice laid it out: *You're strong. You can weather this anomaly. You have gotten your weight down. You're eligible to apply for pilot training for that private license. Quit this 'poor me' attitude. Move the pity party off your calendar. Get yourself out of this funk. Your group friends didn't work the magic. You did. Enough whining!*

Beth hung her head. That small voice was a pain in the ass. But maybe correct. Even in a few months the group had taught her to listen, to be open, to think about moving on and into a better life and a positive attitude. She had come to the river today because this was the last place group had met in person. Well, she, Lee and Connie had met. Today, nobody. She sat on a bench and stared at the river, twisting a face mask in her hands.

She heard a sob. Maybe someone from group was here, just waiting. Leaving the bench, she walked around the screening shrubbery and came upon a lovely young woman, in tears. "Excuse me," whispered Beth, "did you come for group?"

The young woman dressed in hospital scrubs looked at the young attorney. She shook her head. "I came to cry." She was leaning on a railing overlooking the river.

"Can I help?"

"You want to help me cry?" She was using her face mask to wipe her eyes.

Beth stared at the young woman. "You look familiar. Do I know you?"

"I'm Nikki Erhardt, new widow." She dared Beth to say more.

Beth felt intrepid. "I'm sorry. I can't help your circumstances, but I can listen." She had learned a lot from the group sessions about the value of listening.

Nikki gave out a shaky breath. "I'm a nurse." She pulled at her scrubs. "I've been taking care of my husband until he died. I went back to the hospital for my regular job, and I just don't want to be there."

"I know the feeling," sighed Beth.

"You're a nurse, too?"

"No, but I know the 'I-don't-want-to-be-there' feeling. That's why I go to group. I'm looking for where I want to be." Beth gestured toward a bench. "Let's sit. I don't know about you, but I need to talk face to face with someone, not on my computer and not with a mask." Both women shoved masks into their pockets, sharing a guilty smile.

Nikki nodded. "I know that feeling, too."

Beth, the listener in training, said, "Tell me about your husband."

Nikki accepted the offer, not knowing that Beth was an unskilled listener. "I was a nurse in the Army. I met him in evac. He was wounded. I nursed him and followed him here. He was a paraplegic and had more life than anyone I ever met."

Beth's eyes grew big. "The brewery? That guy in the wheelchair?"

Nikki nodded. "You've been to River Dog?"

Beth nodded. "For Mars' wedding reception and with Connie and Doug."

"Barbara's friends!" Nikki thought a moment. She took Beth's hand. "That's the group you were waiting for." Nikki knew that Barbara and Connie were sexual assault survivors.

Beth squeezed her hand. "Yes. I haven't been with them too long, but I've come to value their support. Connie was in my group and there are five others. We tease Connie because she inspired us but doesn't need us since she married Doug. She told us she would always be available if we need her."

Nikki smiled. "Barbara has Zeke now. She's great. Zeke was Eddie's partner. They were in the same explosion. That's where he lost his leg."

"Wow," marveled Beth. "You have a long history with those guys."

"It took my family and Eddie's a long time to believe that we could make a go of marriage. Then they finally saw our love." Nikki wiped her eyes. "It was Lynn."

"Lynn Powers?"

"You know Lynn?"

"This is a small town." Beth sort of grimaced - small town, no secrets.

"Oh, right." Nikki continued her story. "Lynn was helping us deal with the mothers by online meetings. Sara and Kevin helped."

"Kevin's my brother-in-law!" They both laughed.

"Let me finish," said Nikki grinning through her tears. "We had this online meeting and both mothers were hostile, but Sara panned the camera back and they saw me and Eddie when no one was supposed to be watching us. They decided that we really were meant to be together."

"Lynn helped my friend, Dave, with his wedding."

Nikki leaned closer. "Did she really get Meryl Streep's dress for someone?"

"I think so, but it was a wedding before I came back to town."

"You've been gone?"

"I graduated from law school and am in practice with my other brother-in-law." The young attorney shrugged. "I've got three sisters, two brothers-in-law, four nieces and nephews, one dad and one stepmother. I've got more family than I need some days."

Nikki looked at Beth and was silent for several minutes. Finally, she said, "Thank you, Beth, for speaking to me. You've helped me with some of my confusion. Family. I think I need to return to my family and heal before I make any life decisions. Losing Eddie after several intensive weeks of care took all that I had. I need my family around me."

Beth nodded. "I've learned that my family has been very helpful and supportive after I finally told them of my trauma." She laughed. "In fact, I started my healing when I read a stupid book that told me not to be hostage to my trauma. And to set outrageous goals and reaching for them would help me reach my real goals."

Nikki gave her a confused look. "I'll have to think about that."

"Yes, do," agreed Beth. "But in the meantime, family is a great healing potion, if you've got the right kind of family."

Nikki nodded. "I do."

The two young women talked until it was dark on the river. Then each went on to what came next. Nikki would tell the brewers of her plans to return to her family to heal. And Beth would apply for private pilot training. Virus or not, life would move on.

xxx

Beth sat at home thinking about her conversation with Nikki on the river. She was inspired by Nikki's enthusiasm for her goal of getting a private pilot's license. She smiled to herself as she remembered Nikki's encouragement, as the nurse said, "You gotta do it. You're special. You should touch the stars."

Beth thought about that idea, touching the stars. Going to places unknown. Meeting new people. Not being a hostage to her trauma anymore. "I'll do it," she said out loud to no one but herself in her tiny apartment. She sat at her desk and went online to the flight school website. She had bookmarked the site weeks ago and found herself surfing the various links. Tonight she began her flying odyssey in earnest. Following the website instructions she clicked on required reading, clicked on approved medical examiners, clicked to enroll.

The journey began.

CHAPTER 26

Jim ended the last phone call. For several days he had been speaking with old friends and longtime clients, relaying the news of Robert O'Hara's death. "We were together a long time," he said to Marianna as he slid onto the sofa beside her. He rested his head on her shoulder. "We've lost a lot of our friends over the years. But this virus seems to be targeting those of us remaining."

Marianna took his hand and rubbed the knuckles as she said, "We'll hang on so that we can remember all of them. And I think we should take this quarantine seriously."

His head bobbed in agreement against her shoulder. "That's what all those I spoke with said. Everyone seemed to know someone else who had also died." He sat up and patted her knee. "So, my girl, how are you going to entertain me while we hunker down for the duration."

She laughed and kissed him on the cheek. "I think dinner is ready. Afterward we can go to bed and figure things out."

And they figured things out. Jim organized a workstation in the room that had always been designated as an office so that he could continue working with his staff. Marianna took over the guest bedroom and reached out to friends through this new concept called Zoom meetings. And both of them learned how easy it was to shop online and have packages appear at the door in record time.

And imagine Marianna's delight when she learned how easy it was to order dinner online and send Jim out to retrieve the carry-out order, prepaid. Or as she was heard to say, "I haven't cooked for three days, and my waist seems to be growing."

Jim had a solution, when, mask in hand, he eased her out to the street. They walked toward the park, caught the greenway for a mile or two of open-air exercise and at a distance greeted neighbors.

xxx

The guardianship hearing had been an ugly confrontation. Heath had been angry and aggressive. Emily shuddered thinking about his insulting language and his sneering comments about her family. But the children were safe, and Heath was in jail. Dusty had told her that proving Dawson had set the explosives on the cabin and directed Yetta to administer pills might take a little time. The pills Emily had vomited had been tested. She would never have awoken from that dose. Proving it was Dawson's idea would be a challenge. But his DNA was all over Yetta and all over her rental cottage. Dusty was confident Yetta's murder evidence was solid.

Emily had just returned from a final conference with Dusty. She sat on the porch, her meditation place. The dog came running from the trees eager to help her think. She sat on the glider while he sprawled at her feet. She pulled her jacket snug and began to outline her options.

Thirty minutes later, she had developed her plan. But she had to make a few phone calls first. By the time everyone sat down for dinner, she was ready to explain her new course. Clearing her throat she began, "I have some announcements to make." Lynn's family and the three children looked up expectantly. "I don't know how long this virus thing will continue, but I'm ready to get on with my life." That sounded definite. "I am going to buy the Cohen house." The children cheered. They liked life in The Heights. "Carl is going to do some remodeling. He told me we had to move fast. He thinks lumber prices are going to skyrocket. So, we will have a bedroom suite added on the main floor at the back so I won't have to climb stairs. He is finishing the space above the garage because Lucia and her son are moving in with us as household staff."

She sipped her tea and waited for questions. None. She continued, "The children and I are moving back to the other house. Lucia is moving with us. Juan will live at the Cohen house while the workers are there. He's going to be taking some classes online and will also help Abe clean out the house. Lucia and the children are going to help me get my old house cleaned and ready to sell."

The kids moaned. She knew they wanted to stay with Lynn, or more particularly with Jason. She looked at them with affection. "We'll be back in this neighborhood in a few months. Maybe Jason will have time to come out and help us clean." She looked at him.

"Sure," he agreed, and the children smiled. "We'll all be busy with our classes online, but I can come out after lessons."

"You could come out and help me with my multiplications," suggested Amy.

"Yeah, I could do that." He thought he might even miss his temporary siblings. But then he remembered all the questions they asked and all the privacy they invaded. A trip out to visit them in the country was a better option.

"And my Algebra?" asked Meg.

Cody opened his mouth. Jason tousled his hair. "I'll help you all, pal."

It was settled. Emily and the children would move back to the country house with Lucia as live-in housekeeper. Juan would have a job and time to attend classes to begin his CNA certifications and eventual EMT diploma. And the kids would bring as much joy to Emily as she could endure.

xxx

The River Dog Brewery partners sat in the empty bar mourning their own. Eddie Erhardt, the master brewer, formulator of their popular beers, had surrendered to the virus. Eddie had been a paraplegic, confined to a wheelchair. But nothing had conquered his spirit until this illness. He had convinced his friends years ago to take their discharge money and follow him into the microbrewery business. It had become a regional success story.

But now the bar was empty. These were strange times. Everyone was glad that the directives were in place for lockdown. They needed time to mourn and to recover from their loss. Nikki wiped her eyes. "It happened so fast. We couldn't even get him on the respirator. He had given me DNR instructions. I promised him." She sobbed. Barbara and Zeke embraced her. The young widow continued to cry.

"We know, honey," Barbara spoke in a soothing voice. "We all heard him say he wanted to be let go."

"I loved him. He shouldn't have asked me." She continued to sob. It seemed like every day since Eddie's death was another day of mourning, of remembering, of reliving those last days.

"He asked the one person who would listen," said Marilee, Kane's wife. "He knew you loved him enough to do as he wanted." She stepped in as Zeke made space for her to hug Nikki.

Because of travel challenges during national quarantine, Eddie's family had joined the brewers via Zoom for a tearful, joyful celebration of Eddie's life. Nikki's family had also been online to mourn their son-in-law. Friends in the brewery town of Portage had left flowers and cards at the brewery doors, in the brewery parking lot and at the office entrance. Each offering was a sign of the impact the energetic man had on this community. People had marveled at his strength, his vitality, and his optimism. They had celebrated with him when Nikki had become his bride. And now she was his widow.

As a nurse she had tended him through his military injuries, followed him into his discharge and convinced him that they should be together. The two remaining brewers, two wives, one tech support, Darwin and his lady, Shonda, and Nikki the widow, were now working through the impact of the death of the lead brewer. It had been two weeks since they had conducted his funeral. Now what. There were a lot of questions. Especially, what did they do now that the brains and inspiration of the organization had passed?

There was a noise at the door. "Don't folks have any sense?" groused Zeke as he went to chase away customers. But he came back to the group trailed by a young family.

Nikki gasped and rushed to embrace Eddie's brother and his family. The young man looked at his brother's friends. "Mom and Dad sent me. They thought you would need a brewmaster."

The gang exploded. How had they known? How long would he stay?

Lonnie Erhardt smiled at the enthusiastic reception. "Since I'm the youngest," he confessed, "they thought they could do without me." Eddie's family had been brewing beer, a popular national brand, in Pennsylvania for decades.

"That's nonsense," chided Nikki. "Eddie said that after him you were the best brewer in the family." Lonnie grinned and then sniffed, remembering why he was standing at River Dog. Nikki jumped in again. "Where are you staying? How long?"

"We drove down in our camper."

"Then you stay at our place," she said. "We moved the hospital bed and stuff out the other day. I have plenty of room."

Lonnie said, "I'm serious. Mom and Dad sent me. Me and my family," he threw his arm out to indicate his wife and three children, "are here to stay." He embraced Nikki. "You gave him so much and showed us how a person can live with disabilities. Mom says you two were a real love story. She said we have to take care of Nikki and Eddie's friends."

247

"Call Granny," said Darwin, "She's been worried." Granny was babysitting Kane's two boys and Shonda's son. "Tell her to get over here for dinner."

Barbara said, "What a great idea. I'll order from Lao."

And that's how River Dog brewery met the challenge of virus and death - through the power of family.

xxx

Lonnie and his family climbed in the RV and followed Nikki back to the house. He wondered what his life would become in this backwater. He laughed to himself. Eddie had claimed that it was a place to refresh your spirit and to lead a slower life. Lonnie missed his brother more than he had thought he would. They were adults and had been living their separate lives. But they had an attachment. Through the growing up years they had forged a bond as the two younger brothers. Going to camp together, high school athletics, summer jobs at the family brewery, once even dating the same girl. He knew he couldn't replace Eddie, but he was here to help continue what had started out as Eddie's rebellion toward his disabilities and had grown into Eddie's victory. Lonnie would help keep the brewery on track. The house was spacious. But it had to be to allow the wheelchair access to everything. It was nestled among trees overlooking a small ravine that as Eddie had written to the family, contained all sorts of wildlife. Lonnie knew his kids would love the forest adventures in years to come.

"What do you think?" Nikki asked as Lonnie and his wife followed her through the house.

"It's lovely," replied Lonnie's wife, Dana. "But we don't want to move you out. We'll find a place soon."

"But-" Nikki tried to speak.

Lonnie embraced her. "We're here to stay. Mom said we should come after you sent him back to us."

Nikki had respected her mother-in-law's wishes. She sent Eddie's body back to Pennsylvania so that he would be buried in a veteran's cemetery close to his family. She didn't mind. She planned to leave River Bend soon for a few months of recovery with her own family. Then she would move on. She had applied to a visiting nurse program that would be sending her to the virus hot spots. She hadn't told anyone yet. Maybe now was the time.

She moved away from Lonnie. "This is your place." Dana and Lonnie looked puzzled. "I'm leaving," Nikki continued. "I need time away. I'm going back to my family for a bit, then I plan to get a nursing position working with ICU patients struggling with this virus." Tears were on her cheeks. "I learned a lot taking care of Eddie. I don't want to waste my knowledge." Dana and Lonnie hugged her again.

"You're making some big changes quickly." Lonnie knew about quick changes. He was here in North Carolina, a place not even on his radar a month ago.

"I have to go. Too many memories here." They all continued to cling to one another as they watched the children play in Eddie's forest.

xxx

"Everyone's talking about Mars and Trina," said Lynn as she pulled off her sweatshirt. Working from home had caused her to rethink her daytime wardrobe - sweats were winning. "Kew says the community college grapevine is spreading the word."

"Bergy has told Mars that he's claiming grandparent rights." Dusty slipped off his shoes. "Whatever that is."

Lynn laughed as she said, "Bergy misses Janet's kids and wants grandchildren close. He helped raise Mars, so I guess he has a legitimate claim." She stepped into the bathroom to wash up for bed.

Dusty stood beside her at the double sinks and prepared his toothbrush. "Mars is concerned about this virus and wanted to resign to protect Trina."

Lynn gasped. "He's leaving the unit?"

Dusty swished and spit. "No, I told him we would be accommodating." He grinned at her in the mirror. "Danny and Tee are so excited about the baby that he understands that we'll all help him and make sure things work out."

She patted his behind as she left the bathroom. "I know Mars can count on all of you. Looking forward to a new baby may be what we all need in these strange days."

CHAPTER 27

"So Eddie's brother shows up. Says his parents wanted to help Eddie's friends. He's got them up and running again." Mars had stopped by to tell Lynn and Dusty the news.

"But, during this weird time his brother relocated his family?"

Mars shrugged. "He has three small kids. Maybe the oldest is six and his wife does brewery stuff, too." Mars pondered some information. "And," by the tone of his voice everyone leaned in, "Eddie's family is paying the guy's salary. He says his family can't do enough for Eddie's partners. They moved into Nikki's house."

"What's she doing?" Nikki's mom had been Lynn's old college roommate.

Mars shrugged. "I think she went back to visit her family for a while. She told the brewers that she'll move on to some areas where the virus is causing big trouble and lend a hand."

Lynn nodded. "She's a good nurse and she loved Eddie very much. She'll find the nurturing she needs with her folks and figure life out later on."

Jason had been listening to the discussion. "Nikki is like me and my friends. Life just upended everything, and we have to figure it out." Mars nodded agreement.

Lynn listened as Jason and Mars talked about the way things were changing. She saw it every day. People becoming accustomed to masking and to living smaller lives with a closer circle of friends. She saw some interesting things happening, too. A reinterpretation of high school and college graduations and, sadly, redefined memorial services. Online shopping, even grocery shopping seemed to flourish with home deliveries of everything from furniture to pet food. In her opinion the internet was keeping isolation at bay for many. Time would tell how life would come out at the conclusion of this viral interruption.

xxx

Emily sat at Lynn's picnic table in the back yard, or as everyone was calling it, the mask free zone. Connie and Doug, married for two months, sat across from her. Their three children and Emily's grandchildren where getting acquainted as Cody demonstrated his skill in driving them all on the golfcart/vineyard vehicle. Lynn carried out some iced tea and cookies.

"Please join us," said Emily. Lynn took a seat beside her. Emily smiled at Connie, her great-niece. "I'm making another will. I need to name guardians for the children." Connie put her hand up to her mouth. Emily continued, "I know you're newlywed, and you already have children. But you are the only blood relative they have." Lynn took Emily's hand as the old woman said, "I know I won't live forever, but I'll enjoy these kids everyday I'm blessed to be with them. Realistically, I won't see them into college. And with this virus, my time may be even shorter. I want them to stay together, and I want them to have young parents. I want them to have you."

"Aunt Emily, I don't know what to say." Connie had tears in her eyes.

"Let me explain the conditions. I'm sure your handsome husband wants facts before making any decisions. I have a trust for the children. It pays out monthly living expenses. There is enough to see each of them through college and have some money afterward. Lynn, Penny Rawlings, and Babs are the trust managers. My house in the country and the old Cohen house and the house at Hilton Head are all owned by the trust. It also owns some rental property in California and a few other things, plus stocks and securities." She shrugged. "The usual investments in this sort of account. So you

252

wouldn't have to support them." She looked at Doug. "Just love them."

He had been watching the six children playing together. His son Toby seemed to idolize Cody. The older girls were talking with Connie's younger daughters. He had the impression that they would be an affable group. He also looked at Connie who was hanging her head. He had been married long enough to know that she wanted to accept this new role but wanted his buy-in first. He reached over and squeezed her hand, then smiled at Emily. "Ma'am, I think we can accept because you'll be around long enough for all of us to get to know one another better. These kids already seem to enjoy being cousins. Making them siblings in a few years won't be a bother."

Emily smiled in return. "I think you should be calling me Aunt Emily."

His smile broadened to a devilish grin. "Well, Aunt Emily, I think come summer, we all need to take a road trip and investigate this Hilton Head property."

"I like the way you think, young fellow."

And that's how, even in a pandemic, a good family grew into a better family.

xxx

Sean left Will's factory impressed with his boss's solution to social distancing and working. Will had done a survey of workers and negotiated hours. The plant was now running on two shifts with half staffing each shift, but no one losing a job. What delighted Sean the most was that he had trained that young fellow Andy as assistant maintenance and with a little more pay Andy was now working second shift as head of maintenance as well as working his regular floor job at the lathes and milling machines. The young man had confided in Sean that having more day time with his small children was a blessing. Sean had marveled at Andy's faith and appreciation of the small things. Sean wondered if that had been the basis for his mother's faith - different churches, same God - always appreciating the small things.

Sean worked days for Will. The school board had learned about Piper's underground school and closed her down but had reopened all elementary schools four weeks later. So his secret job for Piper had been eliminated. He was back to his pre-virus routine.

It had been six weeks since his last visit from Lee. She had stopped in to tell him about cabins for the Sharing Shelter program and stayed until the next morning. Then she did what she always did - vanish. She didn't return phone calls. She finally sent a text saying, *"Virus taking its toll. Hospice patients need my attention."*

He didn't know what that meant, but he thought he would see her again. She just needed an excuse. He resigned himself to being her boy toy. He smiled at the thought. She would be back. And one of the times she returned he wouldn't let her go. He'd just have to be patient and cunning.

xxx

"There's going to be money coming from the government to pay salaries and things - even for non-profits!"

Lynn was logged into an online meeting with several local agencies. Funny that a few weeks ago everyone thought non-profits were doomed. No clients, no fundraising opportunities. And then these loans were announced. Local banks were advising how to apply, all eligible businesses and services were working to understand how much of the funds they could request; how it could be used; and most important, how much had to be paid back.

"The daycares will be closed," huffed one agency director, "but on the other hand the workers will get beefed-up unemployment. And maybe some moms will be able to afford to stay at home."

Everyone talked about the new way of life. Lynn had sent out her online meeting manners directive, but no one seemed to have read it. She cleared her throat and the little heads on her computer screen sat up. "Not everyone talking at once please." She gave everyone a digital squinty-eyed look. There, that scold should do it, she thought.

Rory, the Arts Council director, laughed. "You are so controlling. But, yes, we got your meeting rules. Raise your hand and wait to be acknowledged before you speak."

"Rule One," shouted all the heads.

She gave them all another squinty-eyed look. "Just remember Rule Two. I have the grant money. I rule."

They all laughed at her. Everyone was feeling a little better. Bleak might be on the horizon, but the horizon was further away than it had been last week. Everyone waved goodbye and clicked on the 'Leave Meeting' button. Soon Lynn was on screen with just her sister-in-law, Salley, director of the domestic violence shelter. "Good job, Lynn. You kept us calm, and things seem to be working out."

"Thanks," Lynn replied. "I appreciate your support, too. I thought earlier, they were going to turn on me."

"That's turn-off you," teased Salley, "you know, hit the 'Leave Meeting' button while you're talking. I think everyone appreciated your manners guide."

Lynn waved to Salley and clicked the "Leave Meeting' button. She sat back in her chair. Meeting online while sitting at her dining room table wasn't a bad option. Everyone was staying healthy and staying engaged. She just wondered for how long.

xxx

"How long will this masking and virus last, do you think?" Lynn asked Dusty as they closed up the house.

Dusty had just come in from taking the dog for his last yard visit of the night. He was thoughtful, the only noise in the

255

kitchen was the dog slurping water from a bowl on the floor. He took Lynn into his arms and spoke into her hair. "I have no idea. There are some crazies who think they have lost their rights to free speech and free opportunities because of this virus."

She chuckled. "I know. I see those folks in the grocery store, unmasked and daring us all to challenge them. But what have you learned from all those CDC communications through your office?"

"The emergency manager suggested that we don't start arresting folks. That made the sheriff happy. I agree. If we all cooperate, this should pass." He hugged her tighter. "I just don't know how long. It certainly has made changes in our lives already."

"That's for sure," agreed Lynn. "Dad and Marianna have adapted to sheltering in place. Your mother seems to be doing well out at the farm. And we got Emily and the children settled back at her house. Each local nonprofit seems to have crafted a work schedule that fits each mission." She picked up a towel and tossed it in the hamper. "Jason is back with us, and Brice is finished with quarantine." She made a mental note to grocery shop tomorrow. "And I heard some gossip."

"How can you hear gossip? You work from home."

She shrugged. "It sort of came up in one of my online discussions." He waited because her eyes were twinkling. "Noah has moved in with Jody." Ta da!

"Damn. He moved pretty fast. Can't say I blame him. She's cute and has a prosperous business." He laughed. "Noah's securing his old age."

Lynn pinched his behind. "It's this virus. People are reorganizing their lives."

Climbing the stairs to bed, Dusty thought about life reorganizing in The Heights. "In a few months Emily and her tribe will be living next door. Those kids will be able to trail after Jason and Jeff again. I think Emily will enjoy this time with those kids, pandemic or not."

As he closed the bedroom door, Lynn threw her arms around his neck to share a kiss. "And you helped Juan get into those classes." He kissed her back.

"I can't understand why it was so difficult to get his records from the prison. He had proof of his GED and some online classes." Dusty had had to lean on everyone at the prison in Buncombe County to get Juan's information.

"You just had to scare someone." She kissed him again. "He's going to be okay and it's because you helped."

"I guess I owed him." He started to undress.

"Owed him?"

"Do you know how much trouble he could have been in by following you into the forest?"

"Trouble?"

"What if you had gotten lost? Or fell and gotten injured? He might have been blamed for putting you at risk."

"But it was my idea."

Dusty scowled at her. "These days you know that a young man with brown skin would have been suspect before anyone listened to the facts." Lynn hung her head. They stood at the double sink washing up. Finally, Dusty said, "You're color blind. I know you never think of these things. But Juan took a risk following you and it might have caused him problems."

They were quiet while they each finished with their nightly routine. Slipping into bed, Lynn sighed, "Should I apologize to him?"

Dusty wrapped her in his arms. "We're even with him. He helped you and I helped him."

She snuggled closer. "He's a good fellow." She kissed Dusty. "So how long will this lockdown and pandemic last?"

"I have no idea," he replied, "but I do think we're going to learn to live our lives differently. Somethings will change

257

for the good and somethings might just be interim steps to new ways."

"You sound philosophical."

"I feel curious. Things are changing at light speed, and I'm interested to see how we adapt." He sighed. "We've already seen how bad guys adapt. Emily's grandson used the pandemic to plot murder. I hope others aren't that opportunistic."

"I agree with you. Things will change and I'm curious, too, about the future."

"One thing won't change." He pulled her closer and kissed her.

About the Author

Renee Kumor has lived in North Carolina for over thirty years. The setting for the River Bend Chronicles series reflects her early life in Ohio and her later years in western North Carolina. She was a stay-at-home mom for several years developing a personal ethic of community service. Through the years as her children aged, she became active in the political and non-profit life of the community. After eight years as a county commissioner, she returned to non-profit service and began writing a monthly column for the newspaper on non-profit management and service issues.

ABSOLUTELY AMAZING eBOOKS

AbsolutelyAmazingeBooks.com
or AA-eBooks.com